MEN OF THE
N #1 ORTH
THE PROTECTOR

ISBN-10: 1548375632
ISBN-13: 978-1548375638
The Protector – Men of the Northlands #1
First Edition
The characters and events portrayed in this book are fictitious. Any similarity to real persons or organizations is coincidental and not intended by the author. Except for Martha Beck and Hera Bosley who have given their consent to being mentioned. Recommended for mature readers due to adult content.
Cover Art by Kellie Dennis: bookcoverbydesign.co.uk
Editing: www.martinohearn.com

Books in this series

The Men of the North series can be read as stand-alone books – but for the best reading experience and to avoid spoilers this is the recommended order to read them in.

To be alerted for new book releases sign up to my list at www.elinpeer.com and receive a free e-book as a welcome gift.

PLEASE NOTE

This book is intended for mature readers only, as it contains a few graphic scenes and some inappropriate language.

All characters are fictional and any likeness to a living person or organization is coincidental except for two women who have inspired me and allowed me to make reference to their work.
Hera Bosley, poet, (barefootfive.com)
Martha Beck, sociologist (marthabeck.com)

DEDICATION

To the mothers and fathers raising boys and girls to understand that no gender is above or below the other, but meant to compliment and support one another.

It's the old story of synergy where 1+1 makes 3.

Elin

CHAPTER 1
Old San Francisco
– Year 2437

"My name is Professor Christina Sanders and I want to express my gratitude to all of you for choosing this class on history," I said softly and smiled at the seventeen students sitting spread out in the large auditorium. Most of them looked only mildly interested but a young man was shooting me a smile that I politely returned.

"This is modern history, and in today's lesson we'll focus on the Toxic War also known as World War III and reflect upon how the world has changed because of it."

A girl in the back raised her hand, and feeling pleased about her interest, I pointed to her. "Yes?"

She sat up straighter and played nervously with her wristband. "Is it true that you'll teach a whole class on the Nmen?"

I swallowed a smile, not surprised by her question. "Yes, it's true. It's a very popular class."

"But is it also true that we have to be here physically or we'll miss it?" she asked.

I leaned against the table behind me and kept my voice soft and friendly. "I know you must find it odd that I insist on doing lectures in this old-fashioned style instead of sticking to virtual reality or holograms like most professors. But I'm a historian and an archeologist – I *like* old school, and this is how I prefer to teach."

The girl chewed on her lip but didn't ask more questions, so I continued.

"If the mysticism surrounding the Nmen will help me draw my students to campus then so be it, and who knows? Maybe you'll find that sitting in a classroom isn't so bad." I smiled. "People used to do it all the time to discuss ideas and learn from each other." I moved around my table and picked up a book on Ancient Greece. Old-fashioned books were a rare sight and the students leaned forward to see better as I held it up. "Ever heard of Socrates?"

When several nodded their heads, I made my point. "He taught like this. In person – face to face."

Another student raised her hand. "Will it affect our grades if we choose to watch the classes from home?"

I shrugged. "Only if you're not here for the Nmen lecture, since it won't be recorded."

"And when is that lecture?" she asked.

Flashing a secretive smile, I walked back to stand in front of my desk. "I'm afraid I can't tell you that. Which is why I would suggest you show up in person to all my classes."

I ignored the discreet sighs from some of them. "Unfortunately, the class on the Nmen and how they came to have their own territory isn't today. Today we're focusing on the Toxic War."

"But is it true that you've been to the Northlands in person and that you came out *alive* with pictures?" the girl asked eagerly.

I laughed and brushed back one of the unruly curls that had escaped my braid. "Surely you can tell that I'm alive and yes, there will be pictures. As for my being there, that's just a rumor. No woman from this side of the border has entered the Northlands for centuries. Not since the peace treaty stopped the Nmen from kidnapping our women, that is."

"Then how did you get the pictures? Isn't it forbidden?" the brunette asked, and a few others nodded as to indicate they were wondering the same thing.

"It *is* true that distributing pictures of the Nmen is normally considered a crime, which is another reason you'll have to be here physically to see the images. But I assure you that I'm not committing any crime by showing you pictures of the Nmen since it's strictly for educational purposes and approved by the council."

"But who took the pictures? And how did the photographer get out alive?" they wanted to know.

I kept my tone calm even though this talk excited me. "As part of the peace treaty we help the Nmen with certain specialized tasks. Being only ten million people, they don't have the same access to specialists, and we've assisted them on different occasions."

Everyone nodded, since it was commonly known that the Northlands was a wild and primitive place and that the Nmen were the black sheep of the human race. No one expected them to be as technologically evolved or as enlightened as us. Teaching the class on the Nmen was one of my favorite things in the world because the students were soaking up my every word, and the element of mystery and adventure spoke to me. I should be getting back to today's lecture but couldn't help indulging myself a few moments longer.

"The pictures I'll be showing you will include a portrait of our very own Michelle Knight standing next to the first president of the Northlands. That photo was taken just after they signed the peace treaty." Always the teacher, I asked: "Raise your hand if you know who Michelle Knight was."

Eleven hands went up in the air, but I nodded to a young woman whose smooth dark skin and frizzy black hair reminded me of my lovely roommate Kya.

3

"Michelle Knight was among the first hundred and one councilwomen to serve the Motherlands, and she was one of the three delegates who negotiated the peace treaty with the Nmen thirteen years after the Toxic War ended," the youngster said matter-of-factly.

"That's right."

"It was lucky that they didn't kidnap her," she added. "Everyone knows that the Nmen kidnap and rape women."

"They *used* to!" I said firmly. "And that's why we made the peace treaty with them and why we secure our borders to the North."

I held up a hand to the five students who had their hands raised. "No more questions about the Nmen. Today we're going to focus on the Toxic War."

The open faces and curious glances that had just been looking at me with their full attention, turned downwards. Not many people shared my passion for the past and most avoided talking about it. We were all raised to focus on the present and be optimistic about the future. Sadly, the past represented grief and regret, and the consensus was that there was no reason to dwell on it.

"You." I pointed to a blonde girl on the first row. "Tell me what you know about the war."

She squirmed in her seat and her eyes looked upward, making me suspect that she had an implant and was accessing the Wise-Share.

"The Toxic War broke out in 2057 after decades of political disturbance across the world. It was the breach of treaties and an escalation of cyberattacks on neighboring countries that made the UN fall apart and former allies attack each other." She frowned as if reading in her mind's eye.

"And then?" I asked to move her along.

"And then it became an endless spiral of retaliation and by the end of 2060 the world was almost completely destroyed."

"True." I nodded my head and pointed to the student to her left. "Can you tell me how the war affected the geography of the world?"

He nodded. "Yes, large areas became uninhabitable because of radiation and pollution from chemical weapons."

"And can you name those areas?"

"Ehhm, it was the area formerly known as Africa, Amia, the eastern part of Russia, and Europe."

"Not Amia… it was called Asia," I corrected him.

"Sorry, Asia."

"And what areas are still inhabitable?" I pointed to the young man who had smiled brightly at the beginning of the class.

"What was formerly known as Australia, New Zealand, South Africa, South America, North America, and the western part of Russia."

"Thank you." I pushed up from the desk and crossed my arms. "And of course one of the first things the council did was to eliminate the old-fashioned idea of countries, so we are now all simply residents of the Motherlands."

I was losing their interest but kept pushing. "Why did the council get rid of country names?"

No one raised their hand so again I had to point to someone.

"I don't know," she said with an uninterested shrug.

"Because it was the mindset of 'them and us' that caused the wars to begin with." I clapped my hands to get them to look at me. "Who wants to tell me what happened after the war ended in the fall of 2060?"

The young man with the bright smile raised his hand and waved it almost enthusiastically.

"Yes?"

5

"The population was reduced from eight billion to only one point five billion – with women outnumbering men twenty-six to one. There was a general blame on male pride and aggression as being the trigger for the near destruction of the planet, and that's why protective laws were made to make sure greedy and power-hungry men can never rule again."

I nodded and pointed to a dark-haired young woman who looked older than the others and had her hand raised. "Yes?"

"Basically what happened was the men almost destroyed us all and we women tried to save what was left," she stated matter-of-factly.

The smiling young man wasn't smiling anymore. Instead he kept his head down, making me feel sorry for him.

"Yes, but let's not forget that not all men were greedy and power-hungry before, and not all women were innocent."

Muttering broke out among the females in the room, so I clarified. "All I'm saying is that the men who survived for the most part supported a transition into a new leadership focusing on rebuilding and nurturing the world."

The mutter only increased, and I knew I was walking a fine line. The last thing I needed was to get reported for being a troublemaker, so I quickly carried on.

"In what ways have we changed our ways of living from before the war? What are the big five?" It was an easy question that every elementary school kid could answer and sure enough; every student raised a hand.

I pointed to another young man in the back. He was wearing a fashionable white jumpsuit with a multicolored vest.

"The big five are: No killing, no greed, no borders, no pollution, and equality for all."

"Exactly. We no longer kill animals to feed on them and we don't hoard to have more possessions than our neighbors, and as I mentioned before, we got rid of borders and the 'them and us' mentality.

Except the border to the Northlands, I thought.

It was, to use a phrase that would probably mean nothing to the students, the elephant in the room that no one spoke about. We had created a society built on equality and tolerance, yet we had a big wall to protect us from the brutal Nmen who refused to live under the rules of the Motherlands.

A sequence of small pinging sounds alerted me that my online students had questions. I ignored them, favoring the students in front of me, and chose a student on the third row. "You have a question?"

"Yes, but it's not related to the war. It's just something I've always been confused about."

"Let's hear it," I encouraged her.

"I know people used to marry, but the more I read about it, the more puzzled I get. Would you please explain how that worked?"

Marriage wasn't on my agenda for today, but it was another area that had always fascinated me so I took the bait and answered the question.

"There used to be a balance in numbers between men and women on earth, and from early on they formed families with one woman and one man coming together to procreate and raise children."

"But how could there be a balance between men and women? Who controlled that an equal number of boys and girls were born?" the brunette asked.

I scratched my head. "Good question. Nature, I suppose."

She waved her hand again but didn't wait for me to give her permission to speak. "But I don't understand how that worked," she said. "Was every family forced to have an equal number of children to even things out? And what if they had two sons already – were they then forced to have two girls too?"

"No, I just meant that nature has a way of evening out the differences. For instance, we know that in some societies they preferred males and would kill their infant baby girls. In that part of the world there would be a lack of women of course, but because women tended to outlive the males around the world the numbers evened out eventually.

"Family unions were formed by one man and one woman, and depending on the culture it was based on either a practical arrangement or passionate love."

Muttering broke out again and I knew it was the phrase "passionate love" that confused them.

"You have to understand that women and men were not as evolved as we are today," I started. "It's mind-boggling to think that the concept of marriage started from an old tradition of a woman's being first her father's property and then handed over by her father to be her husband's property. There was a time when women didn't have the right to vote or pursue a career, and in many cultures it was the custom for a woman to give up part of her identity and take on her husband's name after marriage."

Disturbed looks were exchanged.

"I can see that you're upset about this, but then imagine being a woman living in the parts of Asia and Russia where bride stealing was used."

"Bride stealing?" a male student in the last row asked while fiddling with his pretty long braid.

"Yes, men would kidnap women on the street and force them into marriage."

"Was that legal?" the young man asked with his face scrunched in mortification.

"I'm not sure. It's hard to think that it could have been, but nevertheless we have found solid evidence that it took place as a cultural practice."

The brunette was tearing up and I held out my hand. "Don't get me wrong. Not everyone was forced, of course. But even if you weren't kidnapped or forced there was still a lot of pressure. We know from our research that in general, society placed a high value on the institution of marriage and it forced people, especially women, to feel worthless without it. Some cultures demanded that couples be married in order to have kids. And in some cultures, having children outside of marriage could get a woman shamed or even killed."

Gasps were heard.

"We would like to think that bride stealing was isolated to a small part of the world, but from our studies we know that in large parts of the world women were forced into marriage as children."

"But why?" a girl asked with wide eyes and a look of horror.

"Maybe the family needed money. Maybe it was for political reasons. We can't know for sure, but what we do know is that it was once common among royalty. In the thirteenth century, the King of Portugal married a girl called Elizabeth who was only eleven at the time. In the sixteenth century, Henry the Fourth married off his teenage daughter, Princess Emilia, to a man more than thirty years older than her."

"But why did the women go along with it?" the young man who had been smiling in the beginning asked.

"I don't think they had much choice, or maybe they just didn't know things could be different. Who knows?" I threw my hands up in the air. "We historians can only base our assumptions on the clues left behind and, as you know, much was lost during the war. I encourage you to visit the post-war museum to get a better understanding of the old world. When you do you'll also see the impressive exhibition of extinct and nearly extinct animals. There's a huge one called an elephant that looks really funny with a long nose."

I continued to ask the students questions, and when one of them closed her eyes as if calling for her virtual assistant before answering me, I made a mental note that I'd have to address the use of implants in my class. I would never understand how this new generation could be so reckless. Brain implants had been a huge thing before the Toxic War but it had proven unsafe and an easy target for hackers once the war broke out. Everyone knew that not a single person with a brain implant had survived, and yet these kids thought their implants were safer and that what happened to our ancestors could never happen to them.

After forty-five minutes of teaching my wristband vibrated, telling me it was time to end the lecture. "That'll be all for today. I look forward to seeing more of you for my next class."

Knowing that at least fifty students were watching from home, I said: "And before we end, I'll answer one more question about the Nmen for the students who are physically here." I turned off the transmission and smiled at my audience. "You get one bonus question."

A sea of hands went up in the air.

"Yes?"

The young woman I chose looked excited and flushed red when everyone turned to look at her.

"Is it true that they eat dogs?"

All eyes turned to me. "I'm not sure about their eating dogs, but it wouldn't surprise me if they did, since we know they are hunters in general."

Shocked gasps were heard all around. "They really kill animals?" someone asked with a brittle voice.

I picked up my book on Ancient Greece and placed it in my bag. "Yes, they really do hunt and kill animals, and I'll tell you more about it some other time."

With a smile of satisfaction, I left my outraged audience knowing that by the time I reached the lecture on the Nmen this auditorium would be filled with curious youngsters seeking answers to the mystery they had grown up listening to rumors about.

CHAPTER 2
The Yellow Bike

People mostly smiled when I made my way through town on my yellow bike. It was a replica of how bikes used to look four hundred years ago and even had a basket in front with yellow flowers.

I couldn't help it; I'd always had a fetish for everything historic and quaint. Besides, it might be antique in style, but my bike still complied with the environmental rules and generated power when I rode it. I was a proud contributor of at least half the amount of power I used every day. The other half I earned by teaching at the University and at the senior center, and by volunteering in my building's community garden.

Most buildings had urban gardens growing in row upon row of specially made boxes up the wall of the buildings. It was both beautiful, with all the colors, and practical, as we shared the responsibility of nurturing the plants and herbs with our neighbors and always had seasonal vegetables available.

I pressed harder on my pedals to pass by two slow-moving women who seemed to have all the time in the world. It wasn't that I was stressed; I just wanted to get ten minutes to catch my breath and find my inner peace before my important meeting with the councilwoman, Pearl.

With a smile on my lips I visualized her approving my request to go on an archeological field job again. Maybe even back to the blue area, where the former city of New York offered plenty of fascinating digging sites. The once-huge city had been left in ruins after the war, but a new and more environmentally friendly city had sprung up, and there was always excitement when something from the old world was found and retrieved. Two years ago, I had helped excavate a treasure of old wisdom when the head of a stone lion had been found on a building site. Our team had uncovered the remains of a museum: an incredible find that had provided us with material to study for years to come and made me hungry for more on-site experiences.

I parked my bike outside the city hall and took a second to look up at the intricate design of the vertical garden. Lavender offered a nice purple color to contrast with all the green herbs. I spotted mint, parsley, dill, and rosemary.

"May peace surround you," a passer-by greeted me with a smile.

"And you," I politely returned. Like me she was wearing comfortable clothes in warm colors made of soft fabric, and flat ballerinas.

The minute I opened the door to the large foyer of the town hall, I was met by the soothing sound of running water provided by the impressive fountain in the middle. It had a color-changing feature that played against the water, reflecting beautifully on the walls like a human-made rainbow.

With councilwoman Pearl nowhere to be seen, I took a minute to sit by the fountain and closed my eyes to center myself.

Of course, they'll approve my request. I've done excellent work these past two years and kept out of trouble. It'll be fine.

Smiling, I envisioned walking out of the building with good news, but my lovely visualizations were interrupted by a group of people speaking in hushed voices not far from me. At first, I tried to shut them out and focus on my breathing, but one sentence got my attention.

"It will have to be a male archeologist but so far all have refused."

I automatically squeezed an eye open to see them better.

"It's unlikely they'll find a volunteer; no one is that suicidal," a man with a long black braid proclaimed in a loud whisper. "It's a shame because it would be exciting to get answers, wouldn't it?"

Murmurs from the other four confirmed that, and I was just about to approach them to learn what they wanted answers to, when Councilwoman, Pearl, came walking in to the foyer.

The five people greeted her with wishes of eternal peace and she returned their kind wishes on her way toward me.

"Christina?" she asked politely, her sharp blue eyes locking in on me.

"Yes."

"May peace surround you," she said softly. "I'm pleased to finally meet you." Pearl reached out to hold both my hands in a standard greeting and after the traditionally ten seconds of locking eyes, we let go.

"Let's talk in the greenhouse; the butterflies in there are lovely," Pearl said and walked slowly to the west wing of the city hall. She was taller than me and looked different than I had expected. Of course, I'd been curious about her when I'd been invited to come and meet her in person. It was unbelievable to me that a councilwoman would take time to speak with me and not just let one of her assistants do it. But the video I'd seen on Wise-Share had been a close-up of her face only and it didn't show how tall and fit she was in person.

We didn't speak while walking but politely greeted everyone we passed. Only when we entered a sunroom with an abundance of sunshine, plants, and a lovely smell of roses did Pearl start talking.

"Mind where you sit, Christina, or you might hurt the butterflies," she warned and took a seat on a bench by the large window. I followed her example and sat next to her.

"You know why I called you here today."

I nodded. "My request."

"Yes, you have expressed a desire to get your hands dirty and be part of an archeological excavation again."

I wrung my hands, not liking the grave expression on her face.

"Your request has been discussed, and unfortunately I am the carrier of bad news."

Sucking in air, I held my breath while she told me what I'd been dreading to hear.

"It's not that we don't appreciate your talent and skills within the field of archeology. However, your history classes are very popular and it has been decided that for now, we prefer that you stay and teach."

"But I'm ready to go back in the field. It's been two years, and the students could easily be transferred to Professor Janson's classes. I already spoke to her and she said it was fine."

The edges around Pearl's eyes softened. "I understand your disappointment, but there really isn't an ideal project for you to work on at the moment."

"But what about the project where you need a volunteer?" Not wanting this to be the end of it, I grasped at a straw, referring to the conversation I'd heard in the foyer.

Pearl leaned back and creased her brow. "What project would that be?"

"I'm not sure. I just overheard someone say there's a need for an archeologist and that so far no one has volunteered. Couldn't I volunteer for that project?" My voice was full of hope.

"Ahh," Pearl nodded in understanding. "I think I know which project you speak of and, no, Christina, you certainly don't want to volunteer for *that* project."

"Why not?"

Pearl looked around and although no one was near us she leaned closer and lowered her voice to a conspiratorial whisper, "The site is in the Northlands. They've asked for our assistance to uncover what is believed to be a library."

"They have?" I said unable to hide my excitement.

"Yes, they found books in reading condition and there might be more. Obviously, we're intrigued and hoping to find answers that we've been lacking so far, but we may have to decline since we've been unable to find an archeologist willing to go."

"I could do it!" I said spontaneously without thinking.

"No." Pearl shook her head. "You know our policy. Women are not allowed to enter the Northlands. It's too dangerous."

She was right of course, but somehow I'd been certain my request would be approved and I wasn't prepared to give up on my desire to get back in the field.

"But women have visited the Northlands before; Michelle Knight did it."

"That was more than three hundred years ago. It's been ages since we've had negotiations on their territory or allowed women to enter. It would simply be too risky."

"Couldn't you ask them to guarantee my safety?" I asked, an alarm going off inside me. *I can't let her think me a daredevil or she'll never let me go.*

Pearl watched me closely but stayed silent, so I chose my words carefully.

"I understand that it would be dangerous, but if anyone were to venture into the Northlands to discover what is real and what is myth, it would benefit us enormously. Since I teach classes on the Nmen and I'm considered an expert…" I looked down and took a second before I met her eyes again. "I can't think of a more suitable person than me, and I would be willing to step up and do it for all of us."

"You would consider putting yourself at risk?"

"Yes."

"Why?"

The answer popped into my head immediately. *For the adventure.* But luckily I managed to apply a filter and say what she wanted to hear. "An individual serves the community so the community can support the individual."

It was the words taught to us all from early childhood, and Councilwoman Pearl smiled.

"I see," she said.

"They won't harm me because if they did the repercussions would be severe, right?"

Pearl couldn't be more than a few years older than me but she gave me a patient glance worthy of bestowal upon a child. "Christina, dear. Don't think you know what Nmen would or wouldn't do. They're savages without a conscience."

I nodded slowly. "I understand." My heart was racing with excitement and fear. "But I'm not afraid," I lied.

Pearl raised both her eyebrows. "It's very brave of you to volunteer, but I would need to bring this up with the council before a decision can be made."

"All right."

"Are you absolutely sure you understand what you're asking for, Christina?"

I swallowed hard but remained calm. "I'm volunteering to lead a team to excavate a potential library in the Northlands."

"I'm afraid you're mistaken if you think there will be a team going with you. We can't force anyone, and so far, you're the only one to volunteer. Unless you can find someone to go with you, you'll be on your own."

"But maybe they have some people who could help me with the work. I could teach them how."

She drew in a deep breath with a worried expression. "Maybe, but we can't know what skill level they have nor how cooperative they'll be to a woman."

"Maybe some of my students will come."

Pearl shook her head. "I don't like the idea of women and children going to that awful place."

"My students aren't children; they're all above eighteen."

"Maybe not children then, but young nevertheless."

"If you let me do this, I'm sure I can convince one or two to go with me."

She tapped her finger against her chin. "That would surprise me, but then again, *you* surprise me."

I took that as a compliment, although I'm not sure she meant it as one. "When is the project planned to start?"

"Four months ago," was her short answer. "The ruler of the Northlands contacted us. We just haven't been able to find a volunteer."

"Until now," I added and tried to hide how my hands were shaking.

"Until now," she repeated slowly and studied me. "If you're sure about this, I'll summon the council quickly and let you know."

"Thank you," I said and bowed my head.

CHAPTER 3
Teaching the Teacher

After my meeting with the councilwoman, Pearl, my next stop was the senior center. My yellow bike stood in brilliant contrast to the wall of red tulips that formed a red cross, signaling that this was a place of healing and care.

I liked teaching my history classes at the senior center because unlike my young students, my old students were very knowledgeable.

Today seven showed up, and they greeted me with love and appreciation when I entered.

"Is it today?" My favorite senior, Marie, asked with a hopeful smile that made the edges of her eyes soften with wrinkles.

"Maybe," I said teasingly. "But I won't tell you before you're all sitting down."

Marie quickly got her friends to sit down and pay attention, and a pregnant silence filled the room. The seven seniors were giving me their full attention and when I lowered my voice and said, "Today is the day," excited murmurs broke out among them.

My seniors were no different from my young students. Everyone wanted to hear about the forbidden subject of the Nmen; the men from the Northlands that we weren't allowed to talk about in public.

"What you're about to hear today is for educational purposes only. You cannot repeat what is being said in this class, nor can you record it and play it to others. I trust you will treat this information with great care and secrecy," I said solemnly.

Seven heads nodded back at me.

19

"As you know, we have about one point five billion people left in this world. We all live in harmony and peace, and our only adversaries are the descendants of the original men who opposed the protective laws of banning men from positions of power. Many of them had strong opinions of women being inferior, and they didn't agree with the monetary system being replaced by the fairness system or with the council being women only. Ultimately, they gathered up north in what was formerly known as Alaska and Canada, and after thirteen years of their violating every new law and causing trouble, the council finally decided to let them live the way they pleased and built a border to protect us from their violence and hatred.

"Some women who already lived in that region got caught with them, but because there were so few females the men were desperate enough to kidnap women from the Motherlands. The council stopped that with the first peace treaty.

"We refer to them as Nmen, which is short for Men of the Northlands, but we do not speak of them in public. We do not write about them. We do not allow them access to our lands. They are blocked from accessing our Wise-Share network and we only allow men to trade with them. The Northlands are rich in natural resources, and we supply them with fruits, vegetables, medical technology, and specialized knowledge among other things.

"That's not true," a lady in the back called Martha who was normally quiet during my classes called out in a raspy voice. "It's not only men who trade with them. My friend is a trader and she's a woman."

"Yes," I cleared my throat. "I know there are a few women who trade with them, but a permit is only granted to old women who volunteer for the job," I elaborated.

"That's right. My friend says it's only old crones that can trade with the Nmen," Martha said.

20

I nodded and looked around and smiled at the sight of the seven old people looking intensely at me.

"Nmen see women as less than men, and if they could have it their way men would still be ruling the world," I clarified.

A few of the seniors shuddered at the thought.

I brushed my hair back. "I could talk about them for hours but I know what you're all anxious to see. Pictures, right?"

With a conspiratorial smile, I used my wristband and heard gasps when a picture of two savage-looking men with long beards and bulging muscles appeared above my hand.

Marie leaned closer to see better with her eyes wide open. "Do they all look like that?"

I changed the picture to a close-up of a grave-looking man with a gray beard and a leather tunic.

"It's hard to say, Marie, since the most recent picture we have is this one and it's twenty years old. This is the previous ruler – Marcus, who came into power thirty years ago in a bloody coup."

"How many rulers or kings are there now?" Marie asked.

"Currently only one. His name is Khan Aurelius and he's the son of this guy, Marcus Aurelius."

"What happened to him?" Marie pointed at the image of Marcus.

"He died three years ago and then his son took over."

"Only one man to decide everything?" Maria asked. "Why don't they have a council like we do?"

"I don't think they're very good at making compromises. There have been countless wars for power within the region. In fact, our council has records of a high number of men declaring themselves kings, presidents, emperors, and rulers of the northlands, and often several men at the same time. Most of them didn't keep their title for long, but the current ruler Khan Aurelius and his father before him have stayed in power for more than thirty years combined."

"So, there's no wars now?"

"Not at the moment, and the Northlands are prospering from the peace – which we're pleased about."

"Why aren't there any newer pictures?" Marie asked.

"Because of the law that prohibits anyone from taking pictures of them," I explained.

Martha lowered her voice to a conspiratorial whisper. "I have some."

All heads turned to her and then back to me, waiting for my reaction.

"I'm sorry dear, what did you say? You have some what?" I asked to clarify.

"I have pictures of the Nmen," she said, holding her chin high.

I fiddled with my wristband, unsure how to handle the situation. "That's brave of you to admit, but surely you understand that you just confessed to a crime," I finally said.

Martha shrugged. "I'm one hundred and five years old; what are they going to do about it?"

"Show it to us," Marie encouraged with eagerness, and my curiosity overpowered my duty to prohibit the sharing of unauthorized pictures.

"Only if you all agree to keep it secret," Martha said.

Promises were given and she came closer, walking stiffly on her old legs and taking her time to work her wristband.

"Oh, this cursed thing – my grandchildren got me a new band five years ago, but I'm still struggling to get it to work." She was making commands but nothing happened.

"Maybe you didn't charge it," a man named Carl suggested.

"It's charged from movement," Martha muttered.

"Exactly," he said with a smug smile.

Martha gave him a dirty look before she started banging on the wristband. "Show me pictures."

A picture of a small child came up and it made her light up. "Oh dear, that's Joy when she was a child." Martha paused to admire the little girl until the man pushed at her hip.

"You said you had a picture of the Nmen."

"Yes, yes, let's see." She focused. "Show pictures from the summer of '32," she said and an album came up. "Find pictures from the border."

I took a step closer when a picture came up.

A man dressed in black leather and fur with a serious scowl on his face was in conversation with an old woman. Five more pictures followed of him and two other men.

"Fascinating," Marie whispered. "Look at how barbaric they are. Not only do they kill living beings but they wear their skin like a trophy – or is it a warning to others?"

"What do you mean?" I asked greedily staring at the pictures myself.

"Maybe it's a way to signal that they aren't afraid to kill, you know, to scare potential attackers off." Marie elaborated.

"Could be," I agreed slowly.

There was silence as the pictures flickered from one to another. We were all in this together and collectively knew we were breaking the law by seeing this, but Marie had been right: it was truly fascinating to see something so odd, like discovering a prehistoric primitive tribe.

"I heard they're cannibals," someone whispered.

"I heard they keep women chained in cages," Martha muttered low.

"That's true, I've heard it too," Carl testified.

"They look huge," Marie said and I couldn't decide if it was fear or excitement in her voice.

23

"Martha, where did you get these pictures?" I asked her.

"I visited a friend close to the border and she brought me along to see them."

"I don't understand."

"Her community trade with the Nmen. Since the men aren't allowed to access our Wise-Share network, communication is limited to traders from both sides who meet to negotiate. Once deals have been made, drones make the deliveries. They get fruits, vegetables, electronics and other things from us and pay us with gemstones, wood, and other natural resources."

"And you took these pictures?" I asked, having never seen Martha so animated. The woman usually sat motionless in the corner when I taught, but now her eyes were shining as she had our full attention.

"I took the photos secretly, yes. And I wasn't afraid of the men, if that's what you're wondering."

"How could you not be afraid?" a fragile-looking old mouse asked.

"Because I'm too old for them to take an interest in me. My friend is too," Martha said. "That's why it's only men and old crones that are allowed to trade with the Nmen."

"Did you talk to any of them?"

"No, but I heard them speak and they spoke English like we do, but with an accent."

"Yes, I could have told you that," I said, realizing that I was no longer teaching this class, I was being taught; everyone was looking at Martha.

"Weren't you scared they would kill you?" Carl asked her. "They're unpredictable and cruel, you know."

"Tsk," Martha wrinkled her nose. "Why would they kill an old woman who didn't pose a threat in any way?"

"You can't keep the pictures, Martha; if someone finds out you'll be in big trouble," I pointed out.

"Why are they anatomically so different from normal men?" Marie interrupted me.

"Well…" I turned to look at the pictures of the large males with their long hair, big beards, and muscled chests and arms. "It's not that they are anatomically different from our men, it's just that our men would never be this muscled or be so ungroomed. Nmen look strange to us, since our men take great pride in their appearance and typically have all their facial and body hair removed. In the old days, muscles and beards on men was normal. There was even a time when men were considered physically superior to women because they were bigger and stronger, but these days fit women are often stronger than most men." I looked to Carl. "Why do you think that is?"

He shrugged. "I suppose modern men wanted to separate themselves from the power-hungry Neanderthals who led us into the toxic war." The old man was skinny and held a hand to his sunken cheeks. "I had my facial hair permanently removed when I was seventeen, so I never bothered with a beard, and I would have rather died than have bulging muscles like that. They look like gorillas."

Martha furrowed her brow. "It's a mystery to me why Nmen would need to grow muscles in this day and age. What's the purpose of being strong? Don't they have robots to do the heavy lifting?"

I tilted my head. "As far as we know, they have robots, so maybe their appearance is a fashion statement. It's hard to say."

"My friend told me they import lots of sex-bots," Martha said matter-of-factly.

"Which is good," I added, "Because remember that the peace treaty was made to stop them from kidnapping women for sexual and procreative purposes. Now we supply them with enough boys to sustain their population but not grow in numbers. We also supply them with sex-bots to satisfy their sexual needs. It's a good peaceful way to settle things."

"I delivered a son," a little fragile woman said suddenly.

We all bowed our heads in respect to her. To voluntarily carry a Nchild was seen as a great sacrifice. We didn't have soldiers who fought wars, but we honored the peacekeepers who kept us safe from the Nmen by giving birth to boys already destined to go to the Northlands.

"We thank you," I said and took her hands.

"Can we see the picture of the ruler again?" Marie asked, insensitive to the emotional pain of the other woman. I reminded myself that Marie wasn't a bad person, she was just slipping back into childhood with her lack of manners and disregard for anyone but herself.

"Of course."

I showed the picture of the previous ruler Marcus again and didn't know if I should be amused or shocked that Marie looked almost taken with him.

"He's got beautiful eyes," she muttered low enough for only me to hear.

I starred at the picture feeling that same old curiosity that had landed me in trouble a few years back when I'd wanted to explore the rituals of the Mayan Indians, specifically the part about human sacrifice. It wasn't that I was a disturbed person, fascinated with violence, but more that I wanted to be like my heroes from the past and go on adventures to discover hidden secrets. I had seen old documentaries about archeologists uncovering Viking graves and hidden burial sites of the ancient Egyptians and Mayan Indians. My two favorite heroes were the archeologists from the last millennium whom I had studied and even written my dissertation about. With the content on the old Internet partly lost and partly falsified from cyber-attacks during the war, it was hard to get a clear picture of their lives, but movies had been made to honor their work and I had found video clips that testified to their bravery and adventures. I wanted to be the kind of archeologist that lived in the old days. I wanted to be like my idols Indiana Jones and Lara Croft.

CHAPTER 4
The Northlands

Alexander Boulder

I was circling Khan, my body alert and ready to defend myself against his attack, which would come any second now. Drops of sweat were dripping from his forehead and his right eye was already beginning to swell from the right hook I got in a minute ago.

A displeased grunt escaped Khan as he made a mock attack with his right fist that made me sway back and raise my arms defensively.

"You really thought you could take me in a fight?" He smirked and moved with me as I kept circling him.

"All day, every day," I said fearlessly.

"Tsk." He smacked his tongue and narrowed his eyes, and that was his mistake. I knew his attack was coming because he was as easy to read as he had been when we were teenagers. Back then too he would narrow his eyes just before he came at me full force.

With a swift movement, I turned my body enough to avoid his frontal attack and quickly grabbed his arm to twist it back. Wincing in pain, he didn't stand a chance when I kicked his feet underneath him, forcing him to his knees.

"Do you surrender?" I hissed in his ear and squeezed my arm around his neck.

Unable to breathe, he shot me a murderous look of fury. Khan was a proud man but smart enough to know he had lost this round.

Closing his eyes, he signaled surrender and I immediately let go of my ruler.

We were both panting from the fight and Khan stayed on the ground while I bent forward resting my hands on my knees and taking deep breaths to steady my racing heart.

"Good fight!" I rasped.

"Fuck you," he bit back and slowly got up. "I went easy on you."

"Did you now? Maybe you shouldn't have."

Offended, he snorted and went for his glass of beer on the table. "Don't fucking strangle me again or I'll have you castrated."

I laughed and picked up my own glass, leaning my head back and downing the content. "You're a sore loser, my friend."

Khan emptied his own glass and smacked it down on the table. "Maybe, but so are you."

"Always was and always will be." I picked up a chess piece that had flown through the air when I pushed the game off the table only minutes before. "As I said, you might be able to beat me in chess, but never in a physical challenge. I hate losing."

"Not as much as you're going to hate that you won." Khan had that look on his face that always made me nervous.

"What are you talking about?" I asked and pushed my long hair back.

His tongue ran over his upper front teeth and his hand carefully touched his swollen eye. Khan was a vain man and took pride in his good looks. No wonder he was pissed about his black eye.

"Hey, when you fight you get hurt," I said and shrugged.

He rolled his eyes. "Spare me your wisdom."

I laughed. "You can't be the best at everything. Haven't you learned that by now?"

29

Brushing invisible dust of his shoulders, he ignored me. We both knew that Khan was too competitive to accept being second at anything. He was born to be a winner. Son of a ruler who had mercilessly installed a winner mentality in him, still there were a few things he couldn't change no matter how badly he wanted.

We hardly spoke about it but he absolutely hated that both his younger brother, Magni, and I were taller than him. At six-eight, I was two inches taller than Khan, and his brother Magni had outgrown him at the age of sixteen and become a large man, close to seven feet. Being six-feet-six himself Khan was in no measure a small man, but being the smallest of the three of us bothered him.

"I have a special *prize* for you. Since you're so good at fighting I want you to protect someone," he said.

"Who?"

"An archeologist."

"You want me to protect an archeologist?"

He nodded with a secretive smile.

"From what? Dirt and dust?"

"The Momsies are sending us their finest archeologist, and someone needs to protect the weakling."

I rubbed my scar and followed the line that ran up to my temple. It was a habit of mine and something I did when I was stressed or annoyed. "Do I look like a fucking babysitter?"

Khan turned to face me with his own eyebrow lifted in a perfect arch. "Consider it a great honor that I'm appointing you, to protect the precious gift we're receiving."

"Flattery doesn't work on me, Khan, and you know it," I said and wiped the sweat from my forehead with the back of my hand.

"I'm not giving you a choice. In three days, a frightened archeologist is going to meet you at the border and it's your job to secure his safety while he's in our lands. Is that understood?"

"I'll give you my best man," I said with a nod but that only made him laugh.

"No, Boulder. *You* are personally going to protect him."

Frowning, I picked up my glass of beer. "You know I don't have time for that. I have businesses to run."

Khan stepped closer, snatching the beer glass out of my hand. "It's a fucking order!"

I sighed but bit back further protests, knowing that it would only make things worse. "Yes, lord."

Khan's eyes softened and he placed his hand on my shoulder. "Boulder, my friend, I know it's a shitty job, but I can't walk around with a black eye and not have someone suffer for it."

"You challenged me to fight you," I defended myself.

"I did," he said calmly.

"It's not like I had a choice."

"Exactly, just like you don't have a choice now." Reaching out his arm he pressed his wristband and an image was projected above his arm.

"May peace surround you," a blonde female said and I moved closer to see the recording. The image was flickering and the words changed in volume."

"What happened to the recording?" I asked.

"The messenger insists that it was corrupted before he received it. I don't know what happened." Khan pointed to the woman and started the recording again.

"My name is Councilwoman Pearl. We have selec... one o... our finest archeol... name is Christ... Sanders. We ask that you honor our agreeme... and secure h... safety."

"I can't hear half of it," I complained.

"They're sending their finest archeologist, named Christian Sanders, and you will protect him with your life."

I mumbled low curses under my breath before asking, "When?"

"I already told you. In three days."

"But how long do I have to protect this fucker?"

"Until he goes back."

"And how long is that?"

Khan shrugged. "When the job is done."

I shifted my balance from one foot to the other and folded my arms across my chest. "You might be my oldest friend, but I really don't like you right now."

Khan broke into a wide smile. "Good."

"And my other responsibilities?"

"I suspect you can still do some of them. The digging site isn't far from here and I'm planning to have him stay close to me. Maybe I can learn something useful."

"How close?"

"You'll both sleep here at the Gray Manor. I'll see to it that you have adjacent bedrooms," Khan said and poured more beer into his glass.

"Just so we're clear," I said. "You don't expect me to personally guard this momma's boy constantly, right? I can delegate it to my men."

"Only when you have personal needs or urgent matters. I told you that I expect you to personally see to his safety."

"Now you're just being an ass," I muttered.

Khan pointed a finger at me. "Tread careful or I might make you share a bedroom with him."

I clenched my jaws tightly.

He raised his fingers to feel the swelling of his eye again. "You know, come to think of it, I like that idea. That way he's safer in case of someone preying on his femininity. One can never be too careful."

I bit my tongue knowing the anger I felt would only get me in more trouble. Khan was my friend and ruler, but he could be a real ass, and when he was in this mood the best strategy was to get away before he came up with more of his wicked ideas.

"Goodbye, Boulder," Khan called after me when I stomped out of his suite.

CHAPTER 5
Bad Joke

Christina

Councilwoman Pearl contacted me personally with the good news, and after talking to me about all the council's concerns and telling me that none of my students would be allowed to leave with me because of their age, she made me promise to be extremely careful.

I said all the right things and assured her I would take no unnecessary risks and come home unharmed.

With my request approved, I was finally ready to share the exciting news with my roommate Kya. Beaming like the front light on my bicycle I sank down next to her on the sofa. "They approved me."

"Oh, honey, that's wonderful," she said and gave me a hug. "I'm pleased to see you so happy. When are you leaving?"

"In five days," I said, still smiling widely.

"And did you get the Blue Area again?" Her eyes were on the strawberry in her hand, meticulously picking off the small green leaves. With her peculiar habits, I waited for her to sniff the strawberry like she did with everything before she put it in her mouth.

"No, I didn't get the Blue Area," I said, snatching a piece of melon from her plate.

"The White then?" she asked and sniffed the strawberry. "I would prefer the White Area, it's warmer and their beaches are phenomenal. You can go in the water down there." Kya's large curls were unrulier today than usual, and she blew hair out of her face and raised an arm to lick off drops of strawberry juice from her gorgeous caramel-brown skin.

"I didn't get White either," I said, bursting to tell her. "Actually, I volunteered to do a project in the Northlands."

At first it didn't register with her, but then she looked up with confusion. "Whaaat?"

"You know, the place where the Nmen live."

She blinked her large brown eyes a few times and shook her head. "You can't go there. It's forbidden."

"You're right, but the council gave me a green light."

The triangle forming between her brows told how worried she was, but she said nothing.

"Part of our peace treaty with the Nmen requires that we share information about the past. Apparently, they're in need of an archeologist, so either all their archeologists are working on other projects or they don't have many to begin with. I don't know, but I can ask them when I go there next week."

"Have you lost your mind?" Kya shrieked. "You can't go to the Northlands. I won't allow it."

I sat quietly, allowing her time to digest the news.

"You'll die!" Kya's eyes teared up.

"No, I won't die."

"Then you'll end up as some man's property. That's almost worse than dying if you ask me." Kya was crying now and used the hem of her shirt to dry away her tears while shooting me a glance filled with blame.

"I didn't mean to upset you, Kya, but obviously, I wouldn't do it if I didn't trust that the Nmen would keep me safe."

"Yes, you would. You do crazy things all the time. You don't think about the consequences, Cina," she said, using my nickname.

"Hey, it's going to be all right." I clapped her hand and tried to suppress my own worried thoughts. *Am I making*

34

a mistake and just being too thickheaded to realize that Kya is right?

"How are you going to get there?" Kya asked with her tears still running.

"I'll fly up to the Green Area and take a drone to the border. That's where I'm meeting my contact person. His name is Boulder."

"Boulder?" she exclaimed in a high pitch. "What kind of name is Boulder? Why would you go into unknown territory with a dangerous man called Boulder?" She put her plate of fruits aside and moved forward, placing both her hands on my shoulders. "I'm begging you, Cina, don't do this!"

I was sad to see my best friend so upset, but I wasn't going to back down now that the council had approved my request. This was the adventure I'd been waiting for, and I had to believe that I would come back unharmed.

"Kya," I looked deeply into her eyes. "Thank you for caring so much about me. You're a good friend."

"So, you'll stay home?" she asked hopefully.

"I can't. This is a great opportunity for me. I'm getting the chance to learn more about the Nmen and see a part of the world that has been closed off to us for hundreds of years. Doesn't that sound exciting?"

"No!" She picked up a tissue and blew her nose. "Maybe if it was someone else going, but there's nothing exciting in my best friend putting herself in danger."

"Councilwoman Pearl assured me that I'll have a personal guard to ensure my safety while I'm in the Northlands. Their ruler isn't going to let anything happen to me."

"How do *you* know?"

"Because they know that our council would retaliate with heavy sanctions on their trade business."

"But how long will you be gone?"

"I'm not sure. Probably a few months."

"And is this personal guard of yours the man called Boulder?"

"Maybe. Or he's another archeologist that I'll be working with. I'm not sure."

"And if he tries to rape you? What will you do?"

I caressed her hair and cheek. "He's not going to rape me, Kya."

"Yes, he is." Her voice broke. "That's what they do, Cina."

Rape was a very rare crime in our society. After the toxic war there had been twenty-six women to every man, and even though we had managed to bring a better balance over the last centuries and it was now down to fourteen women per man, it was still unheard of for someone to sexually assault another. Probably because violence in general was almost eradicated, and we had sex-bots for those with perverted tendencies.

"I'm not sure what I would do," I said slowly. "Probably run as fast as I can."

Kya dried her nose and looked at me with teary eyes. "Just promise me that you'll come home safely," she pleaded. "Promise!"

I gave her a long hug and whispered in her ear. "I promise."

CHAPTER 6

By the Border

Christina

The plane ride went smoothly, and my only regret was that I wasn't flying in the early morning or late night. The glass ceiling made it possible to lean your seat back and study the stars, but of course at ten in the morning all I could see were clouds. Hopefully when I returned I would see a sunset and enjoy the night sky.

The drone flight from the airport to the border took a little over an hour flying over forest and fields that were more lush and green than anything I'd ever seen before. I sat with my legs curled up under me and took in the panoramic view with fascination.

The border was just like I'd imagined: a solid wall as far as the eye could see, running in both directions and with an opening in front of me that had two gates. Unfortunately, I couldn't see past the gates so I didn't know if my guide Boulder was waiting on the other side. He should be since it was after noon.

I got out as soon as the drone landed and as I approached the barrier, a scanner lit up red.

"Please wait," a robotic voice informed me and soon a small elderly woman came to meet me.

"May peace surround you," I greeted her and she replied politely. "May peace surround you too."

"My name is Christina Sanders. You should have been informed that I'm crossing the border today."

"Yes, but I didn't believe it," the small woman admitted with worry written across her face so deep that it only increased the churning in my belly.

Don't be a chicken – you wanted an adventure, now get on with it, I scolded myself and thanked the old woman when she let me through.

"Be careful," she warned.

"I will," I assured her and walked on. My bags were rolling slowly just behind me, following the GPS in my wristband. I sure hoped this Boulder man had a large drone, because my equipment and clothes took up three large suitcases.

Waiting on the other side of the border, I scanned as far as I could see but there were no people in sight. I looked back at the old guard, who waved at me from the gate, and then my eyes lifted to the sky, where the drone that had brought me here was returning the same way I'd come.

Unsure what to do, I waited for another few minutes. There wasn't really a road, more like a flat trail leading up a small hill, and I figured that if I walked up to the top, I'd get a better view and possibly be able to spot Mr. Boulder somewhere.

With resolve, I suppressed the nauseated feeling in the pit of my stomach and walked ahead. A buzzing sound made me turn and look up to see a tiny drone hovering behind me. The old woman was no longer by the gate, and I figured this was one of the thousands of drones surveilling the borderline that she and her colleagues supervised. Right now, the drone provided her with a safe way to follow my steps.

I continued walking, unsure what to do if my contact person didn't show up, but then just before I reached the top of the hill an awful noise came toward me followed by the sight of a huge black drone flying at high speed.

My heart was pounding and I tried to steady my breathing and stay calm, but it was impossible. Folding my hands into fists, I prepared to run or fight if the person coming at me was hostile.

The large drone was going so fast that it flew right past me, making a turn so sudden and dangerous that I thought the pitch-black thing would surely crash.

I'd never seen such reckless flying, and suspected the drone was malfunctioning to behave that way.

The horrible noise from before was louder now that the large drone came to hover just an arm's length above the ground right in front of me.

The noise is a type of music, I concluded. Something not far from the aggressive music of the past when foul language and deep bass sounds had been modern.

I couldn't fathom how anyone would voluntarily listen to such awful tones, and curiously looked to see the passenger.

With the sun reflecting on the windshield it was impossible to see him, and so I waited until the door finally opened and the largest male I'd ever seen stepped out, slamming the door shut with such scary aggression that I took a step back.

We were standing apart and taking each other in. The man was huge, with wide shoulders that were exposed in the tight t-shirt he was wearing. My eyes blinked like a camera shooting picture after picture – trying to capture the oddity in front of me. His dark unruly hair stopped at his jaw and wasn't braided or finely combed like the men I was used to seeing. Looking deeply frustrated he scratched his long beard, muttering words that I never thought I would hear in real life.

It was certainly English, but from the forbidden category, and yet he stood there, speaking those words so blatantly.

"What the fuck is this?" As he moved closer, the sun reflected on a thin silvery scar running up to his right temple, and even if he hadn't been scrunching up his face so much, his features were much too sharp and masculine for him to be considered pretty. This man had the most piercing gray eyes I'd ever seen, and they were locked on me with a hostility that made me forget to breathe for a second. I'd never felt so intimidated in my life.

Stand your ground. Show no fear! I chanted internally and forced myself to step forward and meet him with my hands outstretched.

"May peace surround you."

He jerked when I took his giant hands and looked into his eyes as a proper greeting required.

We didn't make it to the ten-second mark, because the large man spoke up. "Why are you staring at me and holding my hands?" he asked.

It rattled me a bit. "It's considered a formal greeting."

"I don't like it," he said and pulled his hands back to place them on his hips. "What I want to know is, who the fuck are you?"

My eyes widened at his rudeness, but I stayed calm. "I'm Christina Sanders, the archeologist your ruler has asked for."

He wrinkled his nose in disgust. "But you're a girl!

The condescension in his last word lit a roaring fire in the pit of my stomach. Never had I been so offended, and I didn't care that I had to lean my head back when I looked the big ogre straight in the eye again. "Do I look like a child to you?"

"No."

"How would you feel if I called you a boy?"

He raised an eyebrow challengingly.

"Exactly. So, don't call me a girl. I've been a woman for more than a decade and will not be belittled by you."

"How old are you?" he asked, and this time there was less disgust and more curiosity in his voice.

"Thirty-one. How old are you?"

"Why?" He narrowed his eyes. "Who wants to know?"

"I do. It's called small talk and it's used to get to know one another," I lectured him.

He gave me a grumpy stare and looked down to my suitcases. "What's this?"

"That's my suitcases. We use them to transport items."

"Don't be a smartass, I know what a suitcase is."

I gaped at him. I'd known him for less than three minutes and he had used more profane words than I'd used in my entire lifetime.

"You can't talk to me that way!" I said firmly.

"What way?"

"That thing you just called me, it's offensive."

"Yeah, you already told me that you're not a girl."

I shook my head. "I meant you calling me a smart-you-know-what. I know what that word means."

The ogre rolled his eyes and walked back toward the large drone. "This is going to be a fucking nightmare," he muttered while I stood paralyzed. I had naïvely thought I was prepared for the worst, and yet I had underestimated how different it was to study something from a safe distance compared to interacting with it up close.

"Are you coming or what?" my guide shouted from the black drone.

"Excuse me, but you haven't introduced yourself," I reminded him.

He had a hand on the door. "My name is Alexander Boulder – now get in the fucking drone, *woman*."

I crossed my arms and pushed my jaw out, letting him know that I would not be disrespected like this.

"What's wrong now?" he asked with exasperation.

"You're being most unkind to me and I don't appreciate your constant use of curse words."

From the way his knuckles changed color to white, I knew he was squeezing the door hard and suspected he was counting to ten in his head.

"I also need help with my luggage, so could you be a gentleman and load them into the drone?"

"Why? I thought you women were all so independent and strong," he mocked me.

"We are," I said quickly. "And we're also very keen to help others. In this case, I'm asking you to help me." While talking, I moved toward him and my luggage followed me.

Alexander opened a hatch and bent down to take the first suitcase.

"Careful with that one, it's very heavy," I warned.

He snorted and lifted the suitcase as if it weighed nothing. I picked up the lightest of my heavy bags, but his drone was too tall and the luggage area much too high for me to reach.

"Could you please help me?" I asked while struggling with the heavy thing.

He did, and judging from his smug smile of satisfaction, he was clearly amused by his superior strength.

"Thank you," I said when all my luggage was loaded aboard the drone.

"Let's go," was his reply and I noted again that he had no manners. I had greeted him kindly when we first met, wishing him peace, but he didn't return the greeting. Now I'd told him thank you and he didn't acknowledge that either. So, it was true then; the Nmen were primitive and rude and didn't have a civilized way of interacting. But then again, they grew up without mothers or female influence, and didn't know any better.

"What am I to call you?" I asked when we sat in the drone and it took off.

"You can call me Boulder," he said and that's when I realized that he was maneuvering the drone around.

"Do you control the drone?"

"Yes."

"Why?"

"Because it's fun."

"But who taught you how to?" I stared at the steering panel with the large screen.

He gave me a sideways glance. "A friend."

"But don't you have automated drones?"

"Of course; this one is a hybrid. I can choose to steer or not."

"But that can't be legal, can it?" I asked skeptically.

"Sure, why wouldn't it be?"

"Because of accidents. Humans get distracted and make mistakes. In traffic that's often fatal. We haven't allowed manually controlled vehicles for hundreds of years."

"You don't have any manual vehicles?"

"No. Well, technically yes, but only in amusement parks. There's one called *The Ranch* not far from where I live. You can ride horses and drive old-fashioned cars. It's really fun!"

"Amusement parks," he mumbled under his breath. "Do you have amusement parks showing off how men used to look, too?"

I gathered my hands in my lap. "What do you mean?"

"You don't have any real men left, so do you see us men as something historical too?"

"No, of course not. It's true we don't have as many men as we would like, but since the toxic war ended we've gone from a ratio of twenty-six women per man to fourteen women per man. That's a significant improvement, wouldn't you say?"

"Hmm." He grunted, keeping his gaze out the windshield.

"You have women here too, right?"

"A few."

"How many are a few?"

"Maybe one for every hundred thousand men. Overall, we have maybe a hundred left in the Northlands.

43

"I wonder what it's like to grow up as a woman in this part of the world," I thought out loud.

Boulder narrowed his eyes as if I had offended him. "At least we let our women be women. You witches castrate your men."

I answered in a high-pitched voice "We do *not* castrate our men! How would we be able to grow in numbers if we did? Where do you hear such nonsense?"

"Everybody knows how you enslave men and make them into little puppets."

"What are you talking about?" I almost laughed at the absurdity.

"I've met men from your part of the world and they look and act like women."

"So? That's the modern man for you. They have evolved into caring, emotionally mature beings with no need to classify themselves as a gender," I lectured him and pushed a strand of my brown hair back.

"That's just a fancy way of saying that you're raising your boys to be fucking pussies."

I clasped a hand to my mouth and gasped out in shock.

For the next twenty-minutes we didn't speak a word. It was clear to me that he was as judgmental toward my part of the world as I was toward his.

"You're staying at the Gray Manor," Boulder informed me. "It's where our ruler Khan Aurelius lives."

I snickered a bit and looked out the window.

"What's so funny to you?" he said grumpily.

"Your names. They're all so pompous."

"You have a problem with our names now?"

"No, it's just funny to me that you would choose to name your boys after great emperors, kings, generals, and gods."

"Why is that funny?

I turned to him and smiled. "Honestly, who does that?"

"You would rather we gave our boys boring loser names?"

"No, but just normal names."

"Normal to who? You?" he asked dryly.

"Seriously though, Khan Aurelius?"

"Yes, after Genghis Khan and Marcus Aurelius, some of the greatest men who ever lived."

"I know who he's named after; I'm a history professor and archeologist," I reminded him. "I suppose you're named after Alexander the Great?"

He nodded with an expression of self-importance. "A name has power – if you tell a wolf it's a chicken it loses strength."

I laughed then. Long and hard. "How exactly would you tell a wolf that it's a chicken?"

"Bad example," he admitted. "But everyone knows that words have power; why else would you object to me calling you a girl?"

That shut me up. He was right. Being called a girl had felt demeaning. I was a grown woman and equal to a man. A girl equaled a boy.

"We honor our boys by naming them after great men because it's a reminder that those great men were once boys too. Every boy has a destiny, and for some of these boys it could be to grow up and rule the world."

I swung my head toward him. "The world?"

"I meant the Northlands," he added quickly.

His words confirmed to me that men were naturally inclined to seek power.

"And what kind of rulers would they be?"

"Firm rulers."

"What kind of ruler is Khan Aurelius?"

Boulder seemed to think about it. "You'll meet him soon enough and then you can make up your own mind. He's excited to meet you, but I should warn you."

"About what?"

"We were all expecting a man."

"But Councilwoman Pearl said she sent a message. Didn't you get it?"

"Yes, but it was of bad quality and we mistook your name as being Christian Sanders.

I tilted my head. "Christian, now that's a nice name for a boy – much better than Khan Aurelius."

Alexander shook his head. "I wouldn't say that to his face if I were you."

CHAPTER 7
The Unexpected

Boulder

I couldn't believe my eyes when I saw a woman walking in the middle of the road. Hardly anyone crosses that border on foot, and certainly not a woman. It was bad enough that Khan was a sore loser and made me babysit some whimsical man from the Motherlands, but I couldn't let this defenseless woman continue without protection.

I brought my hybrid to a landing and got out to approach the woman. It was the most bizarre thing ever. She wasn't an old crone like the people we trade with at the border. She was young.

Because I was a close friend to our ruler, I had seen a real woman before. There were several men in Khan's elite circle that had wives. Still, the women were always kept mostly out of sight, so for me to be alone with one was a first.

Anger filled me. Did she not know what could happen to a defenseless woman? What if I hadn't come across her and some tradesman had found her? The thought was disturbing.

I moved closer and looked her over. She wasn't wearing any make-up and squinted because of the sun. Strands of her long brown hair had escaped her braid and were blowing around her face in the mild breeze.

I was just about to ask her who she was and if she had any idea what an idiot she was for coming here without any protection when she took a step toward me and opened her mouth.

"May peace surround you," she said and smiled at me, her face pretty and innocent.

When she took my hands and gazed fearlessly into my eyes, it took me by surprise and made me forget what I wanted to say. I had never physically touched a woman, and no person had ever kept eye contact with me for that long unless we were fighting and they were trying to read my next attack. The expression in her eyes wasn't hostile, it was friendly – and I was fascinated that her eyes had two different colors, one blue and one hazel-green. She was small and fragile and only reached my shoulder in height.

"Why are you staring at me and holding my hands?" I blurted out, not liking the funny feeling inside of me.

"It's considered a formal greeting," she explained.

"I don't like it," I said and jerked my hands back. "What I want to know is, who the fuck are you?"

"My name is Christina Sanders, the archeologist your ruler asked for."

And that's when I knew I was truly fucked. The archeologist from the Motherlands that I had to protect was a woman, and not only was she a woman – she was a *young* woman that any man in this goddamn place would want to marry. With a hundred thousand men to one woman, women were the highest-priced commodity, and I would need an army if I were to keep her safe from the thousands of men that would demand her for their own.

My mind was racing, trying to come up with a strategy and at the same time talk to her. She got offended easier than any man I'd ever met and was too weak to put her own luggage in the hybrid. How the hell did women survive without men if they were this helpless?

I was happy when we reached the gates of the Gray Manor, and feeling hopeful that Khan would release me of my duty when he realized Christina was a woman.

Only a few guards saw her when I hurried her upstairs to her room. With her safely inside, I locked the door.

"Hey, did you just lock me in?" I heard her protest as I walked away, but there was no reason to explain to her how dangerous a situation she was really in. Women were too emotionally fragile to deal with worries of that magnitude. Khan and I would have to find a way to solve this.

When I found Khan, he was in the garden doing a walk and talk with his brother and advisor, Magni, who was also a friend of mine.

I ran up to them, signaling the urgency, and both men stopped talking and turned to me.

"Boulder, has the archeologist arrived?" Khan asked.

"Yes, but we've got a big fucking problem."

"And what is that?" Khan had both hands clasped behind his back and watched me closely.

"It's a woman. Her name is Christina and she's young."

"A young woman?" Magni exclaimed. "Here?"

"A young *beautiful* woman," I confirmed.

The two men exchanged horrified glances and Khan's hands went from behind his back to his head. "How could the council be so reckless? We can't guarantee a woman's safety."

Magni looked around and drew us closer, "Did anyone see her?"

"A few guards. I took her straight to her room and locked her inside."

"Shit, this is bad," Magni hissed. "Why the hell didn't you just push her back over the border?"

"I didn't know what to do so I followed orders." I looked at Khan. "You told me to get the archeologist and take him back here. I did that; only change is that he's a she."

"That's a big fucking change, wouldn't you say?" Magni argued, annoyed.

"I agree," I said low and looked straight at Khan, "We need to take her back before anyone realizes that we have an unmarried young female here, or you could have an uprising on your hand."

Khan looked down for a few seconds and then he straightened up with that devilish gleam in his eyes that always meant trouble. "No," he said. "We won't send her back. I would like to meet this woman. Who knows? If we charm her, she might want to stay."

"What? Are you insane?"

He gave me a warning glance. "Take me to her and I'll decide what needs to be done."

The three of us walked in a brisk pace back to the large manor and up the stairs to the second floor where I had left her.

I opened the door and we all walked inside the large bedroom to find Christina sitting by the window with the light surrounding her hair like a bright halo.

She stood up and clasped her hands in front of her, watching us with eyes flickering between us.

"Christina Sanders, this is our ruler Lord Khan Aurelius and his brother Magni Aurelius."

Christina bowed her head and said softly, "May peace surround you all."

Khan stepped closer and took her hands when she reached out to him. "May peace surround you too," he said and for the longest time they stood quietly and looked each other in the eye while holding hands. Maybe Khan's father had taught him about this strange greeting of the Motherlands.

Magni cleared his throat, clearly as uncomfortable about this strange custom as I was.

"It's nice to meet you," Christina told Khan with a smile. "I've come to help you excavate the site you've located and I would love to know more." She spoke softly.

"Yes, but before we can get to that, there's an urgent matter that we must discuss," Khan said and signaled for Magni to close the door.

Christina moved behind a chair and stood quietly observing us. Her facial color was paling and I figured she was intimidated by our size. She was a small female and the three of us were all large men. Instinctively I took a stance close to her, wanting her to know that she had nothing to fear as long as I was in the room, but my closeness only made her move back further.

"Why don't we sit?" Khan asked and gestured to the lounge area in the corner of the room.

With a stiff nod, Christina followed his lead and walked over to the lounge area with her head held high and her shoulders tensed up.

"We were expecting a male archeologist, and you're being a woman presents us with a problem," Khan started when they sat down.

"I can assure you that I'm as qualified as any man," she said quickly.

He held up a hand. "That's not what concerns me."

"Oh?"

"I'm puzzled why the council would allow a woman to take on this job."

"And yet, you guaranteed my safety."

Khan exhaled forcefully. "I'm afraid there was a misunderstanding. It's true that we guaranteed the safety of a male archeologist, but I assure you we would have never encouraged the council to send a female. It's simply too dangerous for you to be here."

Christina sat straight and stoically, saying nothing.

"It's a shame, because the job that we need help with is exciting and shows great promise. If it's truly a library, it could provide valuable answers we've all been looking for."

Her eyes expanded with interest and she moved forward in her chair.

"If only you had been a man," Khan added with a tone of regret, and that last statement made Christina crease her brow.

"Isn't there any way for me to do my job and still be safe?"

Khan, Magni, and I exchanged long solemn glances and then Khan spoke. "As you might know, we do have a few women here. My brother..." He waved his hand to Magni, who was standing by the window with a grim expression on his face. "...has a female that he protects and I suppose in theory we could raise you up to the same position as her, which would make it safe for you to work."

"That would be great, what kind of job does she have?"

A snort came from Magni, and I knew he found the idea of his wife working ridiculous.

Khan's smile stiffened "No, our women don't work. Life is made easy for them because we cherish them a great deal."

Christina didn't look impressed. "Really? Then what does she do all day?"

Khan turned to his brother. "I'm not sure exactly. Do you know?"

Magni wrinkled his forehead like he had just been asked a hard mathematical question that needed critical thinking. "Ehh, I believe she does creative things," he said.

"What kind of creative things?" Christina asked.

"Ehh, paintings and dancing, and that sort of thing."

"Can she walk around freely?"

"Yes," Khan lied.

"What is her name?"

"Laura," Magni said quickly.

"And what position does Laura hold exactly?" Christina asked Magni.

"She's my..."

Khan interrupted his brother. "She's his responsibility. Which means she holds the highest position a woman can have in our society. She's what we like to call 'a protected woman.'"

There was a thoughtful expression on her face.

"I see," Khan said slowly. "You thought we mistreated women, didn't you?"

"Well, I..." she trailed off.

"Laura *chose* my brother as her protector. It was entirely her choice," Khan assured her. "You see, the way it works is that the few women who are born in our part of the world are treasured by all men, and when they reach their eighteenth year we celebrate them with a big ceremony where the woman chooses her protector among the strongest and bravest of our men."

"Do you have a female you protect?" Christina asked Khan.

"No." He shifted his balance and pinned his dark eyes on her. "I never participate in those selections – it wouldn't be fair to my men, as my title alone would make every woman choose me."

The skeptical expression on Christina's face made me wish I could read her mind.

"So, what are you suggesting?" she asked.

"That you choose a protector for yourself so we can get you to work." He smiled innocently.

"Fine." She nodded and turned her head to look straight at me. "I choose you then?"

Flames shot up my spine and I felt a little dizzy but Khan chuckled and drew back her attention. "I'm afraid it's not that easy. I can't just announce that you've chosen Boulder. Other men would complain that they didn't get a chance to prove themselves worthy. There needs to be a ceremony."

Biting her lip, Christina's eyes darted around the room. "And how long will this ceremony take?"

"A few days at least."

"A few days? Why that long?"

"Because this sort of thing needs preparation and it takes time for the men to prove themselves."

Christina sighed. "And how exactly do they do that?"

"They fight," he said matter-of-factly and pointed to me. "Boulder, I appoint you as her temporary protector. Make sure she's comfortable and safe," he said and got up to leave.

"Wait a minute, I don't want anyone to fight over me," she objected and got up from her seat.

Khan turned to face her with his brows dropped low. "How else would you know which man is the strongest and who will be most suited to keep you safe?"

"But they're not really going to hurt each other, are they?" Her eyes darted between all three of us.

"Of course they are." Khan and Magni were leaving but on their way out Khan threw over his shoulder, "We're not boys, Christina, we're *men*."

When the door closed behind them she turned to me. "What is that supposed to mean?"

"It means that the games are bloody," I said dryly.

"But surely there must be a non-violent way to settle this small detail."

I didn't tell her that it was no small detail when a woman chose her husband; it was better to leave that out. Clearly Khan didn't want her to have the full picture of what choosing a protector meant.

"Have you ever participated?" she asked me.

I didn't answer.

"Will you do it this time?"

Something was pulling at me. "Would you like me to?" I asked.

She played with the tip of her braid and looked thoughtful. "I don't want you to get hurt or anything, but I wouldn't mind you protecting me. You seem big and strong."

It felt good to hear her say that but I knew she didn't fully comprehend what she was asking of me.

"I'll consider it," I told her, but in reality, I'd already made up my mind. If there was a chance I could marry her, it would give me immense status and I would fight hard for the privilege.

"Thank you," she said softly. "And if you decide to participate, make sure you win quickly because I'm eager to get this nonsense over with so I can get to work."

"Of course."

"Boulder, can you take me to see the digging site today?"

"No."

"Tomorrow?"

"Possibly. Once Khan has made the announcement and everyone knows they'll have a fair chance at winning your favor, I can take you outside."

"And until then?"

"We stay in this room."

"But what are we supposed to do here?" she asked.

A dirty idea came to mind, but I pushed it away and instead I asked, "Can you read?"

"Of course, I can read. Everyone can read in the Motherlands, and I already told you I'm a professor in history."

"Then maybe you would enjoy a book." I opened a cabinet to reveal four shelves with old books.

Her eyes immediately lit up and she came closer, looking positively giddy. "You have antique books here?"

"Yes,

"Any from the late nineteen-hundreds?"

"I don't know – let's see." I was just about to pick out a book when she gave a small shriek.

"Don't touch them."

"Why not?" I asked.

"Are your hands clean? If those books are centuries old they should be handled with extreme care." She turned around and headed for her luggage. "Hang on, I have gloves you can use."

"Gloves?" I shook my head. "It's just books. I'm not going to wear gloves." To demonstrate that I was serious I pulled a stack of books down from the shelves. "Let's see what we have here."

Christina puffed out a loud sigh but gave in and came back to see me put the seven books down on the table.

"Oh, I actually read that one," I pointed to a book with a warship on the front. "It's a Second World War story and there's a lot of violence in it. I liked it."

Christina's fingers gently touched the cover of a book with a woman sandwiched between two men who were kissing her shoulder and neck. All three were topless.

"These books are forbidden," she whispered.

"No, they're not."

She looked up at me with tension written on her face. "They are books of passion and violence."

"Uh-huh." I'd picked another book up with a soldier in full uniform who was holding a woman in his arms. "So?"

It was as if a panic grabbed Christina and she gathered all the books to put them back. "We shouldn't be reading any of them. They're dangerous."

"What the hell are you talking about?" I asked, annoyed, when she grabbed the book from my hands. "Hey, that one looked interesting. The back said it was steamy; I like steamy."

"I'm sorry, but it's better if we pretend we didn't see them."

"You can pretend all you want," I said and moved her out of my way to get the book I'd been looking at. "But if I'm going to be stuck in a room with you all day, I need something to distract me."

"Are you really going to read that?" she asked.

"Yes, I am," I said and sat down.

"Well, lucky for me, I brought suitable reading material so I won't be poisoning my mind with those books."

"Suit yourself," I said and opened the book.

Christina

I didn't want to sit next to Boulder so I took a seat on the bed and waited for it to fit around me, offering me support.

My reader was in my handbag; I put it on like a pair of glasses, activating the library by pushing a button on the side and navigating by looking left, right, up, down and blinking. The book I was currently reading came up in my field of vision and I started chapter nine.

"What are you reading?" Boulder asked me after about forty minutes.

"A historical tragedy about five sisters living in the early nineteenth century. They were oppressed by society, unable to inherit from their father, and threatened with the prospects of poverty if they didn't marry. It's really a very sad story."

"What's it called?"

"*Pride and Prejudice* by an author called Jane Austen."

"Oh, okay, you want to know what I'm reading?"

When I didn't answer him, he suggested, "How about you read me something from your book and I read you something from mine?"

Minimizing my book in the lower right corner, I saw him clearly and felt provoked by his smug smile. "You think the content of your book will shock me," I said. "But I'll have you know that in my work I've seen many shocking things. I'm not an innocent, you know."

"Define innocent."

I removed my glasses. "I've heard and seen things."

"Such as?"

I raised my chin, meeting his piercing gray eyes full on. "Such as secrets things and secret words."

Boulder's smile grew wider. "You've got to be more specific than that."

"Okay," I smoothed the sheet underneath me with my hands. "The words you use... the curse words. I have seen them in historical texts and one time..."

"Yes?"

"One time I was allowed access to the forbidden part of the University's library. I saw things from the department of violence that gave me nightmares for months."

"Like what."

"Killings, torture, terrorist attacks, men and women being beaten, children hit by their own parents." I looked down "And the worst part was the sexual violence."

"Tell me about the sexual violence."

"It was awful. Did you know that the old Internet was full of disgusting videos of people having sex? It was called pornography and for the most part it was males being aggressive to women. I saw a clip with a woman who submitted herself to three men at the same time, and some of them smacked her and called her vile names."

"I know porn, we have it here," he said unapologetically. "Did the woman in the video like it?"

Horrified that he could be so misguided as to think violence in any sort could be enjoyable, I gave him a disapproving glance. "What kind of question is that? How would you like it if people smacked you and called you vile names?"

"I've heard that some women like that," he expostulated.

"You're out of your mind. I've never heard of a woman who likes to be treated like that. It's unnatural."

58

"Are you sure? This book tells a different story, and it's written by a woman. Listen to this," he started reading and I knew I should have stopped him, but my curiosity got the better of me.

"He pinned me down and forced my thighs apart with his knees. 'I told you not to wear that short dress and yet you did. Are you asking to be punished?' he whispered against my ear in a raw masculine voice.

"'No,' I lied, because the truth was that I loved it when he dominated me. The sound of the first smack hitting my butt send shivers down my spine. It didn't hurt much but it excited me to be in his control.

"'Are you going to be a good girl and do as you're told?' he asked in a raw voice.

"'Yes,' I gasped and felt moist heat between my thighs. I was longing to feel his hard cock inside me."

With my heart pounding and my cheeks flushed, I stopped Boulder. "That's enough!"

"Are you sure? Because the good part is just about to start," Boulder teased with a small grin.

"I'm sure!"

"So what do you think?" he asked. "Do women enjoy being dominated or was the author just making it up?"

"Oh, that part is complete fiction. I'm a woman and I can assure you that I know plenty of men and I've *never* felt aroused by any of them. And I can tell you with absolute certainty that should one have the nerve to smack me, I would report him instantly."

Boulder tilted his head with interest. "You've never been aroused by a man?"

"No, never. I think it's a myth."

"What is?"

"The notion that men bring out arousal in women. I know some women claim to feel that way, but it has never happened to me."

"So are you saying you wouldn't be interested in having sex with me if I offered it?" he asked with an innocent smile that quickly grew into a belly-deep laugh.

"What's so funny?"

"You should see yourself. You look like you swallowed a swarm of flies."

"No, I don't," I defended myself, aware that my cheeks were flushed just from the images his questions had inspired in my mind.

"So is that a no?" he asked and winked at me.

"I can't believe you asked me that. Of course, I wouldn't want to have sex with you."

"Because I'm a man of the Northlands?"

Confirming that would be insulting, and I was trained to always choose the considerate answer. "No, that's not why. It's just the whole idea of having sex with a person. It's unhygienic."

"Unhygienic? It should be the most natural thing in the world. People used to have sex all the time."

"And they got sick from all sorts of horrible sexually transmitted diseases," I pointed out. "Sex-bots are a much safer and hygienic solution if you have a physical need."

Boulder shrugged. "I don't know. I would love to know what it feels like to be with a real woman. I've heard there's a big difference."

I couldn't look him in the eye, and felt flustered by the direction this conversation had taken and from the way he sat leisurely on the couch with his thighs slightly spread and his hand resting above his crotch holding the book.

Images from what I'd seen in the forbidden part of the library came to mind, and I wondered if he was anatomically as big down there as he was tall and broad-shouldered.

"I'm not curious at all," I said firmly.

"What a shame," was his only reply before he went back to reading.

CHAPTER 8
The Games

Boulder

We hadn't had a marital ceremony in our area in three years. There had been one big ceremony on the East Coast last year that had attracted thousands of men when Laura and her twin had selected their mates.

The excitement that a woman from the Motherland had come to The Northlands to marry one of us made headlines, and the whole country was buzzing with rumors. Some news sites speculated that women had finally seen the light and soon more brides would follow.

Other more radical theories speculated that women would soon submit to men again and that every Northman would be allowed to have as many as four wives per man.

I worried about what was going to happen when Christina realized that men would be killing each other to prove themselves to her and that she would be forced to marry one of the five winners.

Following my orders from Khan, I stayed with her for two full days and was only replaced by guards when I needed to shower or use the bathroom.

During the night, I pushed the sofa in front of the door and slept on it.

During the day, Christina and I read, walked in circles, and talked a lot. I was as curious about her part of the world as she was about mine.

The things she had heard about us had me shaking my head, and on the last night before the games we had a long talk that started off fine but ended in a big mess.

"Someone seriously thinks we're fucking cannibals?"

"Yes, and murderers and rapists," she said.

"Wow, but I guess it makes sense that people as distorted as you would think that. After all, you're enslaving people and prohibiting free thought.

"Not free thought, only free speech."

"But free speech is important, don't you think?" I argued.

"Not if it's hurtful. Our rules are meant to protect people's feelings. It's best if everyone is kind and caring."

I laughed hard at that statement and asked: "So you would rather have people be kind to you than honest?"

She creased her brow. "Yes, I suppose so."

"That's stupid. Sometimes you've just got to call out people's bullshit."

"You can set your personal boundaries without being unpleasant," she argued.

"Nah, I'm the opposite. My friends can call me an ass and I wouldn't be offended by it. It's how we interact. I call them names and they call me names, it's almost a sign of affection."

"Impossible! How can offending someone be a sign of affection?" she asked.

"I don't know, I never gave it much thought. It's just how things are done around here. I mean we call Magni asshat all the time, and mostly because we're jealous of him."

"Why are you jealous?"

"That's not important; my point is, we call him asshat and he calls us something nasty back."

"Are you saying that no man can insult another man?" she asked.

"Of course they can." I smiled. "And if you ask me, some men are whiners that get too easily offended. Trust me, there are plenty of ways to piss off a man."

She tilted her head and looked intrigued. "Like what? Help me understand how men feel insulted."

I shrugged and scratched my arm, before brushing my hair out of my eyes. "Most of all it depends on the situation and the tone. If we're friends we can get away with most anything, but if someone is getting on my nerves I can tell him things like: you're such a pussy, grow a pair of balls, suck my dick, stupid faggot, are you gonna cry like a little girl? Or I can tell him you're so fucking irrational I suspect you have a vagina."

"Wow," Christina raised her eyebrows, "I see the common denominator here. So basically, to insult a man you have to accuse him of being feminine?"

I thought about it and leaned back against the cabinet behind me. "Hmm, I suppose that's true."

"Because women are weak and less than men?" she asked and started pacing the floor in front of me.

"Of course, everyone knows that," I answered honestly.

"Then why am I here? Why did you ask the Motherlands for help if you're all so superior to us?"

"We didn't ask for *you.* We asked for a male archeologist because we don't have enough."

Her pacing intensified and she was now using her hands to underline her words. "Not only have women brought back more than two hundred species that went extinct when *men* almost killed off the entire planet, but we have found ways to clean up massive areas of land, we've regrown sixty-seven percent of the corals and cleaned up substantial parts of the ocean, utilizing all the plastic waste to create energy. We have invented ways for obese people to donate fat to underweight people and eradicated cancer and other awful diseases, not to mention that we have kept peace on earth for close to four hundred years."

I looked at her, waiting for her to make her point.

"Yet you're saying that you would be offended to be compared to a woman?" she asked.

"Of course I would. Women are too soft and emotional. You don't think rationally and you're suffocating people with your radical kindness shit. Men need to swear and fight, it's in our nature."

"I strongly disagree," she said and placed both hands on her hips. "On our side of the border millions of men live wonderful lives without being violent or foulmouthed. They appreciate the feminine values and live in peace and harmony." Her curly hair was breaking free from her braid and framing her pretty face with those fascinating mismatched eyes.

I got close to her and pointed my finger. "No, Christina, you're wrong. What you have aren't *men*. They're a gender-neutral group of pussies who're afraid of standing up to the women, and they're just waiting for the right man to come along and spark their flame. Trust me, men *will* take back power, it's just a matter of time."

She looked shaken by my sneering and her voice was a bit high-pitched. "Is that what you want, Boulder? To have men back in power when you know how close we came to absolute annihilation?"

"We've done much to clean up our lands too," I said to avoid answering her direct question. "You're not the only ones who made strides to restore the earth."

"Is that right?"

"Yeah," I said and squared my shoulders.

"Interesting – because as I see it, while we've been restoring extinct animals, you've been hunting and killing bears, wolves, and other animals that live here?"

"We have." I nodded.

She narrowed her eyes. "And how is that helping them, exactly?"

I threw my hands up in the air and huffed out air. The woman was impossible and didn't understand anything about our lifestyle. "We're done!" I said and walked away.

65

"Yes, I can see how it would be difficult for you to defend killing," she called after me.

That made me whip my head in her direction, giving her a hard stare and lowering my voice. "I will kill anyone who tries to hurt you. Do I need to defend that too?"

That shut her up.

Christina

My hours with Alexander Boulder were insanely interesting because he gave me answers to things I had always been curious about. He taught me about the way Nmen live, their training as boys, and their strict hierarchies.

"So you arrived here when you were three?" I asked and looked over at his big shape in the supporter. We had something similar at home, and they were very comfortable to sit and lie in with the way the supporter formed around you.

Boulder stretched lazily and turned his head to look at me. "We all arrive when we're three, except of course for the few who are born here. The rest of us are born in Momsiland but fortunate enough to be shipped here and trained as *real* men."

I ignored that last ignorant comment and fired more questions at him while I sank to the floor and crossed my legs in front of me. "And then what? Who raised you? Do you go to school and what happens after school is over?"

"We grow up in schools with other boys and we live there until we're eighteen."

"What? In the same place?"

"No, we go through different schools depending on age and skill set."

"What do you mean, skill set?"

He smiled. "I've never talked about this, since we all do it and understand it. I'm not sure I'm good at explaining it, but from the time we're three to ten we live in one school. After that we move on to the next one, where we stay until we're fifteen."

"Okay."

"At fifteen we take the test."

"What test?"

"It's designed to assess our strengths and weaknesses. It's a week long and every day the focus is on something different. Like one day it's physical to show our speed, strength, and agility. The next day it's academics, and we're tested in everything we've learned in school. The third day is strategy, so we play war games and chess."

He looked up. "Or maybe strategy was day four and teamwork was day three – I can't remember – but anyway, you get the point, right?"

"Yeah, you get a lot of tests."

"Uh-huh, and depending on how well you do on the tests you'll be transferred to what is the right place for you. I excelled in two areas and had to choose one of them, so in the end I went to the business academy because I had a knack for finances."

"What was the other area you excelled in?"

"Physical strength and agility. That's why I'm a good fighter."

"I see. But then what happens when you're eighteen?"

"We go out to get jobs and build our future. I was lucky that a man named Henry hired me right out of the academy. He was a grumpy old asshole, but he taught me everything about running successful companies and in his own way he cared for me."

"By being grumpy?"

"No, by letting me work hard and earn what I have today. I busted my ass for the company, and it paid off and made me a rich man. Of course, it helped that he left everything to me when he passed away five years ago."

"Why would he do that?" I asked.

"It's common for a man to leave his belongings to his favorite. Some spread it out, but Henry chose me and it surprised me as much as everyone else."

"Are you're saying that the Northlands still run on a monetary system and you have poor and rich people."

"Yes."

I thought that terribly old-fashioned and primitive but didn't tell him that.

"What about you?" he asked. "You have a mother, right?"

"I do. We all do, but to be honest my mother is..." I hesitated, unsure how to describe Louise. "Flighty."

"Flighty?"

"Yes. She's a traveler, always on the move with some new intriguing idea to explore. It's a wonder she stayed for twelve years in the parenting unit to raise me. I don't think she's stayed in one place for more than a year since then. Right now she's down somewhere south restoring chorales, and last year she mentored youth on the east coast, and before that..." I sighed. "The list is so long."

Boulder scratched his nose. "How often do you see her?"

"It's been three years – no, actually four, I think." I shrugged. "It's fine. My mom is a wonderful person and I love her. She's sweet, and hugs and kisses me constantly when we're together, but she's just a restless spirit who wants to make the most of her life."

"But if you were only twelve when she left who took care of you?"

"Oh, we all grow up in parenting units so there were always other parents I could go to. There were twelve adults and twenty-two children in my unit when I left, but a parenting unit is an organic thing where people move in and out as the children grow up. Although, Ketti joined when she was twenty and was still living there at seventy-five."

"How many kids did this Ketti have?" Boulder asked and cleared his throat.

"Ketti had seven; she was a peacekeeper, so she only got to keep the girls."

"A peace keeper?"

"Yes, the women who carry and raise the boys that come here. Your mother was a peacekeeper. It's considered a great sacrifice and they are honored among us."

"Wow – my mom was a peacekeeper." Boulder tasted the word. "I like that."

"Yeah, well, anyway, Ketti stayed in the parenting unit even after her own children moved out and she took care of me and other children as well. It's good for kids to be surrounded by adults of all ages."

"Okay." Boulder lifted his shoulders in a shrug signaling that he wouldn't know.

"And in a parenting unit there's always someone who has time for you."

"That's nice. So do you see any of the other parents?"

I drew in a deep breath. "No. I want to, but the thing is that the parenting unit I grew up in is located in a small area of old South Africa. There's a pocket of land still habitable but the quality of life is low, and I couldn't study to be an archeologist there, so I moved a long time ago."

"Have you been back?"

"Once." I looked away.

"And?"

"And I told you: people move in and out of the parenting units, and most of the adults I knew were gone."

"Was Ketti gone?"

"Ketti was there." A lovely memory of her embracing me filled my heart and I laughed. "She tried to convince me to stay and have children of my own."

"And?"

I waved my hands. "I was twenty-four and nowhere near ready, and if I'm ever to have children I would want to have them somewhere else. You know, closer to where my work and my friends are."

Boulder nodded.

We had many more interesting conversations, and he was surprisingly well informed about the world. But unfortunately, his perception of the Motherlands was all wrong. He confused our kindness with oppressiveness and he classified our men's gentleness as being submissive to women.

There were moments when I almost raised my voice at him. Like when he insisted that women were supposed to be protected because we were fragile and inferior to men. Although I suspected he wouldn't report me for improper use of language, I was determined not to lower myself to his level and use strong words that were hurtful and forbidden, but a few inappropriate phrases passed through my mind when we discussed their way of living versus ours.

Since I arrived, there had been several times when I'd felt frightened. Especially on the first day, when Boulder first locked me in and shortly after stormed in with Khan and Magni. One giant of their size was intimidating enough, but to have three of them intensely staring at me at the same time had made me almost pee my pants.

Magni was the tallest of the three and the one that scared me the most. Unlike Khan and Boulder he kept his long hair tied in a hairband; probably to show off the tattoo running up his neck. I thought it was hideous and made him look like a prehistoric Viking. And it was strange to me that Magni and Khan were brothers, since

Magni was dark blonde with blue eyes and Khan was his opposite. Khan's hair color was pitch black, his eyes were a deep brown, and his skin was either tanned or naturally brown. I wondered if the title "brother" was an honorary title because, except for the fact that they were both tall and strong, they didn't share any similarities in looks.

But it wasn't just Magni that had scared me. When nighttime came, Boulder had barricaded the door by pushing the sofa in front of it, practically trapping me inside with him. My heart had been pounding like a woodpecker in my chest, fearful that he would take advantage of the situation and thinking of ways I could defend myself if he did. To be honest, I hardly slept at all that first night, but to my relief, he kept his distance and never touched me.

I kept asking to meet Laura, the woman Khan had mentioned that Magni was protecting. For some reason, she was never available and I quickly suspected that the men were making up excuses. It annoyed me since I had questions for her and would love to hear how she had experienced the ceremony where she chose Magni as her protector.

On the second morning, Boulder agreed to take me to see the area that I was here to excavate. We left before sunrise in order to avoid people. And just as on the day he brought me from the border, he flew himself. I was pretty sure the ten-minute ride in his hybrid as he called the drone would have taken much longer in one of the safety regulated drones that I was used to from back home.

When we reached the destination, it was everything I had dreamed it would be. Like a child in an amusement park I wanted to get my tools and get started right away, but Boulder insisted on a short visit, and so we returned to the manor after only an hour in the early morning sun.

"Tomorrow, you can be outside all day," he assured me, and he was right.

On the third day, the games started and I was told they were happening simultaneously in cities around the Northlands. It frustrated me that it was necessary and that I couldn't just be appointed a bodyguard without all this unnecessary nonsense.

Khan excitedly told me he was happy to get the chance to host a tournament and that it had been years since the last one was held in this area. "It's good for the men's morale," he told me.

"I don't understand why anyone would go through this much trouble to become a bodyguard," I responded. "Wouldn't it be better if the men collectively decided to quit the fighting and just let me do my job? The sooner I can get to it, the sooner we can all have answers and I can return back home."

"In theory that sounds good, but in real life things work differently here," Khan stated and left it at that.

The first fight I witnessed made me almost sick. It was like witnessing something from the medieval days when two men stepped shirt-less into an arena and fought like their lives depended on it.

I stood on the balcony of the Gray Mansion. With Boulder on my right side, Khan in front of me, and Magni on my left side, I was caged in and had to peek around Khan to see anything. The lovely park had an amphitheater, much like the Romans used to have, and it was cleverly designed so that the mansion created a backdrop for the audience and the large balcony we stood on had an excellent view of the performance.

I counted twelve hundred seats and all were occupied, with more men walking around the park or trying to get in.

Khan, Magni, and Boulder were commenting as two savage-looking males entered the arena and the audience cheered.

It all went incredibly fast when one of the men attacked the other and the fight broke out. Shocked by the violence, I gave a loud scream, but the roars from the pumped males overshadowed my cry.

Horrified, I looked up at Boulder. His eyes were fixed on the game and shone with excitement. Magni shouted a loud "Hell yeah" and Khan was laughing.

"You've got to stop this," I pleaded and pulled at Khan to make him turn and face me.

"What did you say?" He laughed.

"Someone is going to get hurt, you've got to stop this," I pleaded again.

He dismissively waved a hand at me. "It's amazing. Look how alive they are. Look at the audience. I've missed this rush of excitement; I think we all have." With an elbow to his brother's ribs, Khan grinned. "We should have these games more often."

Magni nodded but didn't take his eyes off the fight.

I couldn't look when one of the men forced the other to the ground and choked him with a knee to his throat.

Even from this distance I could tell the man on the ground was dying. His eyes bulged out, his face was redder than a ripe cherry, and he couldn't breathe. When he clapped the ground and the attacker pulled back, loud "boos" erupted from the audience.

"Why are they making that noise?" I asked.

Boulder looked down at me. "Because he surrendered."

"He didn't have a choice. That man was killing him," I argued.

"There's always a choice," Magni stated dryly.

"I don't understand."

"He could have chosen *not* to surrender."

"And died for it?" I asked incredulously, receiving nothing more than a shrug from the men.

"Boulder," I exclaimed and placed a hand on his arm.

73

He looked down at my hand and back to my eyes. "What?"

"I don't want you to fight!"

That made all three men turn their full attention on me.

"Why not?" Boulder said, his face hardening.

"You could get hurt, and I don't want anyone to bleed because of me or worse, get killed. How could I live with myself if you died?"

The men exchanged glances and then Boulder pulled me back inside the manor, where it was easier to talk.

"Look, you don't understand. It's really not just about you."

"It's not?"

"No, we've been trained to fight all our lives and this is our chance to move up in rank. We fight for prestige, for power, and for honor."

"Then why do I have to be dragged into it?"

"I told you: the highest honor is to protect a woman, and that means you've provided us with a grand prize."

"But this makes no sense. I'm only going to be here for a few months and protecting me would be a boring job. I'm going to be at the digging site from sunrise to sunset. Don't these people have jobs to go to?"

"Yes, of course."

I rubbed my face. "Then how are they supposed to protect me? Do they know it's just a temporary job? I've seen the guards at this mansion – why can't one of them protect me?"

Boulder looked back to the loud roars.

"This is Khan's plan; you'll have to ask him."

I never got the chance because I was distracted when a woman walked in.

She was young and stopped when she saw me, her eyes expanding in surprise.

74

"May peace surround you," I greeted her, encouraging her to come closer.

"Magni," Boulder called and opened the balcony door.

"What?" The large male looked back over his shoulder and was about to turn his attention back to the games when he did a double take. "Oh!" he exclaimed at the sight of the woman and hurried toward her. "Laura, I thought I asked you to stay in your room."

Her eyes darted between Magni and me. "Who is she?" she asked, telling me that I'd been right. They were trying to keep us apart.

"My name is Christina," I said and got in front of Magni to take her hand. "I asked to meet you several times."

"You did?" she asked with a look of confusion.

"Yes, Khan mentioned you, and I've been eager to meet you and ask you some questions."

"Now isn't the best time," Magni interjected and whisked Laura away with an arm around her, leading her out of the room.

She was looking back and almost running to keep up with him, her long ginger-colored hair falling down her back in soft waves. My eyes narrowed when I turned around to confront Boulder and Khan, who were now inside as well. "What is going on? Why isn't she allowed to speak to me?"

"I don't know what gave you that idea," Khan said innocently while Boulder looked away. "Please forgive my brother for being a bit overprotective of her, but with all the men in the area he prefers that she stays in her room."

"Fine, then I'll go and talk with her in her room." I started walking in the direction they had disappeared.

"Wonderful, but could you wait just a few minutes?" Khan called when I had almost reached the doorway. "I was just about to present you to the crowd." He gestured to the balcony.

I stopped, unsure what to do. Boulder was quick to guide me with a hand on the small of my back, and a minute later I stood between the two large men on the balcony.

Khan fished out a small device from his pocket and handed it to Boulder.

"Are you ready?" he asked me but didn't wait for my reply before he nodded to Boulder, who tapped the round thing and cleared his throat. The sound of his deep voice resounded loud and clear all over the park and arena, making the masses look up to the balcony.

"Men of the Northlands, hear this message from your ruler, Khan Aurelius."

Boulder stood with his back straight and a look of importance. "Men of the Northlands," he repeated and complete silence fell upon the park.

Nervous energy surged through my body as I witnessed Boulder hand the small device back to Khan, who calmly placed it on his leather shirt.

"What a blessed day to be meeting and fighting," Khan started and cheers broke out.

"It is my great honor to introduce you all to Christina Sanders, who has joined us from the Motherlands."

My legs started shaking when Khan pushed me forward. We were on the second floor with all their faces looking up at me some of them smiling, others looking more like hunters watching their prey. It frightened me, and deep down I knew what I saw in their faces was connected to something sexual.

Taking a step back, I was stopped by a wall of a chest behind me when Boulder made sure I stayed visible to the men while Khan spoke.

"Tomorrow night, when the five winners have been selected, Christina will make her choice of champion. The ultimate winner shall be honored with the title of Protector and receive a bonus of one million dollars."

The crowd erupted in wild cheering and Boulder released his hold on me. I immediately hurried back inside to get away from the unwanted attention.

"One million dollars?" I asked accusingly when Boulder followed me inside. Khan was still waving from the balcony to his people.

I brushed my hair back, feeling my hands shake. "Why would you pay someone one million dollars to be my bodyguard?"

"The man you pick wins honor, status, and financial freedom."

"So that's why they risk their lives?"

"Yes," he confirmed. "I'll be fighting in half an hour and I would be honored if you'll cheer me on."

"No, Boulder, don't – what if you get hurt?"

He drew his brows closely together. "Why do you think I was picked to protect you in the first place? I'm a good fighter." His gray eyes locked with mine. "You asked me to fight for you."

"Yes," I said, finding it hard to breathe with his intense gazing into my eyes. He looked fierce with his long hair pulled back and his broad shoulders visible in a tank top that revealed he had several tattoos on his shoulders.

"Christina, you asked me to protect you."

"Yes, but..."

"Then stay with Khan and watch; I must prepare for my fight." With those words, Boulder left us.

CHAPTER 9
Powerful Words

Boulder

My first opponent was no match for me, and I took him out in mere minutes. I hardly broke a sweat and went back to my duty of protecting Christina, receiving a pat on the shoulder from Khan, who was delighted by the whole thing.

I fought my second match the next morning, facing a young, aggressive male who made the mistake of overestimating his own speed. I took him out in less than five minutes too.

My third opponent wasn't much harder and it didn't surprise me, since I always suspected that Khan had influenced the games to make sure the right people went all the way.

In the end, I stood opposite, Nelson, a man around forty who had a fierce reputation of making his opponents suffer painfully before killing them. I remembered him from when I was a teenager and our paths had crossed. Being six years my senior, he had once trained me and my peers, and I would never forget the way he did it. The man was a sadistic asshole who had tortured us in the woods for weeks. I raised my head, searching out Khan on the balcony with Christina and Magni by his side. The expression on Khan's face told me it was no coincidence that Nelson was my opponent. I had told Khan about my experience as a young man and he was giving me the chance to get my revenge.

In an exaggerated gesture, Nelson bowed to Khan and blew Christina a kiss. That last part made my insides twist in a knot. I'd spent three days with Christina and my view on women would never be the same. She might be naïve, small, fragile, sensitive, and easily rattled, but she was also intelligent, sweet, and innocent, and there was no way I would ever allow a monster like Nelson to get close to her.

With revenge and protectiveness as my fuel, I stormed against him. He turned his head at the last minute and managed a surprised "The fuck?" before I knocked him to the ground.

The fight was dirty and brutal. The audience loved it and cheered in a blood rush as we fought like lions.

After getting in some really good punches, I thought I heard Christina scream my name and in the second it took for me to look up, Nelson had my left arm in his grip and wrenched it backward. Massive pain shot up my arm when it snapped and I knew it was broken.

"Which limb do you want me to break next?" he roared at me.

I managed to break free and move back, protecting my arm with my body. Nelson came at me again like a wild boar and I made a quick decision. Rolling my body to get under him, I swallowed the hellish pain of landing on my arm and managed to trip him over and get a hold of his hair with my right hand. Jerking his head back I swung my legs around his neck and squeezed.

Nelson was arching up and reaching back, but he couldn't get loose from my death grip, and his pounding on my hips only made me squeeze my knees tighter, completely suffocating him.

Roars of excitement rose from the audience, who were on their feet shouting for me to kill him. I waited for Nelson to pound the dirt, but he didn't. Foam was forming at his mouth and his facial color was almost blue. His hands were waving uncoordinated, slapping at me without force, and I knew it was a matter of seconds before he would pass out.

Among all the noise from the audience, I heard one plea in a high-pitched scream. "Have mercy."

I looked up to see Christina with both hands clasped in front of her face in a display of horror and cursing under my breath, I let go.

Nelson deserved to die, but Christina wouldn't understand that and I didn't want her to resent me. A few clapped because of my mercy, but most booed with disappointment.

As I walked away, medics came running to check on Nelson. I honestly couldn't care less if he lived or died, but supported my left hand with my right and cursed the motherfucker for breaking my arm.

Christina

I don't know what was worst – the brutality in front of me or the fact that the crowd encouraged it. Disgusted, I watched Khan, Magni, and the crowd beneath us cheer for Boulder to kill the man trapped between his legs.

My heart was racing so fast I felt close to a heart attack. This was madness and I had to do something. As loud as I could, I screamed for Boulder to show mercy, and received annoyed glances from both Magni and Khan.

"What did you do that for?" Khan asked me in irritation when Boulder released his opponent.

"I don't want Boulder to become a killer."

The way they both raised their brows made me suspect that he already was.

"Has he killed before?" I asked in a mere whisper because part of me didn't want to know.

Khan pursed his lips and seemed to consider his answer. "I'll let Boulder answer that question himself. For now, let's rejoice that the winners have all been selected and that tonight you'll be able to pick your champion."

"A shame about Boulder, though," Magni said distractedly and waved at someone he knew below.

"What about Boulder?" I asked.

"I think his arm broke. That means you only have four to pick from."

"Why?" I asked, slightly panicking. I was used to Boulder now and I didn't want some other big man in my room.

Magni shook his head at me. "Well, obviously, you can't choose a protector with a broken arm. That should be fucking obvious."

"But don't you have bone accelerators?"

"Yes, but it'll still take at least a week for him to heal."

I didn't respond to that but kept my questions for Boulder, who came to see me in my room after he had been seen by a doctor.

"How serious is it?" I asked with a nod to his arm.

His arm was covered in blue accelerator spray like the one we used back home.

"It's broken," he said grumpily.

"I'm sorry."

He shrugged. "It's not your fault."

"It feels like it is. Can you forgive me?" I asked with all the humbleness I'd been taught from an early age. "Although I did not directly cause you this injury, I fear it was my reckless decision to volunteer for this journey that led to the outcome and ultimately your suffering. You have my deepest apology." I bowed my head and waited for his forgiveness.

When nothing came, I looked up again.

"Are you done?" he asked, annoyed.

"Done?"

"Yeah, with that girly sensitivity shit. I fought a scumbag and he broke my arm. You had nothing to do with it and your apology only annoys the shit out of me."

"I'm sorry," I said, perplexed by his hostility.

81

"God damn it, Christina, I told you not to apologize. I swear, if you don't stop, I'll use my right hand to stuff your mouth."

"Stuff my mouth?" I gasped.

"Yeah, so I don't have to listen to your idiotic nonsense."

"I was trying to be nice."

Boulder rolled his eyes. "If you wanted to be nice you could have told me I fought bravely or that you appreciate me taking that fucking sadist out of the games so you won't end up with him."

"You think he was the sadist?" I asked. "You almost killed him."

"Of course. If I hadn't he would have killed me. And he would have enjoyed doing it by taking the time to break every bone in my body first."

My eyes teared up. "That's horrible. Someone like that should be detained and helped. Clearly he must have a personality disorder."

"Nah, he's just a mean motherfucker. He's also one of the highest-ranked police officials in the Northlands."

I was dumbfounded.

"What?" he asked

"Nothing, I just didn't know you still had a police force."

"Yes, of course. What do you have?"

"Mediators."

His raised eyebrows told me he wanted me to clarify.

"Mediators are specially trained to calm down people who are upset. If someone snaps and becomes violent, a team of mediators will quickly secure that person with non-violent methods and take them to a safe facility."

"Like a prison?"

"No, like a place of reflection. We don't have prisons, Boulder. Instead we have nice places that resemble hotels with green gardens and nice staff to help them find inner peace."

He snorted. "Of course you do, but can they leave?"

"No, not until they've been deemed harmless to themselves and others."

"So it's a prison disguised as a hotel?"

"It's a place of reflection," I insisted.

He scoffed and rolled his eyes again. "That's just a nice word for a mental institution."

I sighed over his obstinate attitude. "The point is, we don't have police officers."

"Because you're all a bunch of brainwashed bobbing heads living in fairyland."

"At least we don't kill each other for money," I said in a low hiss and instantly covered my mouth with both hands.

Boulder creased his brow and looked at my hands. "What's wrong?"

"I hissed at you," I said.

"So?"

"It's verbal aggression and should be avoided."

"Why?"

"Because it's hurtful and unnecessary."

Boulder shifted his balance from one foot to the other and huffed out air. "You know what your problem is?"

"What?" I asked and forgave him for being in such a foul mood; surely his broken arm was upsetting to him.

"You give away too much power."

"I beg your pardon."

"You worry about what you say and you get offended too easily. Hell, I can make you react just by using a swear word and that makes you vulnerable."

"I disagree. I'm an emotionally strong person, and I'm very good at setting my personal boundaries," I stated as calmly as I could.

"Bullshit. You're fragile as hell." He frowned and moved closer. "I wish I could protect you, but tonight you'll be in the company of another man and it will take him less than ten minutes to realize that he can confuse and upset you by using the right words. That makes you easy to manipulate, Christina."

I opened my mouth to speak but he cut me off. "Words only hold the power you allow them to. You know that people used to speak different languages in the world, right?"

"Of course,"

"So if I spoke a different language, I could call you a hideous cocksucker and you wouldn't be offended because you wouldn't understand."

My eyes expanded, but I understood his point. "But if I learned the meaning I would be deeply offended," I pointed out.

"Really?"

"Most certainly," I insisted.

"So let me ask you this." He looked around and pointed to the bed. "If I called you a bed, would you be offended?"

"No."

"Why not? I might mean it as an insult. It might be an inference that you're lazy or big and bulky."

I made a dismissive chuckle to lighten the mood. "I wouldn't be offended because I'm not a bed. That's just ridiculous."

"Did you ever suck a man's cock?"

"*No!*" I shrieked as my hand flew to my chest.

"Are you hideous?"

My cheeks were flaming red and I was losing my patience with him. "What are you trying to say?"

"You wouldn't get offended if I called you a bed, because you're *not* a bed. So why would you get offended if someone called you a hideous cocksucker, when you're *not*?"

"Those are horrible words."

"Yet, they're just words."

"Words hold power," I argued.

"True, but only the power you give them." He moved even closer and was in my personal space now. "Please, try to adapt, Christina. Don't give away your power so easily."

"I'm not giving away my power," I said, mostly to convince myself.

"Yes, you are. You're allowing me to use my words as weapons against you, and every man will figure out your weakness if you're not careful."

"Why are you telling me this?"

He sighed loudly. "Because it's the only thing I can do to protect you in some small measure."

"But you won your fight – you could still be my champion, couldn't you?"

Boulder scoffed again and this time it was a hoarse, pained sound. "A champion with a broken arm? I don't think so."

"But I've gotten used to you and you're…"

He waited for me to continue. His gray eyes locked on me. "I'm what?"

"Not *entirely* bad for an Nman."

"Thanks, I'll take that as a compliment," he said with a laugh that sounded bitter. "You're not entirely awful yourself… for a Momsi, that is."

After that, we didn't speak for more than an hour until a dress was brought to me.

"You need to put this on, and maybe you can do something about your hair too," Boulder instructed.

I thought about protesting, but the crimson dress was beautiful, like something from an old movie, and I secretly wanted to try it on. I went to the adjacent bathroom and smiled in the bathroom mirror at the sight of the silky material against my skin. Spinning, I watched my reflection in the mirror from all angles. The dress was sleeveless and went all the way to the floor following my natural curves, and with fabric thin enough to reveal the outlines of my half globes on the lower back and the upper front.

I undid my braid and sighed when my hair puffed out in all directions. And then I remembered my roommate, Kya, and how she was always proud of her voluminous hair. My big curly nougat-brown hair would have to do.

"What about shoes?" I asked when I stepped out from the bathroom.

Boulder looked up from the book he was reading and from the way his eyes grew big, I got the feeling that he thought me presentable enough.

He cleared his throat and moved in his seat. "Magni brought those." He pointed to the floor where two different pairs stood. "They belong to Laura, but maybe they'll fit you."

I moved closer and squatted down to look at the shoes. They were like something from a museum and had me smiling with glee. I'd always wanted to try on high-heeled shoes and now was my chance.

CHAPTER 10
Christina's Choice

Boulder

It was impossible not to stare!

In front of me on the floor sat a flesh and blood woman with nothing but a thin layer of silk between me and her nakedness. I don't think she was aware that when she bent down and leaned forward her dress shaped her ass perfectly.

Swallowing hard and fisting my hands, I told myself not to touch her, but everything about her lured me in. Her feminine scent was strong, her hair looked soft and inviting with the sexy curls falling down her back, and when she first walked out from the bathroom I had seen her from the front. Fuck! I knew she was pretty, but the woman was curved in all the right places and had the cutest freckles.

Next time I go to a sex-center I'm getting a sex-bot with freckles and curly brown hair, I thought to myself.

I watched in wonder as she tried on the shoes and I automatically moved forward to support her when she almost fell.

"They're much harder to walk in than they look," she said and held on to me.

My heart was pounding harder than when I fought that prick Nelson. It was her strong grip on my shoulder and the closeness between our bodies that was messing with my head. Any time now we would have to go down to the ceremony and she would marry another man.

The thought alone made it hard to breathe. I'd been so close to becoming her champion and protector – if only that fucking sack of shit hadn't broken my arm. A bit of rage welled up inside me and I regretted not killing him for coming between me and the chance to spend more time with Christina.

"Christina," I said in a solemn voice, and unsteady on her feet she turned her head and looked up at me, her hand still holding on to me.

"There's something I should explain to you before we go down."

"Yes?"

"It's just that, once you've chosen your champion, I can't speak to you unless he allows it."

"Why?"

"It's a rule that helps the protectors. Imagine if any man could strike up a conversation with you. It would be incredibly stressful for him to keep you safe from that much male interaction."

"But, you're the only friend I have here," she said, her voice dripping with sadness.

I closed my eyes and clenched my jaw, regretting even more that these were my last minutes with her. "I just want you to know that if I see you again and I don't look your way, it's not because I wish to ignore you. It's how things must be."

I was surprised to see Christina's eyes grow moist. "You'll ignore me?"

"I'll have to."

"But what if I speak to you?"

"You shouldn't," I said. "It would upset your… champion." I almost slipped and said husband and felt heat rise in my cheeks.

I wasn't sure how Khan thought this was going to go down peacefully. Christina would surely refuse to marry an Nman once she understood what Khan's plan was. And even if he somehow convinced her to go through with the ceremony, he couldn't keep her here against her will. The council would request her return to the Motherlands and most likely enforce strict sanctions on our trade if he failed to return her.

Had he informed the other winners of the games that the marriage was only temporary?

I didn't think so. In fact, I was convinced that every winner in that room was already planning their wedding night in detail.

It enraged me to think that Christina might be pressured into having sex against her will. There wasn't much I could do about it except maybe speak to the man she chose and ask him to go slow with her.

Christina blinked away her tears. "I'm sorry that I'm being emotional. I know you don't like that, but it's just that we've been together night and day for three days and I feel like I know you. That you're my friend."

An invisible iron band formed around my throat and I looked away, uncomfortable with the emotions she brought out in me. "I did my job and kept you safe; I'm glad you consider me a friend but I'm afraid this is where our friendship ends," I said, low.

"Can I hug you?" she asked with a sad expression and looked down on my arm. "I'll be careful."

My minuscule nod was all the encouragement she needed, and I forgot to breathe when she pressed herself against me, snaking her arms around my waist and placing her head against my shoulder.

Her hair tickled my nose but I slowly placed my right arm around her and took a second to enjoy my first hug with a woman, which was completely different from any hug I'd ever had with a man. Men's hugs were quick and often involved slapping on the shoulders or backs. This hug was warm and long.

Without releasing her arms around me she leaned her head back and looked up at me with those fascinating eyes of hers. "I'll never forget you, Alexander."

I don't know why she called me Alexander at that moment, when so far she had called me Boulder, but her closeness and my name on her lips made me act on instinct.

I leaned in and kissed her. She gasped and pulled back, her fingers shot to her lips, and her eyes filled with confusion.

"I shouldn't have done that," I said quickly to apologize, but we didn't get a chance to discuss it further when a knock on the door alerted us that it was time to go.

"Are you going to wear those shoes?" I asked to change her focus from the failed kiss.

She looked down and shook her head. "I would break an ankle before I made it down the stairs. They're beautiful but I can't wear them." She took them off and went to pick up her own flat shoes, which were simple in design and neutral with their charcoal gray color.

Christina

My head was still spinning from what had just happened between Boulder and me.

He had kissed me!

I'd never been kissed before.

At least not by a man and not on the mouth. My friends and I were huggers and would kiss each other's cheeks on occasion, but Boulder's kiss had been different and made my body buzz with confusion. My reaction had been to pull back immediately but in all honesty, the kiss hadn't been unpleasant.

I was on Boulder's right side when we walked into the arena. Maybe he was puffing himself up or walking taller than usual, because I'd never felt so small next to him as I did now. I was only a bit below the average height of women. Still, he was more than a head taller than me.

The white noise from the audience settled down as we came to stand in the middle where Khan and four other men waited for us.

My pulse raced and my eyes flickered around, taking in the huge audience of men and the four large males that had to be the other four winners.

Every one of them scared me, just like Boulder had scared me in the beginning too.

"Our games have successfully resulted in five winners," Khan said and faced the audience. "It is time for Christina Sanders to choose her champion."

It was stupid that I felt so nervous about picking my bodyguard, but the set-up of the whole thing was so over the top that it made the responsibility weigh heavily on my shoulders. The man I chose would get a higher rank and financial freedom – something these men had risked their lives for.

With all eyes on me, I cleared my throat and said. "I can't choose fairly, when I know nothing about these men. Am I allowed to ask them questions?"

Khan frowned. "No," he said, "but I'll allow them all to briefly present themselves."

I nodded and listened carefully when the first man stepped forward.

"I'm Napoleon and I supervise lumber-bots in the area called Old Alaska," he said.

"Okay, but you do understand that..." I started but was silenced by Khan.

"No questions," he said.

The next man stepped forward and it almost made me want to take a step back. He was badly bruised, with a big black eye and a crooked nose that looked like it had been broken more than once and never healed right. He presented himself as a mining engineer from somewhere – I had no idea where it was – and informed me that he was forty-two years old.

91

The third man was young and good-looking. His hair was nicely braided and he only had stubble instead of a full beard like most of the Nmen I'd seen. He even smiled at me when he stepped forward. "My name is Archer Rex and I'm twenty-eight years old. I'm a Mentor."

"What kind of mentor?" I asked quickly and after getting a nod from Khan, Archer explained.

"I teach boys in both academics and survival skills. My title is Mentor."

"Oh, like a teacher," I exclaimed.

The last man stepped forward and mumbled something I couldn't hear.

"Speak up," Khan ordered but the man pointed to his mouth and repeated something in a mumble.

"He broke his jaw. It's hard for him to speak," Archer, who stood closest to the man, translated.

I turned my head to meet Boulder's eyes, wondering why he stood by Khan's side instead of in the line of men. "And you?"

He shook his head. "I hardly need to introduce myself, and with a broken arm you don't want to choose me."

I gave him a long glance, silently asking if he was sure. Boulder's chest rose in a deep sigh and then he looked at Archer – giving me his answer.

I took a deep breath and studied Archer closer. He was the obvious choice: young, strong, and smiling.

"In that case I choose you," I said and pointed to the tall man.

Archer's fists flew in the air and he jumped with glee. "*Yes!!*"

Applause filled the air from the audience. I gave a last glance at Boulder and didn't like the way his head hung down.

"Congratulations," Khan told Archer and shook his hand. I figured this would be the place to greet the winner properly so I walked over and reached out my hands to him. He didn't take them but instead he grabbed me by my waist and lifted me in the air, carrying me around like a trophy.

"Let me down," I demanded and when he did I smiled stiffly at him. "I feel bad about taking you away from your students."

He shook his head. "Not at all, we'll go back tomorrow and you'll meet them all."

My smile vanished.

"That's not possible. I have a job to do and I need to get started right away."

He frowned. "A job?"

All the color left my face and I turned away from him, moving fast to face Khan. "Why does Archer think I'm going with him? And why does he not know about my job here? Did you not explain to him that he's merely my bodyguard?"

Khan looked down his nose at me with a smile I didn't like. "I'm afraid, I haven't been quite honest with Archer. After all, I expected you to pick Boulder. How was I to know he would break his arm?"

Archer had moved closer and asked, "What's wrong?"

With a hand in the air, Khan silenced the audience. "As you all know, this is a different ceremony than previous ones."

Absolute silence fell and I had my eyes fixed on Khan as he spoke.

"Normally the woman is born and raised among us – Christina Sanders is not.

"Another thing that is different about her is that she has a profession and she's here to do a job."

I scanned the audience when unease spread among them.

"Christina has chosen Archer to be her protector while she leads the excavation of an important archeological digging site. Now it's up to Archer if he'll take the money,

93

prestige, and stay to make sure she's safe while she works."

Archer looked furious "What kind of fuckery is this? I have obligations with my students and I was expecting to take my wife home tomorrow."

"Wife?" The word came out of me as a high-pitched scream and my head whipped from Khan to Archer and back, but Khan didn't look the least bit shaken.

"A champion is the woman's husband," he said, loud and clear. "It's the oldest tradition of keeping women safe in history. I'm sure I've mentioned that to you."

"No, you *never* mentioned the word *wife*," I forced out, feeling my heart run in circles of sheer panic.

He shrugged. "It's a minor detail really. The contract is still the same."

"What contract?"

"The marriage contract."

"I'm not marrying any man – *ever!*" I practically screamed.

The audience got up from their seats and were visibly upset about the situation.

Khan's hand went up again and it calmed them.

"No man here wants to marry a woman without her consent, so if you're adamant that you don't want a protector we'll have to respect that."

"I'm here to do my job and you said I needed a bodyguard," I accused him.

"That's true. It would be very dangerous for you to be here without protection. Still, it's your choice and you're free to leave anytime you want."

"What about the job?" I asked, my voice shaking.

"I already told you it would be impossible for you to work without having a Champion. No one here would touch a married woman – it's punishable by death."

The men on stage nodded in agreement.

"However, a single woman without protection… That's a completely different story."

I bit my lip and felt like exploding from the pressure inside me.

"Maybe you'll make it to the border, but I wouldn't count on it," Khan said with a calculating smile on his face.

"Are you saying I have to marry Archer or you'll send me back without protection?"

"Of course not. I already assigned Boulder to protect you, but he's one man with a broken arm and now that the whole country knows you're a single woman…" Khan trailed off and walked close to Boulder, who looked down. A pat on his shoulder and a sad smile from Khan came before he drove in the last nail in my coffin. "To be honest, I hope you won't ask Boulder to take you to the border because he'll surely die protecting you, and he's my friend."

I was shocked and enraged that I'd been lured into this trap. This was like choosing between jumping into a pool with one large crocodile or a pool with many. Either way I would be chewed up.

"And if I marry, what happens when I've finished my job? Can I still go home?"

Khan tilted his head. "Hopefully you'll want to stay, but I give you my word that if you want to leave after the excavation is finished, you can."

"What?" Archer exclaimed. "My wife can leave me?"

"I'm counting on you to make her want to stay," Khan responded.

Archer leaned forward crossing his arms. "And if she's already pregnant?"

I almost fainted then and there. Clearly this stranger was expecting us to have an old-fashioned marriage and not just a contract of protection.

Reacting on instinct, I ran straight into Boulder's arms with eyes full of fright. "I won't do it!" I repeated over and over.

He pushed me behind him and faced all the men, speaking loud and clear. "Christina will marry *me*!"

"No, she chose *me*," Archer shouted.

"And now that she understands what her choice involves she's changed her mind," Boulder roared.

"Christina," Khan called loudly.

I moved to Boulder's side but stayed very close. "Do you wish to marry Boulder instead of Archer?"

"Yes," I said quickly, trusting that Boulder would willingly let me go when I was done working and that he wouldn't expect anything sexual from me. We had spent three nights together without his touching me, after all.

Archer was cursing and objecting but Khan silenced him with a hard glance. "You are young, Archer, and I promise you this: Next time we have a tournament you don't even have to fight. You have a spot as one of the five winners and a chance of being selected."

"But that could take years."

"It won't, and to compensate you, Boulder will give you half of the prize money."

Archer was clearly frustrated but stepped back and left the arena when Khan announced that he would now be performing the ritual to unite Boulder and me.

I was numbed from the shock I was in. Boulder held my hand and guided me through the ceremony and before I knew it, we were declared man and wife.

Marriage, a tradition that had been outdated for hundreds of years because of its predatory nature toward women and yet here I was, married to Alexander Boulder, the first Nman I'd ever met.

I couldn't smile when Boulder picked me up and kissed me in front of a cheering audience!

CHAPTER 11

Laura

Christina

Boulder was wise enough to keep his distance and give me time to digest what had just happened. He complied when I asked him to take me back to my room and leave me alone.

Being in a haze, I was unsure if I should be furious, curious, or scared out of my mind.

Everything I had learned on my first year in college about the institution of marriage was coming back to me, and I kept hearing Kya tell me that I shouldn't go and that I would end up some man's property. I had wanted an adventure, but not *this* kind of adventure.

When a soft knock sounded on my door, I turned my back, unwilling to talk to any of the cunning Nmen who had tricked me.

"Hello," a soft voice called out and got my attention. A woman!

I pushed myself up on my elbows and turned my body to see her, and recognized Laura as she stood by the door with an insecure smile on her face.

"How are you doing?" she asked.

"I'm angry at Khan for tricking me," I said but waved her closer. "Did you sneak in here, or do they know you came?"

Laura looked pretty with her blue eyes, ginger-colored hair, and a blue dress that enhanced her slim waist. "Boulder asked Magni to let me come see you," she said and stopped next to my bed. "He's right outside your door."

"Who, Magni?"

"No, Boulder. He looks pissed."

I widened my eyes from her use of the P-word. It was such a contradiction to see such beauty and innocence and then hear such foul language. Patting the mattress, I encouraged her. "Please take a seat."

I waited for her to sit down before I continued. "I'm relieved to see a woman in this awful place. And obviously now I know why they kept us apart. Surely you would have warned me that they were planning to make me marry one of them."

"Why? Are you against the marriage? I don't understand."

My jaw dropped.

"What?" she asked, her brows drawing closely together.

"Why am I against marriage?" I didn't wait for her response, but answered the question myself. "Because it's a ridiculous old-fashioned thing that went out of fashion hundreds of years ago."

"It did?" Laura asked with great interest.

"Laura, sweetie, you grew up here so you have no idea, but in the Motherlands men are kind and gentle, not like these barbarians. And the women... we're all educated, and not one would ever marry a man."

"You wouldn't?"

"No. It's an antique way of thinking from back in the day when women needed men for protection, financial security, social standing, or procreation. Women don't need men for *anything* anymore."

"But who protects you then?"

"There's no crime in the Motherlands – we don't need protection."

"But being married isn't a bad thing. Is it because you don't like Boulder?" Laura asked and looked so young.

I ignored her question and asked my own. "I suppose this means that Magni is your husband then?"

She smiled vaguely. "Yes, I was lucky that he fought for me."

"Lucky?" I said incredulously.

"When he was one of the winners, I had no doubt that he was my first choice," Laura explained. "I think he's very handsome and I like his name. Did you know Magni was the name of Thor's son?"

"No."

"Among the old Norse gods, Magni was the god of strength."

"Really?" I shook my head. "I don't know, Laura, I think it's all a bit silly how they name their boys after heroes and gods."

Laura's eyebrows shot up. "But it was Erika, their mother, who named Khan and Magni."

"They have a mother?"

"Yes, they are some of the few who grew up with a mother. Erika is one of the ancestors of the original women, just like me."

"And Erika lives here?"

"Yes, she's been under the protection of Khan ever since her husband died, and she's very respected by all us women here."

"All? How many women are there?"

"Only she and I live here at the Gray Mansion. But there are other women in the area. The rest are spread out around the Northlands."

"Do you know exactly how many women live in the Northlands in total?"

She nodded. "Currently we're one hundred and seven." A smile erupted on her lips. "But Laila Michelle is pregnant and expecting a girl."

"Is she a friend of yours?" I asked.

"Yes, she's a close friend."

"But doesn't it seem strange to you that the males are all named after heroes and gods and the women..." I trailed off. "You're named ordinary names like Laura, Erika, and Michelle."

Laura bit her lip. "Actually, Erika means eternal ruler and my name means the favorable one. It comes from the old traditional in the Ancient Rome where they created victors' garlands from leaves of the laurel tree." She looked up as if thinking hard. "I can't remember what the meaning of Michelle is; I'll have to ask her."

"It's okay," I said and grabbed her hand, a more urgent question pressing on my chest. "Laura, what does marriage mean here?"

"What do you mean?" she asked.

"Well, I have no experience with marriage and I'm scared. Will he expect to have sex with me and if so will he demand to have me circumcised?"

"Circumcised?" Laura scrunched her face. "I don't know what that is."

"When part of your womanhood is cut off."

That only confused her more, so I chose to say it without a filter. "In parts of the world men used to refuse to marry a woman with her clitoris still intact. They considered her unclean, promiscuous, and they would suppress her sexual desire by cutting away her clitoris."

"How awful," Laura exclaimed.

"So, they don't do that here?"

"No!" She blinked her eyes. "I don't know why any man would think that way."

"But will he force me to have sex with him?"

"Probably. Magni and I had sex on our wedding night, that's normal."

"Did you resist him?"

"No, of course not. It's my duty as his wife, everyone knows that."

I paled and closed my eyes. "This can't be happening to me," I muttered.

"I'm sure he'll be gentle if you ask him," she said and squeezed my hand. It made me open my eyes and lock eyes with her.

"Tell me the truth, how awful is it?"

"The sex?" she asked and I gave a solemn nod preparing myself for the horrible truth.

"I like it."

"You *like* it?"

"Yes. It feels good."

I couldn't believe that she would actually say that, but I had to ask. "So he doesn't force you? You do it voluntarily?"

"Uh-huh. Sometimes I'm not in the mood, but once we get started it's nice."

My mind was exploding and I knew I had to change the subject away from sex. "And what about last names? Did you have to take his last name?"

"Of course. My maiden name was Laura Metz, but now I'm Laura Aurelius." She looked proud when she spoke the name and it made me shake my head in frustration.

"I'm not giving up my name. No way will I be Christina Boulder, that's just ridiculous."

"What's your last name?"

"My middle name is Sara and my last name is Sanders."

She tasted my name "Christina Sara Sanders. I like it."

"Exactly. I can't be Christina Sara Boulder. Even if it's just for a few months."

"What do you mean?"

"I mean I'm not staying, Laura. I'm here to do a job and as soon as I'm done, I'll be gone."

"Oh!" She pulled back. "Does Boulder know?"

"Yes." As soon as I said it a welcome feeling of calmness spread. The initial shock was subsiding and my haze was lifting. "Boulder knows and he also knows that it's not a real marriage, so I'm sure he won't expect any sort of intimacy."

Laura got up from the bed. "Well, in that case you have nothing to worry about."

"No, I don't think I have," I said and got up from the bed too. "This is all just a big storm in a glass of water, and soon I'll be excavating all day long and laughing about the whole thing."

Laura bowed her head. "It was very nice to meet you."

"When can I see you again?" I asked quickly.

"If you'd like, I could introduce you to Erika; she's coming back from the east coast tomorrow morning."

"That would be lovely, thank you, but I'm hoping to get started with my work as soon as possible."

"I'm sure I could convince her to go on a picnic close to your digging site. That way we could have lunch together." She smiled.

"I would like that," I said, but secretly I feared the mother would be like her sons.

CHAPTER 12
The Wedding Night

Boulder

When Laura came out she nodded politely to me.

"How did it go?" I asked.

"Fine. I find Christina very interesting," Laura responded.

"But what did she say?"

"We spoke about marriage and she had questions for me."

I stepped closer to her and was happy Magni wasn't there to stop me. "What kind of questions?"

"Intimate questions."

"Like what?" My eyes were boring into hers as I wished I could read her mind.

The door opened and both Laura and I turned our heads to see Christina standing in the doorway with a hand on her hip.

"If you want to know what I said, why don't you ask me?"

Laura looked a little surprised by Christina's tone with me, but she hurried along while I faced my new wife.

"Are you coming?" she asked and opened the door.

I didn't like her running the show and had felt like a fool waiting outside my new bride's room when everyone would be expecting me to be busy with her inside. I knew very well that women from the Motherlands oppressed men for a pastime, and I sure as hell wasn't going to let her do that to me.

"How about we go for a walk instead?" I asked to regain control. Surely, she wouldn't fight with me in public, and we'd been cooped up in that room for too long anyway.

"All right," she said and stepped out in the large hallway. "A walk in the garden then?"

"Yes." I swung my arm for her to follow me.

We didn't talk much in the beginning, her staccato steps indicating that she was still upset and unwilling to look at me.

"Do you regret your choice?" I finally asked.

"What choice? I didn't have a choice," she said sourly.

"You could have stuck with Archer."

"And been pregnant within a month," she scoffed. "I don't think so! He would have taken me to get inseminated next week if he had anything to say."

I wondered what she meant by that, but left it for now.

Five more minutes of walking in silence and we reached a water fountain. "Just so we're clear," she said. "I object to being married."

"Why?"

"Because it suppresses women," she said and folded her arms and looked away.

"How the hell did you come to that brain-dead conclusion?" I asked.

That made her spin around, and for someone from the Motherlands I knew she had to be fuming on the inside when she sneered through gritted teeth. "In case you didn't know this: men dominated and mistreated women for thousands of years. There was a time when women were the property of men and practically treated like slaves. They had no power, no voice, and could be raped by their husband without anyone to help them."

I chuckled. "Whoever wrote your history books must have been poorly informed. That's all lies made up by women."

"It's true," she said and lifted her chin.

"No, it's not. Women were never property to men. They were highly cherished members of society. And a father protected his daughter until he carefully chose a man worthy of protecting her for him."

"Maybe in some cases," she admitted. "But where I come from, women don't need men to protect them. And you're missing the point. If women were so cherished then why weren't they allowed to have a political vote or have a profession?"

"You're talking about something that happened thousands of years ago."

"No, I'm not; women only gained basic rights within the last five hundred years."

"You don't know that for sure. And it doesn't change that you have an obscure way of looking at males as the evil ones, when we're anything but."

"You almost ruined the world," she blamed me in a harsh whisper.

I squared my shoulders and narrowed my eyes, feeling extremely tired of her feminist shit. "No, *I* did not ruin the world and *I* will not take the blame for what men did hundreds of years ago. You're a historian, so why don't we take a look at all the horrible things women did throughout history? If you think women are any better than men, then you're naïve."

"Can you point to one female dictator?" I defended myself."

"Don't be stupid. Dictators are always linked to military power, and women never came to power that way. Female prime ministers and queens could be just as heartless and brutal as any man. There was no difference."

"Only because they were navigating a male-dominated world. They had to be tough."

I buried my hands in my pockets and rocked on my feet. "Women are fully capable of murdering or taking advantage of others. Just like men. It's human nature!"

"No, it's not," Christina protested. "I think the Motherlands have showed that we've evolved beyond such appalling behavior."

"Or maybe you're so strongly regulated and controlled that you never get the chance to explore the darker part of your personality," I provoked her. "My point is just that *I* refuse to take the blame for the men who mistreated women in the past. I can't imagine it was the norm at any point in time, and if it was then I'm happy to tell you that we men have evolved since our ancestors."

"Have you?" her voice was seething. "You still kill for greed."

I clenched my jaws.

"The only reason all those men fought in the tournament was greed," she claimed. "You want more. Men always want *more*."

"That's not true."

"Really? So they weren't motivated by the million-dollar reward or the prestige that came along with it?"

"Some of us did it for honor and to protect you."

She gave me a long hard look. "Can you truly say you did it to protect me?"

Our gazes clashed. "Yes!" I said loud and clear.

That left her silent.

"You have all these ridiculous ideas about men being women's adversaries, but we're not. We're meant to live together, that should be fucking obvious." I couldn't hide the frustration I felt. "You speak of marriage as something awful but I've read stories describing love between men and women. And passion."

"The forbidden books," she breathed.

"Yes, Christina. People used to fall in love and marry because they couldn't stand the thought of being separated. They were partners, mates... do you understand?"

"That's not what I've heard."

"Well, did it occur to you that you might not know everything and that there's a reason those books are forbidden?"

"They are forbidden because they create unwanted emotions in people and in some cases depression," Christina explained.

"Yeah, I can relate," I said and raised her chin to make her look at me. "But it's only because reading those books will make you long for how it used to be between men and women, I always wanted to experience it, but we're cut off from the women living in the Motherlands and even if we could go there, you've all been brainwashed to think of love and passion as something wrong."

"We have love," Christina defended. "I feel great love and affection for my friends."

"I'm not talking about that kind of love." I took her hand and lifted it to my heart. "I'm talking about the passionate kind between a man and a woman."

For a second we stood close, her hand on my chest and my hand over hers.

"Remember when you called me your friend? And when you ran into my arms at the ceremony?"

"Yes."

"Doesn't that tell you something?"

"What?"

I sighed, annoyed that she couldn't see what I was seeing. "You trust me and you feel safe with me."

She pulled back a little. "I wouldn't say that."

"Then what would you say then?"

"That of all my options at that time you were the least frightening."

I let go of her and started walking again. She followed me in silence toward the Gray Mansion and remained quiet after that.

The situation was awkward. We'd been together day and night for days and had talked and learned from each other, but now she was closed off to me. I treated her like I would treat a distrustful animal and advanced slowly.

It was only nine thirty when she went to bed. "What are you doing?" she asked when I joined her.

"I'm tired too. It's been a long day and fighting Nelson took a lot out of me."

"But you sleep on the couch," she said and pulled the cover to her nose.

"Not anymore," I said and made myself comfortable next to her.

"Don't think we'll be having sex," she said quickly.

I turned on my right side, facing her, and arranging my pillow while trying to find a comfortable position for my broken arm and a solution to my predicament. I wanted to move slowly so as not to scare her, but I also couldn't give in to her idea that we would never have sex.

"Is it because you're afraid of hurting my arm?" I finally asked.

"No," she said quickly. "It's because I don't like the idea of sex at all."

"You'll get used to it," I said, "And if it's any consolation I'm a virgin too."

Christina held up a palm. "I'm going to stop you right there. You might as well get the notion of our having sex out of your mind, because it will never happen. If I wanted sex I could have stayed with Archer."

"But you didn't," I stated. "You married me and you are now *my* wife."

She shot me a dirty look. "It's a practical arrangement only."

I ignored that comment and asked a question of my own. "Don't men and women have sex in the Motherlands?"

She shrugged. "I suppose some do. I have friends who are coupled. Theresa and Dan have been together for years, but I never see them touch each other, and most people live in community buildings where we share meals but have our own rooms. I live with Kya."

I scrunched my face. "You live with a woman?"

"Yeah."

"Is she your lover?"

"No!" Her answer came quickly and then she gave me a curious smile. "Kya is my best friend. Why? Do you have sex with any of your friends?"

I shook my head. "No – I mean, sure we experimented when we were teens, but I can honestly say that I fantasize about women only – I've just never been with a real woman," I elaborated.

"Whoa, whoa, slow down. What do you mean you experimented when you were teens?"

I bit the inside of my cheek. "Nothing."

"Is that normal?" she asked like she was onto something profound. "For teenage boys to experiment sexually? Do men experiment too?"

I rubbed the bridge of my nose. "I don't know what other men do, and I'm not in the mood to entertain you with my teenage memories."

"Just tell me if you..." She trailed off, unable to ask the obvious question.

"No," I said.

"No, you didn't, or no, you don't want to answer the question," she asked.

"Christina, just let it go." I sighed.

"No, I'm trying to understand the culture among Nmen, and you just gave me a very interesting piece of information."

"What? That teenage boys are constantly horny and experimenting? That's hardly groundbreaking research right there. It's been like that since the beginning of mankind. I don't think we were any different than generations before us."

"But what did you do?"

I looked away. "The usual."

"And what would that be?"

"You really want to know?" I puffed up my pillow again and liked that I was in the same bed as her and not on the sofa.

"Yes, I'm very curious," she whispered.

"We masturbated together, compared sizes, some of the guys jerked each other off; others did more, but I wasn't one of them."

Her face was completely flushed and she was watching me so intensely that it felt intimate between us.

"So you never?" she asked.

I waited for her to speak the words but again, she couldn't.

"Did I fuck another guy?"

Her breathing stopped for a moment.

"Does it matter?" I asked.

"No!" She blinked. "No, of course not, I'm just trying to understand how society works in the Northlands."

"I already told you, I wasn't one of the guys who did more, but I don't judge the ones who did. It wasn't like they could have a girlfriend, and sex-bots weren't on the menu very often."

"So you've had sex with sex-bots," she asked.

"Of course. Lots. You have sex centers too, right?" I asked.

"Yes," she said, low. "We have physical centers where you go to take care of your physical needs. The one close to me is pretty big. There's a gym, a spa, a hairdresser, a nail salon, all sorts of physical therapy and healing places, a medical clinic and a pleasure parlor with sex-bots."

"How practical," I said dryly. "And how often do you go?"

"It's recommended to go twice a month, so that's what I do."

110

"Okay." I placed my hand between our pillows and noticed that she wasn't shielding herself with the cover anymore. "I go a few times a week."

"You have sex several times a week?" she asked in a disbelieving whisper.

"Uh-huh, if you count the times I have sex with the sex-bots. If you count the times I have sex with myself it's..."

"You don't have to tell me that," she cut me off, color rising in her cheeks again.

"It's fine. I'm not shy about masturbating. Every healthy man does it at least once a day."

Her eyes widened. "They do?"

"Yes. How often do women masturbate?"

"I don't know. I've never asked my friends so I can only speak for myself."

"So?" I asked.

She wrinkled her nose, and it made the cutest expression on her face. "That's private," she said with a smile of embarrassment.

"Just give me a rough estimate. Once a day, once a week, what?"

Christina raised her head up and supported it with a hand. "I can't believe we're having this conversation but in the spirit of mutual curiosity I'll answer you honestly." She took a deep breath. "For me it varies. Sometimes I can go weeks without and other times it's several times a week."

"Really?" I smiled. "So we're not so different. And what do you find arousing?" I asked her. "I'm curious because you said that you've never met a man that arouses you, and you just admitted that you're not aroused by women either, so what turns you on?"

The color of her face told me this was a difficult subject but I admired her for not backing down. "Mostly things from the past. Things I've read or movie clips I've seen."

"Like what?"

111

"Like..." She played with a lock of her hair. "People kissing and such."

"Kissing turns you on?" I gave her my most charming smile and moved my hand closer.

She didn't move.

"Did it turn you on when I kissed you?"

"It was too quick for me to really feel much," she said pragmatically.

"That's because you pulled away."

"You surprised me."

"Can I kiss you now?" I asked and touched her hand while moving closer. "I promise I won't do anything but kiss you."

Christina looked undecided when I slowly leaned in and kissed her. This time she didn't pull away but she didn't kiss me back either.

Carefully caressing her face, I deepened my kiss and felt her respond a little.

Enough, a voice of reason said in the back of my mind while parts of me wanted to roll on top of her and sink myself inside her.

I pulled back and looked at her. "How was that?"

Christina touched her lips and drew a deep breath as if suddenly remembering that she had to breathe.

"That was..."

"What?"

"I don't know."

"Then maybe I need to do it aga..." I was already kissing her again and letting my hand slide up and down her arm, getting closer to her breast. This time she raised her arm and touched my shoulder, which made instant heat spread down my spine. It was all the acceptance I needed to do what I'd always wanted to try. My fingers weave into her hair and when my hand was behind her neck, I opened my mouth and licked her upper lip. Her eyes had been closed but they flew open and she gasped,

112

opening her mouth just enough for me to enter and touch her tongue with mine. I'm sure she would have pulled back if she could, but my hand was in position to keep her in place and I didn't budge. I had read about French kissing and longed to experience what it would feel like.

Christina

You can't be an archeologist if you're not curious by nature. By definition you're digging to find secrets and understand how people used to live. I had come to the Northlands in the hope of finding a library full of information. Instead I was experiencing with my own body what I had never known in my own life. Boulder was like a time traveler who didn't know what living in the year 2437 meant. He broke laws every day with his improper use of language and disregard for my warnings not to read emotionally provocative books, but then, the laws didn't apply to the Nmen, who had their own set of rules to live by.

My first reaction when I was forced to marry Boulder was to have him take me to the border. The only reason I didn't ask him was the thought of all the "I told you so" comments I would be facing back home and the fact that there was still so much more to learn from this place.

Boulder wasn't the monster of an Nman I'd been warned against. He wasn't pinning me down and forcing his will on me, and his raw masculinity didn't frighten me as it had in the beginning.

I had let him kiss me out of curiosity and now his tongue playfully touched mine like an invitation to a dance. It was highly unhygienic of course, but I'd read about this old custom and knew that some couples still did it in private. Lara Croft wouldn't shy away from a hands-on experience like this and neither would Indiana Jones. I could be brave like them and see it as an experiment.

Slowly I pushed back against his tongue with my own, circling it, and starting a new and exciting dance of ours. Boulder tightened his grip on the back of my head and lifted his broken arm up before he rolled on top of me. I didn't mean our kiss to get this far, but I didn't stop him either when he pushed my legs apart with his knees, while still kissing me.

It's okay, he's wearing pajama pants and I have my long t-shirt and underwear on; nothing is going to happen, I calmed myself.

"It feels so good," Boulder moaned into my mouth and ground himself against me.

He's hard! The thought both frightened and excited me, and I couldn't decide if my body was burning hot because of all the heat he was throwing off or because the situation aroused me. I'd fantasized about being in a situation like this, but not with someone like him.

"Remember we're not going to have sex," I said to make sure we were on the same page.

"Uh-huh," he said and kissed my jaw.

Growing bolder, I let my hands explore his strong torso and didn't protest when he pulled his t-shirt over his head. I'd never seen him topless and was fascinated by his hard muscles.

He tugged at my t-shirt, silently asking me to take it off, but I shook my head and was grateful when he didn't pressure me further.

Boulder planted kisses down my neck, my jawline, my nose and I got the feeling he was exploring like me. And all the while he was grinding against me, simulating intercourse.

"Ahh!" I couldn't help the small eruption of a moan because it felt good.

"You like it?" he whispered into my ear and gently bit my earlobe.

"A little," I admitted.

"And this?" he asked and took me by surprise when he lifted my thighs around his waist and made a long circular movement with his hips. Tingles and moist heat spread in my lower parts and my breathing became faster. He looked enormous, towering over me with eyes full of lust.

"I want you so fucking bad, Christina," he growled and pressed against me, holding himself up on his elbows.

For a long moment, we looked into each other's eyes and I knew he was silently asking me to make love to him, but that was a whole different experiment that I wasn't ready for.

"I like kissing," I said and gave him a small smile.

"Me too." He touched my nose with his and pressed another kiss to my lips and slowly, while holding our gazes locked, he pulled back and slid his hand under my t-shirt. The feel of his hand on my naked skin was forbidden, and felt so different from my own touch when he slid it over my thigh, my hip, my belly and finally made a sound in his throat when he cupped my right breast. "A perfect handful," he muttered and kissed me again. "One day, I'll kiss your nipple and bury my head between your breasts."

I opened my mouth to protest but he cut me off with another kiss and released my breast. "Don't say anything," he muttered against me, and from the way he was breathing harder and moving faster I knew he had accepted that this was as far as I'd let him go.

Boulder was making love to me on my conditions. He wasn't inside me but he was grinding himself against me and moving up and down my body while we were kissing.

"Fuck," he said and pumped harder, pressing my legs further apart and grunting into my ear. "You're my wife, and soon I'm gonna fuck you so hard."

His words freaked me out, but with his large body pressing me into the mattress and his state of arousal I couldn't do much. Fortunately, it only took a few seconds before he stiffened and leaned his head back roaring "Fuuuuck, yes."

I pushed at him then and was relieved when he rolled onto his back away from me.

"What did you do? Why did you scream like that?"

Boulder had his eyes closed and was panting. His broken arm resting on his chest and the other on his forehead.

I looked down at myself and noticed a wet spot on my front and then my eyes flew to his pants. He had a large wet spot in front too. At first I was confused because I'd never experienced a male sex-bot behave like Boulder just did, but then I realized what had just happened. "You ejaculated."

He replied with a deep exhale.

"I've learned about this in school. Men have a component needed to create babies, and they take it to fertility clinics where women ready to take on the role of motherhood will receive that gift."

Boulder opened his eyes and turned his head to look at me. "Children are supposed to be a creation of love," he said. "I read that in a book and I like to imagine I too was a creation of love."

"Of course you were," I said quickly. "We grow up with dedicated parents who care very much about us, and even Nboys are loved fiercely while they're with us. I guarantee that your mother and other adults showered you with love and care before you left the Motherlands"

"I don't remember, but one thing is for sure, Christina," he said and got up from the bed. "Now you know."

"Know what?"

"What kissing feels like."

I sat up too and pulled my knees to my chest. "That thing you said, you didn't really mean it, did you?"

"What thing?" He walked to a closet and picked out a new pair of pants.

"The last thing, about me being your wife and you wanting to do a certain thing to me."

"What? Oh… that." Boulder scratched his head. "That's just dirty talk."

"Dirty talk?"

"Yeah, you know, something you say when you're horny."

I closed my eyes taking a deep breath. "I know what horny means," I said. "But does that mean you didn't mean it?"

He chuckled and came closer. "Are you asking me if I would like to fuck you hard?"

"No." I looked away.

"Hey," he sat down on the bed next to me. "Don't worry about it."

"Just tell me you didn't mean it."

"I can't."

"Why not?"

"Because I really want to."

My head snapped back and I stared at him with a defiant glance. "But *I* don't!"

"Yet!" he said with a smug smile and got up. "I'll be right back."

CHAPTER 13
The Picnic

Christina

The day after our wedding I started working at the digging site. I wish we had precise maps of the area from before the war but all I knew was that this area was built on top of what used to be Vancouver, Canada.

Bombs and fires had destroyed the old city and the progressive mentality of the decades that followed the war had been inclined to bury the past and start again – I didn't blame the survivors of that time, since the traumatic experience they went through explained in full why they chose to bury the ruins with the billions of people that lost their lives around the world.

But as an archeologist I wished we had a clearer picture of the world before the war. In many ways we'd been forced to start over and re-invent things that were lost to us. With so many people dead, important knowledge had been lost and priorities had shifted from pre-war space programs to restoring the world. In the Motherlands we had reinvented the Internet and had carefully selected what could be part of it. The Wise-Share, as we called it, was strictly governed by librarians who made sure no content of a violent nature could be uploaded. Just as in real life, improper communication wasn't tolerated, and anyone who broke the rules of interaction would lose privileges like electricity, permission to travel with public transportation, food rations, or, worst case, end up in a place of reflection.

Here, the men had simply built on top of the old Internet, and it made for a confusing mix of outdated or false information that I found hard to navigate. We knew much of the original Internet had been deleted or falsified by hackers during the Toxic War, and no matter how much I searched I couldn't find a detailed map of this area.

Khan had provided me with most of the items on the list I had given him. He'd even found seven men to help me excavate – two of whom I had a strong sense were anything but volunteering for the job.

Boulder stayed close enough to see me, but was busy working too. According to him he was a businessman and owned logging and mining companies among other things.

I didn't ask him many questions about it since I was too focused on my own job.

We had our first challenge when he didn't like me talking to my helpers.

"I have to teach them how to do the work properly or they could ruin something of value," I argued.

"I don't like them being too close to you."

"That's too bad because they're my colleagues, and colleagues on digging sites have to work side by side."

Grumpy and unsatisfied, Boulder resolved to having a serious conversation with each man, imparting all the gory ways he would kill them if they ever touched me.

I rolled my eyes, something I would have never done at home, but then at home no one would threaten another with ripping their heart out through their behind.

The men didn't seem to think Boulder crazy. They just shook his hand and gave their word without hesitation.

At lunchtime Laura arrived with everything for a picnic, and it forced me to take a break although I really wanted to continue my work.

"I packed two lunches," she said and took my arm, leading me away from the site and toward a group of trees. "One for Magni and Boulder and one for you and me."

The men watched until we sat down on a blanket she had brought. Laura waved at them and received a nod in return.

"What about Erika? I thought you were going to bring her," I asked.

"She wasn't feeling well, and I told her she could meet you another time." Laura was unpacking the lunch and placed a plate in front of me with a pie, some meatballs, and a salad.

"Are these normal meatballs?"

"Yes," she confirmed.

"So no animals died to produce them?" I asked to be certain.

"What do you mean?" She looked puzzled.

"We have replaced meat with plant-based products that taste the same, and for those who insist on real meat they get cultured meat."

"Really?"

"Yes." I pushed the meatballs away. "And the pie, what's in the pie?"

"Oh, just vegetables," Laura said. "I think it's leek and potatoes."

I thought about Kya when I sniffed it carefully before taking a small bite. I didn't detect any meat.

"Since our talk, I have a million questions for you," Laura began and flicked her long hair behind her shoulder. "That's why I made two lunches. I didn't want the men to hear us."

"All right. What do you want to know?"

"What you said about women living in freedom. Being educated and unafraid. I want to know more."

"Well..." I finished chewing. "It's a completely different life, Laura, you would love it there. You would be surrounded by other women and you wouldn't have to hear men barking at each other. The men there are pretty and gentle."

"Pretty how?"

"They typically don't have beards but some of them have long hair too. The difference is just that it's soft and cared for and often braided in beautiful ways. They also manicure their nails and smell wonderful, of soap and perfume."

Laura had stopped eating. "They sound like women."

"We don't care much for gender roles. People are people and it really doesn't matter what sex you were born as."

"Yes, it does." Her big blue eyes studied me. "We're very different creatures."

"You only say that because you grew up here and you don't know what it's like for women in the Motherlands."

Laura looked over to Magni and Boulder, who were talking and eating. "But the thing you said about education, what did you mean?"

"I'm a professor at a university. I teach history and archeology. Others are doctors, social workers, artists, anything you can imagine."

"Are any warriors?" she asked with another nervous glance to the men.

"Warriors?" I leaned back. "I'm not sure I understand."

"I want to learn how to fight."

"Why?"

"Because I think I'd be good at it."

I bit my lip. "We don't have soldiers and fighters like in the old days, but we do have people who practice martial arts as a hobby and to stay fit."

"You do?"

"Yes."

"Magni is really good at martial arts, but he won't teach me. He says women aren't meant to learn."

I made a small snort.

"What?" she asked.

"Laura, of course he won't show you. If you could protect yourself he would be redundant, wouldn't he?"

She bit her lip. "I suppose so, but I watch him practice in the mornings and it looks amazing. Sometimes I try to do like he does when he leaves."

"If you lived in the Motherlands you could train as much as you'd like. That's what I meant by freedom. No man will ever tell you how to live your life there; you could pursue any career you want and walk around freely."

We ate for a while, Laura's mind spinning almost loud enough for me to hear. "Maybe you could take me with you when you go back. You know, just for a visit," she said.

"You think Magni would let you go?"

Her shoulders dropped. "No. He's very protective."

"I would call it possessive," I muttered. "He sees you as an inferior, you know."

She frowned. "But men are by definition stronger than women."

I scoffed loudly. "Women are as smart and capable as men. Don't for one second believe otherwise. I've seen women compete with men and win plenty of times."

"You have?" Laura sat up on her knees and leaned forward. "How?"

"I've seen women and men apply for the same job and the woman get it because she was better qualified. I've seen women and men race in track and a woman was the fastest. It happens all the time, Laura."

Laura's eyes were shining but she was shaking her head as if she couldn't believe it. "Incredible. I would love to beat Magni at something but he's so good at everything."

"Yeah, especially at bossing you around."

She looked down. "He can be a bit much sometimes."

"They all can. Not least his brother," I said dryly. "Khan tricked me and I don't think he even feels bad about it."

"No, I don't think he does. Khan is very intelligent and known to be superior in intellect. That's why he's such a good ruler."

"Is he now?"

"What are you talking about?" a deep voice asked and we turned our heads to see Magni and Boulder approaching.

"Oh, just what a good ruler Khan is," Laura said innocently.

Boulder gave me a questioning look but I nodded my head, confirming what she had said.

"He'll be glad to hear you think so," Magni noted and crossed his arms. "Laura, it's time to pack up. I have business to attend to and we need to go."

She looked down at her half-eaten pie and gave me a low sigh. She clearly didn't want to challenge him so I did it for her. "We're almost done eating; just give us a few more minutes and Laura will be right with you," I said.

He muttered a grumpy "hurry up," and walked away with Boulder.

"I couldn't stand someone bossing me around like that – you have to set your boundaries, Laura," I whispered.

Laura took a big bite of her pie and looked after Magni with her eyes narrowed and a thoughtful expression.

CHAPTER 14
Spies

Boulder

"So, how was the wedding night?" Magni asked me before stuffing his mouth with a large piece of chicken.

"Good," I said and popped a meatball in my mouth.

"Did she submit to you willingly?"

"Sort of."

"What's that supposed to mean?"

"We kissed and fooled around but she didn't want to go all the way."

"And you gave her a choice?"

I scowled at him. "You didn't give Laura a choice?"

"No, of course not. She's my wife and I fought for her; I took her on our wedding night and I certainly didn't ask for her permission."

"Did she fight you?"

He snorted. "That would have been futile, she's a tiny thing compared to me."

"Are you saying that you raped her?"

"Of course not. Laura was raised properly. She gave herself to me like a proper wife should."

I threw a meatball in the air and caught it with my mouth. "Yeah, but Christina isn't like Laura and unless I want to scar her for life, I have to take it slow with her."

Magni looked over at the women. "I told Laura to teach Christina about our ways, I'm sure she's putting in a good word for you."

I followed his gaze to the two women and hoped he was right.

When we got back to the mansion late in the afternoon, Christina wanted to take a shower so I placed guards outside her room and went to find Khan to have a word with him.

"I want to take Christina home to my place," I said.

Khan sat in front of his chessboard and pointed to a free chair.

"I don't wanna play."

"Afraid of losing?" he said without looking up.

"Chess isn't my game."

"True, but beating you in chess is so much fun."

"Did you hear me? I want to take my wife home."

"I heard you," he lifted his gaze, "but my answer is no."

"Why?"

"Because I'm intrigued with her and I like having you both here."

"But you hardly talk to her."

"Ahh, and yet I learn so much from her." The smug smile on his face made my spine tingle. It was a sure sign that Khan was up to no good. With my hands forming into fists I sank down on the chair and leaned forward. "Tell me that you're not tapping our room?"

Khan raised his head and looked straight at me. "Of course I am," he said without any sign of shame.

My voice rose, "You've heard everything?"

"And seen everything too," he added.

I pounded my fist down on his chessboard, making all the pieces fly in the air.

Khan calmly leaned back in his seat and pointed to the board. "Look what you did, Boulder."

"You have no right to invade my privacy like that."

"Do not tell me what I can or cannot do," he said in a hard tone. "You're my friend but I will not tolerate you dictating to me."

"Nor will I tolerate you spying on me. On us!"

"You have nothing to be ashamed of. I think you're doing a decent job of seducing her. Your wedding night was entertaining."

I exploded and knocked the table aside, grabbing onto his collar with both hands and staring him straight in the eye. "You fucking asshole."

Khan arched a brow and remained calm. "Let go, Boulder, or you'll be sorry."

I pushed back from him, growling in frustration. The man was a clever bastard with too much power, and I should have known he would do something like this.

"And the bathroom? Have you seen her naked too?"

He nodded and got up to stand behind his chair. "She's a beautiful woman."

Rage filled me and I wanted to kill him for having seen my wife fully naked. Even I hadn't seen Christina that vulnerable.

"Relax, look at the bright side – I could have insisted on her marrying *me* to study her up close. Instead I gave you the honor. Wasn't last night nice?"

My jaw was clenched and I had nothing kind to say to him.

"So you see, I want you to stay here so I can continue to keep an eye on her and learn more about the Motherlands."

I crossed my arms, "Why don't you just fucking ask her what you want to know?"

"Because you're doing such a good job at it." He smiled.

"I'll tell her."

"No, you won't." Khan tilted his head. "Defying your ruler never ends well, and I'm sure that once you've calmed down, you'll see that you're completely overreacting."

"How many have seen us?"

"Only me."

I spun around and stomped toward the door.

"Better luck with tonight. I hope she lets you undress her," he called after me and I replied by flipping him a finger. I could hear him laughing as I left the room.

Christina

Boulder was in a bad mood when he came back.

I was dressed and ready to go down for dinner, but he told me that he didn't feel like it.

"It's okay, I can go by myself," I said but he insisted that we order some food to our room.

Half an hour later a large tray arrived with wild mushroom risotto and freshly baked bread for me and a large steak with a baked potato and salad for him.

"Doesn't it bother you that an animal had to die for you to eat?" I asked.

"It's natural."

"How is it natural?" I asked, provoked by his lack of conscience.

Boulder pointed his knife at the window. "Why don't you go and ask the bird why it eats worms, or ask the wolf why it eats cute little rabbits."

"They don't know any better," I said with a frown. "They don't have a conscience, but you should have."

"How the hell would you know anything about how animals feel or think?"

"I know they don't feel sorry for killing another species."

"Exactly – because it's called nature. We're part of nature too and for thousands of years we've hunted and eaten animals. Nothing new about it, nothing wrong about it." Boulder took another bite.

"It's a crime in the Motherlands."

"I know, you told me so the first time you saw me eat meat, but you Momsies are all softies and you don't know what you're missing out on."

"We still get the taste of meat. Ours is just grown in laboratories and no animal had to die for it."

"Are you done?" He gave me a hard stare. "I'm trying to enjoy my steak here, and this deer tasted excellent until you started ruining my appetite with talk about laboratory meat. That's just disgusting."

"You seem very tense."

"Yeah, well, maybe I am."

"You can tell me if I'm getting on your nerves or something," I said, trying to figure out what I'd said wrong.

"It's not you."

"Then what is it?"

"I want to go home and take you with me but Khan denied my request."

"Oh, I see." I put down my fork. "Where do you live?"

"I own an island west of here. It's called Victoria Island and I have it all to myself, except for a few staff members."

"Is it far?"

"About fifteen minutes in the hybrid."

"And why did Khan want us to stay?"

I got no reply and went back to eating my risotto.

Boulder was quiet. He seemed to have a lot on his mind and kept scowling around the room.

Tired from a long day of digging I went to bed early, bringing my reader, and continued my novel, *Pride and Prejudice.*

Boulder chose to watch a movie and put on his movie glasses and earpiece while stretching out on the supporter.

"What are you watching?" I asked.

"What?" He pulled out an earpiece and popped the glasses up on his forehead.

"What are you watching?" I asked again.

128

"Oh, just an old movie."

"What is it about?"

"War."

I scrunched my face, "That doesn't sound very nice."

"I like it." He grinned. "Lots of blood and gory details, it's cool. But you know what always amuses me in these old movies?"

"What?"

"The fact that every time our ancestors envisioned the future and made a movie about it, like this one" – he pointed to the glasses – "the future was either a complete hell with burned-down ruins or something super boring and sleek."

I nodded. "I know, Kya and I talked about that too. It's always so clinical and colorless, as if we wouldn't appreciate art and colors as much as the generations before us."

"In this movie everyone wears white and walks like they're cyborgs or something. And their food is these disgusting packages of optimized nutrients. Who the hell would want to live like that?"

I smiled. "Not me."

"You know what's also completely unrealistic?"

"What?"

"There isn't a piece of trash anywhere. It's hysterical."

I frowned. "Well, actually, we do keep our streets very clean in the Motherlands. At least where I live."

"Yeah, all right, but what about your homes? Don't people have messes at home?"

"Of course, Kya and I aren't the tidiest of people, but she says it's what makes our apartment cozy." I pointed to his forehead with the glasses. "You get back to your movie; I'll be quiet now."

"It's okay, I've seen it at least ten times." He put the glasses back on, and soon his head was moving around and I knew he was taking in the virtual reality the movie offered. "It's one of my favorites because of the cool visual effects," he said and when two minutes later he raised both hands defensively I figured someone was attacking and sighed. Movies like that were disturbing and could cause emotional distress, but of course, he wouldn't listen when I told him that.

My eyes drifted to the cabinet with the antique books. What had happened between us yesterday was playing in my mind and curiosity was making me come up with arguments to justify why skimming one of those books would be all right.

1: It's not illegal in this part of the world and therefore I'm not technically breaking any laws.

2: I'm an archeologist, so studying what our ancestors considered entertainment is actually part of my job.

3: I've already proven that I can conduct social experiments and not succumb to emotional distress. After all, these past days have been very challenging; I've heard horrible language and witnessed violence up close.

4: Nothing in those books can be more damaging to my mental state than an Nman on top of me sticking his tongue in my mouth.

Without making much noise, I put my reader aside and got out of bed, tip-toeing slowly past Boulder to the cabinet. I knew exactly which book I wanted, and picked out the novel with the woman sandwiched between two men.

Like a child stealing apples, I hurried back to the bed and placed myself on my side letting my body hide the book, just in case Boulder took off his glasses to look over.

Twin Lovers, the book title read and eagerly I opened it up and started reading.

The plot had me intrigued. A woman was aboard an alien spaceship with thousands of humanoid aliens living there and two of them were trying to seduce her in any way possible.

My eyes widened when they tied her down and took control of her body until she cried out their names and begged them to fill her up.

My mind was bursting with questions, and I wish I could ask the woman who wrote the book if she based this on an actual experience or it was pure fiction. Surely no woman would like to be tied down and feel powerless, and I couldn't imagine how frightened she would have been with two men touching her.

As far as I knew humans hadn't made contact with aliens, but it was an ongoing discussion among my colleagues as there were several witness descriptions saying otherwise. And now this. Could it be based on something real or was it just a figment of the author's imagination?

I bit my lip and squeezed my thighs tighter when the woman surrendered to the good-looking twins in the book. They were described as large and ripped with muscles so I couldn't help comparing them in my mind to Boulder, although the twins had fangs, which Boulder luckily didn't.

The graphic description of the sex and the woman's pleasure had me aroused and so completely engulfed in the story that I didn't hear him walk up behind me.

"What are you doing?" Boulder asked in his deep masculine voice.

Flustered and embarrassed, I hid the book under the cover. "Nothing," I lied.

Boulder's face split in a grin and he crawled up on the bed reaching for the cover. "You're hiding something."

"No, I'm not." I tried pushing him away but I might as well have pushed at the wall.

In no time, he had the book, which was still open to the page I'd been reading.

With humor in his eyes, Boulder held the book in his outstretched hand so I couldn't take it from him and I was mortified when he read aloud, "*I arched my back and opened my mouth in a silent moan when his tongue licked my pussy and sweet agony filled my body.*" Boulder's smile grew. "You call this nothing?"

"Just give it to me." I reached for the book but he continued reading.

"*'Submit', his brother whispered in my ear, squeezing my nipple in painful pleasure. Spreading my thighs, I signaled that I wasn't going to fight them any longer. I was in their power and I wanted to be.*

"See," Boulder teased, "women like to be taken by men. It's in your nature to submit to us."

"Nonsense," I protested.

He put the book away and focused on me instead, his eyes full of mischief when he raised his hand to my lips. "Christina,"

"Yes?"

"Say that you'll submit to me," he said and looked more serious than before.

"Never!"

He didn't look away when he pulled me in for a kiss and I didn't fight it.

"I want you, Christina," he whispered.

I didn't respond with anything but my kiss.

"Say that you want me too," he coaxed.

"I like kissing you," I admitted and allowed him to push me gently down on my back.

"Tonight you'll let me see your body," he said and tucked the cover over us.

"That's not up to you," I argued with a small smile.

Boulder rested his forehead on mine and spoke in a low voice. "Please, Christina, I want to touch your naked chest and feel a real heartbeat."

"Maybe my breasts aren't as perfect as what you're used to with the sex-bots."

He pulled back and took me in. "Don't ever compare yourself with a sex-bot. I swear to you that I'll love your breasts whatever the shape or the size."

"You already know the size; you touched me yesterday."

The way he closed his eyes and drew in a deep breath before he boldly pulled at my shirt alarmed me a bit. Boulder was determined to see my body, and I needed to know that I was safe.

"Stop!"

The word made him freeze. "What's wrong?"

"You're going too fast."

Without breaking eye contact, he slowly pulled my shirt up, his hands touching my skin and his mouth opening slightly when the shirt was up to my armpits. He knew it, I knew it, my breasts were exposed and all he had to do was lower his eyes to see them for himself.

His Adam's apple bobbed in his throat for another second before his eyes dropped down to my perky breasts pointing straight up at him.

It was almost amusing to see his eyes expand and his lips lift up in a smile before he buried his head between my breasts and touched, licked, and gently nibbled at them. The sounds of wonder that he made had me laughing.

"What's so special about breasts?" I asked and felt a surge of heat spread down my belly when he twirled his tongue around my left nipple and suckled at it.

"They are just perfect, soft, amazing…"

I was getting affected from his playing with my body and weaved my hands through his hair. This wasn't such a bad experiment, and I was beginning to see why men and women used to do this regularly.

"Your beard tickles," I said.

"Because your skin is so sensitive." He smiled up at me with more mischief in his eyes, and making sure that I was still covered with the bedcover he moved lower, kissing my belly button and opening my pants.

"You promise you'll stop if I ask you to?" I asked and received a nod as confirmation.

"Lift your butt," he said and pulled down my pants. I had the cover over my head and was looking down at him trying to understand what he was up to. The first kiss on my inner thigh gave me an idea, and I flushed red thinking about what we had just read.

He's not going to actually kiss me there, is he?

Boulder licked and kissed his way closer and closer to my triangle, and by now the scratching of his beard felt good.

No one should know about this when I go back home. It's just a scientific experiment and he won't hurt me, I convinced myself when Boulder's fingers removed the last piece of clothing between him and my complete nakedness.

CHAPTER 15
Average

Boulder

I'd been so fucking close, but again Christina had stopped me before we got to actual intercourse. I had touched her, kissed her, licked her, tasted her and it had been fucking amazing.

Her body was soft and delicate, fragile and fine. She didn't have scars or tattoos like me. Hair didn't grow on her chest or in a line down to her belly like it did on me. Christina only had a sweet triangle of dark curly hair on her pussy that made me absolutely insane.

She was all woman, and I loved everything about her body. Finally, being able to bury my head between her thighs and tasting female nectar for the first time was everything I thought it would be. I had read about it and seen movie clips of men and women doing it, but this time I'd experienced it in real life, and it was the biggest turn-on to hear her breathing become faster and deeper in response.

With the hardest boner in my pants, I'd been so ready to go all the way and finally find out if it was true that being with a woman was much better than a sex-bot.

I'd ground against her, enjoyed the sight of her brown hair spread over the pillow and her beautiful eyes looking up at me with warmth. Everything was going so well until I opened my pants to let out my instrument, which made Christina freak out and push at my chest to get away.

"What's wrong?" I asked

"Your thing."

I looked down and saw the tip of my cock pointing up at her belly. Everything looked normal to me.

"It's way too big," she complained and furrowed her brow.

"What are you talking about, I'm completely normal."

She made a sound indicating that I had to be delusional. "You're.... you're huge."

Since my best friend was frightening her, I tucked him away and rolled down next to her. "What did you expect?"

"In my local sex center the sex-bots' penises are adjustable to your preference. I always choose medium, and what you have doesn't come close," she said and looked almost accusingly at me.

"Why would you have sex-bots with small dicks?" I asked confused.

"They're not small. They're just the right size. If they were bigger it would be painful, and nobody likes that."

I closed my eyes and exhaled. "Christina, trust me, I'm very normal for a man."

"How do you know – have you ever compared yourself to others?"

"Uh-huh."

She widened her eyes. "Right, I forgot about your teenage experiments."

"It wasn't just that. But we showered together and shared rooms at the academy, I saw plenty of other guys to know my size compared to others.

"And you're average?"

I propped myself on my elbow and she did the same, facing me. "Yep, I'm perfectly normal. Khan is tiny," I lied and grinned. "It's crooked too but don't tell him I told you so." I placed a hand over her hip and lifted my middle finger, hoping that Khan would both hear and see my protest of his spying on us.

"Why would I speak to Khan about such intimate matters?" she asked with that sweet triangle forming between her brows.

"Oh, you know, he's not big on personal boundaries, so I'm sure he wouldn't be offended if you asked him to see his small crooked dick. Believe me, he would have no qualms asking to see your naked body."

She pulled her cover higher. "I would never let him see me without clothes on, and I certainly have no interest in seeing any part of him naked."

"Good."

"I don't trust him," she said.

"Who, Khan?"

"Yes, he's trying too hard to be polite to me. I mean he definitely has a silver tongue and a charming smile, but the way he tricked me was awful."

I lifted her hand and kissed it. "I don't know, I'm kinda liking being your husband."

She lowered her head and spoke softly. "Just don't forget that I'm only staying for a little while."

I didn't like to think about it and kissed her to stop her from saying any more.

Christina

We fell asleep holding hands and woke up with my head resting on his chest. I think it made Boulder happy, because he was whistling when we went down to have breakfast.

Magni, Laura, Khan, and Erika were already there when we joined them.

"Christina, may I please introduce you to my mother, Erika," Khan said with a cordial smile.

I walked over to offer the older woman my hands. "May peace surround you," I said and although she looked at her sons with slight confusion at first, she eventually took my hands and returned my friendly smile.

"It's a great honor to meet a woman from the Motherlands," Erika said and gestured for me to take a seat between her and Khan.

"Boulder, there was a message from the Motherlands this morning. They're expecting a status report from Christina as soon as possible." Khan was looking at Boulder.

"Excuse me, but why are you talking to Boulder when the matter clearly concerns me?" I asked Khan.

Laura gave a small gasp and Erika put a hand on my arm. "Matters of the state aren't for us to concern our pretty heads with. The men will take care of it."

I gave her a stiff smile. "I'm sure they will, but I wasn't raised to obey men and I'm fully capable of speaking for myself."

Erika squirmed in her seat and Laura sat quietly with her shoulders up and eyes looking down at her folded hands.

"If only the Momsies didn't block us from connecting to their network we could just send it from here, but I'm afraid we'll have to record a message and deliver it to the border," Khan complained.

"Do you have a messenger?" Boulder asked. "Christina wants to go digging and I plan on working from there."

"It's fine, I didn't expect you to go. I'll send one of my guards." Khan picked up a pastry and finally addressed me. "Will you kindly make a recording that assures the council that you're being treated well?"

I nodded and scooped up another spoonful of the delicious rhubarb yogurt, hoping that it truly was non-dairy as they promised me the first morning.

After breakfast, I held up my wristband and recorded a message for Councilwoman Pearl.

138

"Thank you for your concern. I hope this message finds you in peace and comfort. I'm pleased to report that I'm in good health and finally working on the digging site, which is looking promising. It took me a while to get started because selecting the right bodyguard turned out to be more problematic than I'd ever imagined." I left out the details and continued by introducing Boulder. "This is Alexander, who has been kind enough to dedicate his next few months to keeping me safe. Say hi, Boulder." I swung the wristband in his direction and my big scary-looking friend raised a large hand in greeting.

"Hey, council Momsies, come see us sometime," he said with a crooked smile.

The rest of the day I spent at the digging site, and it wasn't until we returned that we understood something was very wrong.

CHAPTER 16
Bad Influence

Boulder

The roaring from Khan's office made me run to get there.

"What the hell is going on?" I shouted at the sight of Magni throwing things around like a crazed bear.

Khan was trying to get close to Magni, who stood with a chair lifted over his head and eyes bulging in rage. On Khan's signal, I moved to the left and waited for Magni to turn his back on me before I tackled him and knocked him to the floor.

"Calm the fuck down and tell me what happened," I screamed at him and tried to protect my broken arm when he kicked me off him. Agile and strong, Magni leaped up again and pointed at Khan, roaring, "I'm not going to sit quietly and wait for them to return her, I'm going after her – and I swear on our father's grave, if I have to start a war to get my wife back, I will. She's *mine!*"

"What happened to Laura?" I asked, baffled by Magni's outrage.

He was panting, and spun on his heel until he eyed Christina, who stood halfway hidden behind the doorframe, looking in. "You!" Magni stormed up to her and grabbed her by the shoulders.

Protective fear fueled me to quickly get between them, pushing him away from her. "Back away," I said, low and threatening. "And tell us what troubles you."

Magni's chest rose and fell in rapid intakes of breath, his lips were pressed into thin lines, and his eyes narrowed with thunder. "Your wife is a bad influence. She helped Laura get to the Motherlands and now she's gone."

"Wait – what?" I swung my head to face Christina.

"I swear I had nothing to do with Laura's disappearance," she exclaimed. "Are you sure she went to the Motherlands?"

"Yes! I'm fucking sure," he roared. "She tricked me, telling me she was tired and needed a rest. I trusted her and left her for a few hours but when I came back I found that letter." Magni pointed to the floor where a piece of paper lay. He bent down and picked it up, holding it in the air and sputtering in contempt. "She wants to do martial arts." Magni's voice was booming with blame and his eyes were shooting daggers at Christina, who hid behind me. "Did or didn't you tell her she could train in martial arts in the Motherlands?"

"Ohhh." Christina bit her lip. "I… might have."

That admittance set Magni off again, and it took both Khan and me to hold him back from Christina. "I told you to stay the fuck back," I warned him and delivered a punch to his hard abs to underline that I was serious.

He growled and bent over in pain. "Your woman is fucking poison and she made my wife leave me."

"Maybe she wouldn't have left if you had only taught her martial arts instead of treating her like a piece of property," Christina said accusingly, but that only made him lift his head and shoot her a frostbitten glare.

"We'll send a message to the council and ask them to return her," Khan said loudly and walked Magni back to his desk with a hand on his shoulder. "I feel your pain, but you'll get Laura back, be sure of it."

Magni rolled his shoulder to shake Khan's hand off and hissed. "You're damn right I'll get her back, but I'm not going to sit here quietly, I'm going to get her back right now."

"You can't get into the Motherlands," Christina pointed out. "You'd be detained at the border. There are thousands of drones and they're armed.

"So much for being pacifists," Magni said mockingly.

"With numb-guns," Christina explained. "They won't kill you, but you'll be pacified and detained.

Magni pushed away from Khan and me. "I'll take my chances. If Laura thinks she can escape me, she's mistaken. She *belongs to me!*"

"I'll go with you," I offered Magni solemnly, but Khan shook his head.

"You two are not going to bring war on us because of a woman. We'll solve this my way."

"The hell we will," Magni exclaimed with force.

"You'll stay here and that's an order!" Khan replied and signaled for me to leave. "Take Christina out of his sight for now. Magni needs time to calm down."

Christina and I left. Clearly shaken, she looked up at me. "I didn't tell Laura to run away, really I didn't. How did she even get to the border?"

I scoffed. "I'll bet she was a hidden passenger with the guard who went with your message today."

Christina nodded and then a hint of a small smile spread on her lips. "Good for Laura."

I stopped abruptly and hissed, low. "What did you say?"

"I mean, did you see Magni, the way he went berserk? The man clearly has anger issues, and I've seen how he bosses Laura around. I'm happy that she escaped him if she wasn't happy."

I leaned closer and spoke in a low firm voice. "If you think he was angry then you don't want to see me if you did something similar. He's her protector and now she's out of his reach. He's worried."

"No, he's possessive of her."

"Because he cares," I argued.

142

Christina tilted her head back to look up at me. "Sorry, Boulder, but I don't think Magni or Khan cares about anyone but themselves. Laura means nothing to Magni other than the prestige that comes with having a wife."

I pointed a finger at her. "You know nothing about how he feels, and I won't let you judge him or his actions."

"Fine!" she said and continued up the stairs.

I followed with a knot in my stomach, feeling great sympathy for Magni and a troubling suspicion that Christina *was* somehow responsible for Laura's disappearance.

CHAPTER 17
Surrounded by Men

Christina

After Laura's disappearance, I wasn't allowed to speak to any other women unsupervised. I saw Erika at breakfast and dinner but she refused to speak to me, so I figured she blamed me for the incident too. After all, Magni was her son and only a day after Laura left, he'd vanished too. Khan had sent several messages to the council, demanding that they return Laura at once, but so far there had been no reply.

Four long days passed with everyone in the mansion tip-toeing around their troubled and irritable ruler. The good thing was that Boulder's arm was fully healed and didn't cause him more pain. The bad thing was that the atmosphere around the mansion was incredibly tense.

Each day I spent as long as possible at the digging site. At least there I was distracted by my work and didn't have time to worry about the situation with Laura.

Boulder was quieter than usual. In fact, we hardly spoke, and yet, every night he would want to be physical with me. I missed my friends and felt homesick, and maybe that's why the physical part of my relationship with Boulder became so important to me. He was my only friend in this foreign place and despite his grumpy mood, huge size, and lack of manners, I felt safe with him. The way he had shielded me against Magni's wrath had proven he truly was my protector, and when he touched and kissed me at night, it made me forget all the craziness that surrounded me. I was even starting to wonder what it would be like to go all the way with him and if I could justify it as a part of my scientific approach to this adventure.

On the fifth night after Laura ran away we were upstairs preparing for bed when the sound of a woman screaming outside made us move to the windows to see what was happening. It was too dark to get a clear view, and all we could see was a small figure being dragged by a large man while kicking and screaming.

"Is it Laura?" I asked worriedly.

"Stay here," Boulder muttered low and got dressed again. "I'm just going to see what's going on."

As soon as he was out the door I dressed too and sneaked out quietly, tip-toeing all the way down to the first-floor landing where I hid in the dark shadows to follow the spectacle taking place down in the foyer of the large mansion.

Magni was back, and with him was Laura in a white cloak fighting to get away from him.

"Stand still, woman, or I'll tie you down again," he threatened.

"Hey." Boulder moved closer. "Take it easy, can't you see she's frightened?"

Khan came to the scene and with a furious scowl, he took a masculine stance with his legs and shoulders spread wide. "Magni, what part of my orders didn't you understand?"

Magni cursed under his breath, but Khan kept talking. "I told you to stay here and yet you went anyway."

"I fucking had to," Magni hissed and jerked at Laura to make her stand still.

"And how exactly did you get Laura back?" Khan asked with a nod to her.

"I didn't. I searched for Laura but couldn't find her."

The surprise on Boulder's and Khan's faces spoke volumes, and their eyes grew large when Magni pulled the cloak back and revealed a woman I'd never seen before.

Covering my mouth, I swallowed a gasp when I saw the mark on her face. *A priestess!*

"Son of the devil." Khan's voice was shaking with anger. "What the fucking *fuck* did you do?"

"I told you I couldn't find Laura, and until they hand her back to me, I'm keeping this one hostage."

"You fucking moron." Boulder had both hands in his hair. "You kidnapped a woman and broke the peace treaty. What the hell were you thinking?"

Taking one large step, Magni stood nose to nose with Boulder, hissing at him. "You would have done the same thing if your wife had left you."

I blinked, confused by those words. Surely Magni's possessive rage had made him forget that my marriage to Boulder was always meant to be temporary and a practical solution only.

"Break it up," Khan ordered the men and walked closer to the woman. "What's your name?"

Raising her chin up and meeting Khan's stare, she answered him. "My name is Athena."

"Welcome, Athena." Khan bowed his head to her. "I regret that we meet under such unpleasant circumstances. My name is Khan Aurelius and I'm the ruler of the Northlands."

"Wonderful," she said in a voice trained to be kind and polite like mine. "Then I'm sure you'll be more than willing to return me safely back home."

"No!" Magni roared. "Not until I get Laura back."

Khan drew in a deep breath and turned to Boulder. "Will you please stay with Athena for a moment? I wish to speak to my brother privately."

Boulder nodded and the two other men walked away.

For a few minutes everything was silent, I watched the priestess and Boulder standing together. Athena had her eyes closed and it gave me time to study her. She looked very young – I guessed her to be around twenty – and I knew that with time the small mark that she had between her brows and up her forehead would become bigger as she advanced as a priestess. I was too far away to see what symbols were already there.

She almost reached Boulder's shoulder and had long red hair like Laura, only where Laura's was almost orange this woman's hair was a dark auburn in the most magnificent color that contrasted with her long simple green dress.

"Are you hungry or thirsty?" Boulder asked her.

"Thank you, but no," she said and opened her eyes, looking straight up at *me.*

With my heart beating like a drum I pulled further back into the shadows, hoping she wouldn't betray me to Boulder.

"I'm just not happy with the situation," I heard her say.

"I understand" was his short answer.

"What is your name?" she asked him.

"Alexander, but everyone calls me Boulder."

"What a shame," she said softly. "Alexander is a beautiful name."

"So is Athena."

"Thank you."

When Magni and Khan returned, they brought Finn with them. I had met him at dinner a few times, as he was one of Khan's good friends and was currently staying at the mansion. He was a genius at making the men laugh and didn't seem to take anything too seriously, and right now the idiot was smiling – as if there was anything good about this situation.

"Athena," Khan started. "This is Finn MacCumhail. He's a good friend of mine and I've appointed him to be your personal bodyguard while you're in my house. Given the circumstances you arrived under, I doubt you would feel safe with my brother."

Magni stood quietly with his arms crossed, while Athena looked at Finn without returning his wide smile.

"I'll let the Motherlands Council know that you're here and that you're safe. Hopefully, Laura will be returned to us quickly so you can go home." Khan was less grumpy now and a vague hint of his usual charm had returned. "You might be pleased to hear that we have another woman here from the Motherlands. She's an archeologist who is helping us excavate an old library." His lips pursed upward. "It's late now, but tomorrow, I'll let you meet her and hopefully she can testify that we're not as horrible as you might think right now."

Athena didn't respond but stood stoically still.

"Finn, please take Athena to your room and make sure she is safe and comfortable tonight. I'll see you both tomorrow morning." Khan clasped his hands behind his back and left the way he'd come.

"This way," Finn said and swung his arm to make Athena go first. She didn't move.

"You heard Khan, I'm your appointed protector so you have to come with me," Finn explained, his smile gone.

"If you think I'm willingly going with you into your room, you're mistaken," Athena said and crossed her arms.

Finn looked to Boulder and shrugged before he bent down and simply picked the small woman up on his shoulder like a sack of potatoes.

"Let me down," she insisted but he just started up the staircase and when she wriggled, he smacked her butt.

Magni and Boulder were following right behind them and quiet as a mouse, I sneaked back up to my room, my heart still pounding and my mind racing with how I could help the priestess escape and get back home.

Boulder

I watched the small woman being carried down the hallway by Finn and felt bad for her. At least Christina had come of her own free will.

Finn was a good guy, but Athena didn't know that and although he wasn't as big as me and Magni, he was still a solid man who would be intimidating to all Momsies, especially someone as young and petite as her; the woman looked to be nothing more than a big teenager.

Taking a deep breath, I entered Christina's and my room unsure how much I should tell her. She was on the bed with a hard expression on her pretty face.

"So?" she said.

I scratched my beard. "Ehhm..."

"Don't 'ehhm' me."

I cleared my throat. "It wasn't Laura."

"No, I know. I saw her."

"Ahh, so you didn't stay here as I asked you to?"

"No, I saw the whole thing, and I doubt Magni understands what woman he has kidnapped."

"What do you mean?"

"That mark on her forehead – do you know what it represents?"

"No, I thought it was just a tattoo."

"You thought wrong."

"So? Is she royalty or something?" I joked.

Christina shook her head. "You know we don't have royalty anymore."

"Then what's so special about her?"

She lowered her voice. "Athena is a priestess."

"What?" I scrunched my face. "What kind of priestess? Didn't you say Momsies weren't religious?"

"We're not. Our priestesses are theologians, philosophers, and spiritual advisors. They don't hold a doctrine over people's head telling them how to live their lives."

149

"Then what do they do?"

Christina got up and paced the floor. "They guide anyone seeking a spiritual connection, embracing the core of every religion, which was always love to begin with."

"Okay, but then why do you call them priestesses if they don't follow a specific religion?" I asked, wishing she would stand still. "At least our priests only preach about the Bible."

"I don't know," she said in agitation. "But I do know that we don't have many priestesses and that they are seen as highly treasured. My people will take this as a declaration of war and the council will have to come back at you full force."

"Fuck!" I exclaimed in understanding, feeling even more angry with Magni now.

"You think we're just a bunch of sweet women, but that nickname you have for us..."

"What – Momsies?"

"Yes." She lowered her brows and scolded me. "The Momsies are going to be very angry with you boys and you won't like it."

"Don't call us boys," I said offended. "And you know what, Christina?"

"What?"

"If you want to threaten me, at least have the balls to do it with some curse words. I can't take it seriously when you scold me as if I'm a child."

She looked like she'd sucked on a lemon. "Did you just ask me to grow testicles?"

I turned my back on her with an exasperated sigh.

"I see, so we're back to the insults now, are we?" she said sourly. "But let me tell you something, Alexander Boulder; your fellow Nmen might feel offended when you accuse them of being feminine, but I can assure you that I take it as a compliment. And from what I know of the male physiology I would think that statement is complete nonsense anyway."

I rubbed my face. "What?"

Testicles are fragile, and I've seen men cry when they're hit hard in the crotch.

"So?"

She tilted her head. "I don't follow your logic. Women's private parts seem more robust and can take a hard pounding. They even have to endure giving birth – which isn't easy, I've been told. So, why would you ask me to grow a sensitive, fragile body part and not a tough one like a vagina?"

I groaned at her logic. "It's just a saying and unlike you people, we don't have time to fucking sit and meditate on the deeper meaning of everything we say."

"Well, maybe you should."

"Oh, give me a break, woman."

"Fine... so what are you going to do about Athena?" she asked.

"Me?" I pointed to my chest. "Why would *I* do anything?"

"Because your imbecile of a friend Magni has kidnapped a priestess, and that's deeply wrong."

"Sure, but it's Khan's problem, not mine."

"Of course it's your problem. Aren't you supposed to be a real man?"

I squared my shoulders and narrowed my eyes, signaling for her to elaborate but tread carefully.

"A real man doesn't allow women to be mistreated. Isn't that what you meant when you said men had evolved since the time when they oppressed women?"

"We have!" I expostulated.

"Then show it to me. Free her."

I took off my clothes again and got under the covers. "I'm not doing shit, Christina. My only concern is making sure you're safe, and if I did something stupid like crossing my ruler, I'd be killed and you'd be without a protector."

Emphatically, Christina turned her back on me and curled up in a fetal position.

I put my arm on her shoulder and moved closer but she shook my hand off and hissed, "Don't touch me."

"Hey," I muttered and kissed her shoulder. "It has nothing to do with us."

Christina looked back and met my eye with tears in hers. "Until you help Athena, I won't let you touch me."

That stung! For the last seven days, we had ended our days with kissing and touching, and that shit was addictive as hell.

I lived for it and spent my days fantasizing about finally letting myself sink myself inside her.

That night hadn't come yet, but I would gladly take the feeling of her naked chest rubbing against mine and her legs wrapping around my body, while kissing her long and deep.

The sounds she made when she got aroused, the feeling of her soft curves and the little cries when I made her come with my fingers and tongue... Christina was all I could think about, and the disappointment that she would deny me the highlight of my day made me tense up. "We'll see about that," I said, low, and turned my back on her as well. Christina might not be the initiator of our make-out sessions, but she was definitely enjoying them. *I'll give her a day until she's begging me to touch her*, I thought. But man, was I wrong!

CHAPTER 18
Athena

Christina

The morning after Magni had brought Athena to the mansion I asked Khan if I could bring her breakfast.

His slight nod was all I needed, and ten minutes later I was balancing a large tray full of fruit, bread, juice and tea.

Finn opened the door in his pants only, and I drew in a breath at the sight of his naked torso. I couldn't believe what I was seeing. The man was a cyborg, and I stared at his abdomen where his skin was peeled back and revealed the machinery underneath. I had seen plenty of people with robotic limbs, but never one who had his whole abdomen cybernetic.

He laughed at my expression and slammed his belly. "Don't worry, it's just a tattoo."

My eyes expanded and I took in the artwork that had fooled me. It looked so incredibly realistic.

"Is that for me?" Finn asked and winked at me with a grin while tying his long wavy hair up in a bun.

Like Boulder he was muscled and had a bit of hair on his chest but it worried me that he was only half dressed. *If he's abused Athena in any way I'll make sure he regrets it,* I swore to myself.

"No, the food is for Athena," I said firmly and took a step forward when he opened the door wider.

I almost dropped the tray at the horrible sight that met me. Athena was on the bed, tied down with her legs and arms spread out to the four posters.

"What did you *do*?" I exclaimed with shock.

"It's nothing. I just kept her safe."

I quickly put down the tray and ran to get to her, my fingers frantically pulling at the knots of the ropes to free her from her restrains.

"You animal," I accused him.

Finn didn't look offended but leaned down to pick up a t-shirt from the floor. "I'll give you two a few minutes," he said and put the shirt on before he pointed to Athena with a smug smile. "And you, sexy, don't try anything foolish again or you'll be back in ropes in no time."

Athena didn't even flinch until he left the room.

"Thank you," she muttered when I untied the last rope.

"I'm Christina, the archeologist they told you about last night when you arrived," I explained.

When I helped her sit up, the cover fell down and revealed that she was naked.

Swallowing hard, I asked the question that was burning on my mind. "Did he...? I mean, you can tell me if he..."

"Raped me?" she asked softly.

"Yes."

I was biting my lip when she looked at me with a calm expression. "No, Christina, Finn didn't rape me."

"Oh, thank god." I sighed.

"He and I had a discussion and in his lack of verbal ammunition he used other means to intimidate and dominate me, but you shouldn't worry about me. I'm not easily intimidated."

"But, did *he* undress you, or did you?"

"It matters not," she said in a voice that somehow was too deep and mature for her age. "He's just a young boy."

I frowned. Finn had to be in his early to mid-thirties. He was *not* a boy; it was a strange thing for her to say.

She smiled. "I'm older than I look."

"All right, and how old are you then?" I asked and admired the symbol on her forehead with the elegant mark of a priestess.

"I'm thirty years old."

I couldn't help a small laugh. "No, you're not. You can't be more than twenty; you look very young."

"I *am* young!" She smiled vaguely. "So are you."

"How can you be my age?" I was looking at her flawless skin, apple cheeks, and clear green eyes. Everything about her shouted youth.

She shrugged and took my hand. "My dear, do not let your eyes fool you. Not everything is what it seems."

"I know that," I said and felt a slight irritation. I was the one coming to *her* aid and she behaved like she didn't need it.

"I smell something nice," she said and gave me a bigger smile.

"Oh, yes, of course." Bringing the tray to the bed, I said: "I brought you breakfast."

"That's very kind of you; please, let us share it."

"It's okay, I just ate downstairs."

"Good, then tell me about this place," she said and picked up some grapes.

"Okay." I crawled up on the bed and took a seat with my legs crossed. "This place is called the Gray Mansion and it's the home of the ruler and his family."

"Khan Aurelius?"

"Yes. His mother, Erika, lives here too and his brother Magni." My voice grew brusque. "Magni is the beast who kidnapped you."

While she ate, I spoke. "I'm with Boulder... Or I mean, he's my protector."

"Okay."

"There are other men here at the mansion. Guards, staff, and friends of the ruler, but no other women. Only Erika, Laura, and me."

"And Laura went missing." It wasn't a question. Athena already knew this part.

155

"Yes. And when Magni found out, he lost control of his emotions and threw things around in a rage," I explained. "He wants her back, badly."

"Hmm. Do you know why she left?"

I looked down. "Probably because I told her how much freedom she would have in the Motherlands. She wants to learn martial arts."

"Really?" Athena set down her glass. "How interesting that she wants to learn how to fight. I wonder if she wants to know how to protect herself or if she's motivated by the need to harm someone."

"Someone like Magni, you mean?"

Athena lifted her shoulders in a small shrug.

"I don't know." I blew away a loose strand of hair from my face. "Magni is a dominant and moody man, and I get the sense that he sees Laura as his property; but when I first met her she was happy to be his wife."

"Until you started describing a different life to her."

"Yeah." I looked down.

Athena reached out and lifted my chin. "People are put in our path for a reason, Christina. First you crossed the border to come here, then Laura crossed the border to go there. It makes a balance somehow, wouldn't you agree?"

"Not really, because then Magni kidnapped you and now a war might break out."

She tilted her head. "Yes. You make a good point, but then again..."

The secretive smile on her lips made me sit up straight. "What is it?"

"It's an exciting time we live in, wouldn't you say?"

"I don't know."

Athena popped a grape into her mouth and chewed it. "For someone as adventurous as you this is a great chance."

"How do you know I'm adventurous?"

She gave an untroubled laugh. "You came here, voluntarily. That surely suggests a sense of adventure, I'd say."

"Fair enough," I agreed.

"You've got a chance to be part of something bigger."

"What do you mean?" I asked, but she just patted my hand with a knowing smile without elaborating any further. Confused by her talk, I turned the subject back to the main point on my agenda. "We need to find a way to get you out of here."

"You want to help me escape?" she asked.

"Yes." I picked up a rope. "I'm not letting that bastard tie you up in here."

"Christina," she said reproachfully. "Your language."

"I'm sorry. It's because I've been adjusting to their crude talk."

"I understand, but do try and use proper communication."

"Yes, I apologize." It hadn't taken me long to come to respect her. Athena was charismatic and when I offered to fetch her clothes, she surprised me by pulling aside the cover and getting out of bed stark naked. Unashamed, she walked across the room to her pile of clothes and started to dress.

"How is the excavation going?" she asked.

"Good. We've found thirty-five books so far. Only five of them were in good condition, but I have a feeling that today we'll find more."

"That's wonderful. Can I be of assistance while I'm here?"

"That would be wonderful, but they won't let you walk around freely."

"No, probably not, but maybe we could convince Finn to keep an eye on me at the digging site instead of in this room.

"No!" I said in a small shriek. "That's not a good idea."

157

"Why not?"

"Because… ehm…" I didn't want to tell her that I'd had to marry Boulder to get to work.

"It's just that if you ask Khan, he will offer to find you a permanent protector and arrange a tournament for men to fight over you to prove themselves worthy. It would mean men killing other men. I had to go through that and I don't recommend it."

"How barbaric," Athena exclaimed with a worried expression.

"I know. And besides, you won't be here long. I'll get you out one way or another."

Athena walked back to the bed where I sat and leaned down to look me into my eyes. "Christina, I sense great bravery in you, but this is not your battle."

"No, I know, but I'm still going to do whatever I can to help you."

"Thank you, dear." Athena placed her hand on my head while closing her eyes. "Bless you, child."

CHAPTER 19
Bargain

Christina

Determination is good if you want to help someone escape, but unfortunately you need more than that. I had no experience with how to help someone get out of a hostage situation. I didn't have the negotiation techniques of a mediator or the skill set of a warrior. I was just me – a history professor and archeologist. After three days of searching for a way to help Athena I was getting desperate.

"You have to help her, Boulder," I pleaded with him. The house was quiet and it had been over an hour since we had gone to bed. To me it was another day wasted without finding a way to free Athena.

"What?" he whispered, his voice revealing that he wasn't sleeping either.

"You heard me." I turned on my side to face him and he activated the light. It was a faint glow, but enough to see each other in the darkness.

Boulder was on his back, his arm resting across his forehead and his eyes on me.

"It's not right, and you know it," I said low.

He sighed. "Athena is a strong woman; I honestly feel worse for Finn than her."

"Are you serious?"

"Yes. Have you seen him? He used to be smiling all the time, now he's anything but. You know she cursed him, right?"

My brows flew up. "She cursed him?"

"Yes. I don't know the specifics but he's furious about it."

I swallowed my scoff. I didn't believe in curses and was surprised that Boulder and Finn did.

"Alexander, I'm begging you. Take Athena home."

"No." He turned on his side and propped himself on his elbow, looking calmly at me. "I told you, my concern is you, not her."

Desperate, I played a trump card with a low seductive voice. "I'll let you touch me if you take her home," I said in desperation.

"Why? Do you miss making out with me?" His smug smile provoked me.

"No!" I lied. "I only made out with you as a social experiment."

"Really? I was under the impression that you enjoyed it."

"Who said a social experiment can't be enjoyable?" I pointed out, still whispering. "Look, Boulder, I know it could cost you your life if they found out you helped Athena escape, but I have a plan."

"Hmm..."

"You could teach me how to fly your hybrid. If you could create a distraction I could get Athena out and take us to the border. Khan and Magni would know I did it, but better me than you since I'd be out of their reach."

He didn't like my plan. His expression told me that much.

"And what about your work here? I thought it was important to you."

"It is and I'll be sad to miss out on the rest, but saving Athena is more important."

"I don't want you to leave," he said low.

"I know, but you always knew it was just a matter of time."

160

Boulder's eyes grew stormy and dark. "Is it so awful for you to be here with me?"

"No, but Athena is a hostage. Don't you understand?"

He rolled onto his back, exhaling with frustration.

"Boulder, please," I begged and moved closer, touching him.

"You're leaving me, aren't you?" he asked solemnly.

"Yes," I muttered.

His sadness pulled at my heartstrings. Boulder was my friend and I liked him. I wanted to touch him and show him that I cared, but how could I when I'd told him I wouldn't let him touch me until he helped me free Athena? I couldn't break my word – it was a matter of principle.

And then an idea hit me. "Boulder," I said, my heart pounding a little faster.

"Uh-huh."

"Do you still want to make love to me?"

His eyes flew to me. "Is that a trick question?"

"No."

There was a pregnant silence between us and I cleared my throat to elaborate. "What if I told you I would be okay with it?"

Slowly, he sat up in the bed with his eyes wide open. "Are you messing with me?"

"No, I'm serious. I only have one condition."

"Which is?"

"You'll teach me how to fly your hybrid and you'll create a distraction so I can get Athena out of here."

He sat perfectly still for a few seconds, contemplating my offer, and then he spoke. "Only if *you* don't cross the border."

"How could I not? I would be punished here if I stayed," I argued.

"No," he stated firmly. "I wouldn't allow them to punish you. I'd protect you."

I bit my lip and he continued in a low whisper.

161

"I'll teach you to fly my hybrid and create a distraction, but *only* if you promise to wait for me at the border. I want more time with you."

I want more time with you too. I don't know where that thought came from, but it was the truth. *It's because I want to finish my project,* I concluded and pushed aside the warning that I was getting too attached to Boulder.

Slowly I nodded my head. "All right."

His mouth opened and he drew in a loud breath. "You mean it?" he asked with hope in his voice. "You'll stay with me?"

"Yes. Until my project is done," I confirmed.

"And you'll..." His Adam's apple bobbed in his throat. "You'll have sex with me now?"

Again, I nodded, butterflies swarming around my belly.

There was a quick smile on his face before he pulled me on top of him, kissing me hungrily.

My body was humming with excitement and nervousness.

"Promise that you'll be gentle. I'm still not sure you can actually fit inside me," I warned him.

Boulder was panting and undressing me with eager hands. "I've missed touching you," he mumbled with his mouth against my collarbone.

I had missed touching him too, but I didn't tell him that. Instead I let him undress first me and then himself. I was nervous when he placed me on my back and spread my legs. Boulder sat back on his heels between my legs and gazed over my naked body, always making sure the cover was draped over us. Everything about him was masculinity personified: his muscled chest, shoulders, beard, ruffled hair, burning eyes, and of course his massive phallus pointing straight at me as if aiming at its first prey.

This would be my first time having intercourse with a flesh-and-blood man and it would be Boulder's first time with a real woman. I wondered if he was as nervous as me.

Placing his large hand on my pelvis, he locked eyes with me. "You're so unbelievably beautiful, Christina, and I'm honored that you'll allow me to enter you."

I didn't know whether to be disturbed or flattered by that statement so I said nothing.

Boulder leaned forward, pressing his naked body against mine and his erection directly into my opening.

Boulder

My body was pumped and ready to experience what had been described to me as paradise. I pushed against the entrance that Christina had guarded so well since I first met her. I was the first man to ever enter her sacred cave.

She was nervous and tense, her pussy dry and unwelcoming. Impatiently, I pushed a little more and heard her make a noise of discomfort.

I knew what I had to do, but I just wanted to skip that part and go straight to the fucking. Most of all because I was terrified that she would change her mind and pull back her offer.

Be smart about it. Make sure she enjoys it so she wants to do it again.

Making a quick decision, I pulled back and spread her legs wider with my hands on her inner knees, while lowering my head to lick her.

Christina made a gasp when my tongue ran over her clit, but this was my fourth time doing it to her and I'd gotten rather confident.

"Ohh," she moaned and weaved her hands into my hair.

She tasted sweet and delicious, and it only took a few minutes before I deemed her ready for penetration.

Time to claim my wife!

The thought made me want to fucking bang my chest and howl. I had fought for her and she was my prize. This was my reward – to sink myself balls deep into the softest place in the world.

Time to fill her with my cum!

I had fantasized about this moment since the first night I slept in the same room as her. Dreamt about what it would be like to plant my seed in a woman and have a child with her. There was no greater treasure than to produce a child, especially if that child was a girl. Naturally I was smart enough not to share my impregnation fantasy with Christina but still I wondered why she would take such a risk. There was no way Khan would let her leave if she was pregnant. Hell, there was no way I would let her leave!

Before she could change her mind, I moved up her body and just like a missile locked on its target, my cock quickly found her soft folds. I was panting into her ear now, closing my eyes and letting my tip press against her. She stiffened a little and groaned from the pressure, but I pushed in further, holding my breath and taking in the wondrous feeling of her snug pussy.

Her breathing was shallow, and I paused for a second before I couldn't hold back anymore and pushed all the way in. "*Fuck!*" I moaned, my spine on fire and my hands finding hers and intertwining our fingers.

"Easy," she whispered.

I did my best to be gentle and allowed her time to stretch for a few seconds before I started rocking in and out of her.

"Ohh, shit." My voice quivered with delight and I pulled back to look at her while I moved to create the

164

wonderful friction that felt much better than anything I'd ever tried before.

"How does it feel?" I whispered.

She exhaled with a breathy "Good," her chest rising up and down, her mouth opening in a silent "Ahh"

Driven by a primal need to fuck my woman, I intensified the pace. She had promised me that she would come back to me after freeing Athena, and in my mind, that meant I would get to do this again. But for now, all I could think about was planting my seed in her. Next time I could take it slower, but this time I wanted to get to my finale before she pushed me away.

Christina panted in my ear when I made sure I had secured her under me, my chest pressing her down into the mattress, my hands holding hers in a tight grip. I closed my eyes and focused on my cock ejaculating deep into her womb, creating new life, and the thought alone did it for me. Five long last pumps to make sure every drop was delivered inside her, and I was the man with the biggest smile in this mansion. I had fucking done it! And the best part was that she had let me.

"You're crushing me," she complained and I lifted a bit of my weight off her. She was pushing at me, but I stayed on top of her, wanting to make sure my cum didn't run out of her before it had done its job.

"I'm sorry I didn't last longer," I said and placed a kiss on her nose. "But I've been dreaming of this moment since I was a teenager and I couldn't control myself."

"It's okay, just give me some space to breathe."

"But you didn't come. I'm going to remedy that," I said and moved a bit inside her. She felt wet from my cum, and the thought excited me enough that I remained hard.

"What are you doing?" she asked softly.

"I'm making love to you." I smiled. "And this time I want you from behind." She didn't protest when I pulled her around and placed my hands on her lovely ass, pulling her cheeks apart. Even in the dampened light I could see a bit of my cum dripping from her, and I hurried to push inside her again.

She was marvelous as she crouched on her hands and knees and allowed me to take her. I would have done anything for her at that moment. Fucking anything!

Leaning forward I snaked a hand around her waist and down to her clit, circling the magical area that got to her every time.

Her moans got deeper, her hips started pushing back at me and meeting my thrusts. It blew my mind to experience this glorious moment. She might have done it to save Athena, but Christina was enjoying it – enjoying being fucked by me – and that fact made everything twice as good.

"Say my name, Christina," I breathed.

"Ohhh," she panted back.

"Say my name," I ordered and kept moving rhythmically inside her.

"Alexander," she whispered in a raspy voice.

Fuck me – the way she moaned the four syllables of my name was the sexiest thing I'd ever heard.

I was doomed and I knew it. There was no way I could let this beautiful woman leave me. My heart had already decided that she was mine and I was hers.

CHAPTER 20
Flying Lessons

Boulder

I kept my word to Christina. The morning after she made love to me, we took off in my hybrid and spent the morning at the digging site. According to plan, she complained that she wasn't feeling well just before lunch, and I told her team members that I was taking her home.

A mile away I put the vehicle down on the ground. "All right, your turn to fly," I said and switched seats with her.

Christina reached out to touch the steering panel but couldn't reach it. "This won't work." She sighed. "This thing was built for large men, I think."

"You're damn right it was."

"You knew this?" She narrowed her eyes and I caught her accusation. "Is that's why you agreed to this deal? Because you knew I would never be able to fly your drone?"

"The seats are adjustable," I said dryly. "They probably are in your drones too; you've just never needed that function since you didn't have to fly them." I showed her where to find the button and watched her position her seat just right.

"Now what?" she asked.

"Now you turn on the engine and we get going."

"All right." With a look of concentration, she followed my directions and pushed the accelerator gently. Still the drone jerked with uneven movements that made me hold on to my seat.

"I'm sorry," she said and stopped. "Since it's a hybrid; couldn't you teach me to make it go automatically? That's probably for the best."

"I could," I said and paused, "but I wouldn't recommend it."

"Why not?"

My brows dropped. "Think, Christina!"

"What?" she asked with that sweet innocence of hers.

"What happens if someone steals a drone in Momsiland?"

"Why would anyone steal a drone?" she asked with an open expression.

I rolled my eyes. "Because they need a quick ride or saw a cool drone."

Christina blinked in confusion. "But who would they steal it from? No one owns the drones, they're public transportation."

I wrinkled my nose up. "No one owns them?"

"No, of course not."

"So it's true then?" I couldn't hide my disdain when I crossed my arms. "It's all fucking communism."

"Communism?" Christina raised her voice a tiny bit. "Hardly."

I snorted. "Sounds like communism to me. I couldn't live in a place where I couldn't own my land, my house, my drones."

"Excuse me, Mr. Capitalist, but you clearly haven't the faintest idea of the fairness principle that we live by."

"The fairness principle? Oh, please, just the name makes my throat burn – I think I'm going to vomit."

Her cheeks flamed red and she turned her head to look straight ahead. It was time to get back on track.

"The reason you can't put the hybrid on automatic is that flying it manually is the only way to make sure it can't be overruled by others."

"What do you mean when you say overruled?"

"Let me break it down for you, Christina," I said patiently. "First, I create a distraction, then you and Athena take off; and soon after, Finn is going to find out she's missing. Never mind that Khan will fucking kill Finn for losing sight of her, but the whole mansion will be a beehive of frantic men. The minute they realize my hybrid is missing, they're going to ask me to redirect it to come back." I tapped at my wristband.

Her eyes expanded in understanding. "Ahh, you can override the vehicles computer from your end."

"I can," I said with a rhythmic nodding. "Unless it's being flown manually."

"I see."

"Good, then you better try again – and this time go easy on the accelerator until you get the touch of it."

Christina eventually did get the touch but she flew slow and was clearly nervous about navigating.

I gave her directions and steered her toward my home, flying across water and vast areas of forest.

Once we got there I asked her to fly up to the large estate and park.

"Who lives here?" she asked curiously and leaned forward to see better.

"A handsome, wise, and very sexy man," I answered with a wink.

To my surprise she didn't catch on that I was talking about me. Humor definitely wasn't her strongest suit.

"Come on," I waved her with me up the stairs to the impressive double doors.

"Is he a friend of yours?" she asked a bit nervous and looked up to the rooftop – three floors above us.

"Oh, he's a very good friend of mine," I said and laughed.

"This house looks pre-war; how is that possible?" she asked.

"Because it was built in nineteen twenty-four."

"It was?" she whispered and licked her lips. "Are you sure?"

"Yup, this house is one of the few that wasn't bombed or torn down. I suppose its location outside the city made the difference.

Christina scanned the grounds and I could tell her eyes were lingering on the pretty pond with the ducks floating peacefully. "It's very pretty here with the forest and the water."

"You think?"

"Yes, very idyllic – like something from an old movie."

Butterflies made my belly tingle with a speck of hope that maybe, just maybe...

"Stop – what are you doing, Boulder?" She interrupted my thoughts with her protest when I opened the door and walked in.

"Don't you want to see what the house looks like on the inside?" I tempted. "As I said, it was built in nineteen twenty-four; that makes it..."

"Five hundred and thirteen years old," she breathed, her eyes wide as she took in the extravagant staircase.

"Exactly." I laughed. "So you're good at math, are you?"

Christina wasn't listening, she was walking toward the staircase with her hands outstretched.

"Beautiful, right?" I said.

"It's gorgeous," she whispered and touched the banister as if it was fragile.

"Yeah, they were good at making pretty houses back then. Not like the cubes you live in, huh?"

She nodded but seemed speechless.

"Feel free to walk around. The interior is modern of course, but the house itself is original... or almost original. It's been upgraded a bit to make it more energy-efficient."

"I can't believe it," she muttered and greedily scanned the room, taking in every little detail.

"Go ahead." I swung my arm out wide, signaling for her to investigate.

She walked as if in a daze from one room to the other and when she entered my study she gasped. "Books... so many books."

"I know," I said with a satisfied smile on my lips. "Some of them are really good and steamy."

Her hands were practically shaking when she gently touched the back of a few books, reading their titles.

"It's okay, you can take them out and look at them."

There were hundreds of books and her chest rose visibly when she said. "Were these all excavated?"

"No, they came with the house and have been an excellent source of information."

Again, she licked her lips and it made me smile. Her expression was similar to mine when I had a large, well-cooked steak on my plate.

She was hungry! Hungry to explore my estate and all the history that it contained.

"You like it?" I asked.

"I love it! It's like time traveling. This should be a museum for the rest of the world to see. It's so rare to see something this old and beautiful."

"I know. It takes a lot of money to maintain old properties like this one. That's why no one does it."

Her hand was running over a curved doorframe with delicate carvings in it. "Such craftsmanship," she muttered and walked inside the room.

"What is that?" She stiffened.

"The kitchen," I said and followed her eyes to the glass wall behind which meat hung on large hooks to age. "Oh, you mean the hanging," I continued. "It's just a culinary process to improve the flavor."

"Those are dead animals," she said in a brittle voice.

"That's right. There's deer, cow, and wild boar. I shot them myself."

Her eyes closed, she turned away, and it took her a while to gather herself, but to her credit she didn't address it further.

"Why is this kitchen so modern?"

"Because I like modern kitchens."

She shot me a curious look.

"Christina," I said and waited for her to meet my eyes. "You know it's my house, right?"

"But you said..." She tilted her head.

"That the owner was handsome, wise, and sexy," I finished. "That should have given you a clue." I laughed.

"Hmm." She shrugged and continued the tour, but I quickly caught up to her in the dining room and stopped her with my hands on her hips, turning her around to face me.

"What's 'hmm' supposed to mean?" I demanded.

"Nothing."

"Nothing?" Insecurity was a new thing to me, but then everything about her was new to me. "Are you saying you don't find me handsome, wise, or sexy?"

She leaned her head back looking up at me. "I'm used to pretty men. You're not exactly that."

"*Pretty?*" I spit out the word. "I would be offended if you called me pretty."

Her eyebrows were raised. "Okay, well, in that case it's a good thing that I don't find you pretty."

My jaws tightened and I walked her back to the dining table, pressing myself against her. "Just answer me this: do you find me attractive?"

She swallowed hard and leaned back to get some distance between us.

With my index finger, I lifted her chin and made her look at me. "Last night, Christina, when we had sex – did you find me attractive."

"I didn't find you unattractive," she answered.

"It's not good enough." I shook my head a single time. "I've told you a million times that I find you beautiful. Now it's time for you to tell me the truth: do you find me attractive?"

"Boulder, I..." She trailed off.

"It's a simple question. Yes or no," I insisted.

"You're very masculine but I like the way you..." She looked down.

"No, look at me," I demanded.

She did and took a deep intake of air. "I like it when we're together."

"Sexually or in general?"

Her answer came as a whisper. "Both."

It gave me some satisfaction but I'd already suspected that much. "You still haven't answered my question."

"Why does it matter what I think?"

"It matters because I'm a vain motherfucker and I want to know if you find me attractive," I said impatiently. "Would you say I'm sexy and handsome?"

Hard-pressed, she finally whispered, "No."

"No?" I took a step back.

She placed her hands on her cheeks. "I think it's the beard. It's too much."

My hands flew to my beard. I was proud of it. I'd been one of the first among my peers to grow a decent one and now she was saying she didn't like it.

"And your hair, it's... well, uncombed."

Before I could react, she added. "But I like your eyes, they're full of life and the bright gray color is unique."

When I walked away from her she called out. "I'm sorry, I didn't mean to upset you."

I had always considered myself handsome but apparently Momsies had a different taste in men than what I represented. I knew a few men who didn't have a beard but they looked boyish to me, and in the wintertime it was practical wearing a warm beard.

It annoyed the hell out of me that she didn't find me handsome because I wanted her to fall in love with me and stay. She loved my house, and she had already allowed me to claim her sexually. I was getting in too deep to let her go, but the only way I could truly keep her was if she chose to stay.

"Boulder," her voice rang softly and I felt her hand on my shoulder.

Turning slowly, I spoke, "So you prefer pretty men, huh?"

Her brows drew closer together. "I didn't say that. You know I don't think of men that way."

"That's right," I grumped. "You think the notion of a man bringing out arousal in a woman is a myth, isn't that what you said?"

She didn't answer, but the hunter in me wanted this kill and with a hand around her waist I drew her close to me. "So you're saying that I'm not attractive and I can't arouse you." It wasn't a question but a statement.

Christina watched me carefully.

I leaned in and kept my lips hovering just in front of hers when I spoke in a low and raspy voice. "I'll bet I could make you scream out my name and have you beg me to fuck you if I wanted to."

Her hands pushed gently at my chest but there was no resolve behind it and I didn't pull back. Instead I placed both hands under her behind and lifted her onto my hip. We were eye to eye now and I smiled when she held on to my neck.

"Your men might be pretty as women but they don't know how to fuck like we do," I growled, low.

"Put me down," she said but of course I didn't.

I walked back to the dining room and lowered her to the table. "I think I'm in the mood for a snack," I told her and started undressing her.

174

"Boulder, stop it," she panted and pushed at my hands. "I don't want to..." The rest of her words were swallowed by my open-mouthed kiss.

Her struggle of resistance was weak and more for show. I didn't stop my attack on her and slid my hand under her shirt, finding her delicious globes and smiling when I felt how hard her nipples were.

She gave a small moan: "Stop it, Boulder."

"I'll stop," I groaned into her ear and bit her earlobe gently, "if you're not wet for me."

She protested when I opened her pants and snaked my hand down between her legs.

My smile grew wider when I felt how warm and moist she was. Holding her gaze, I slid my finger inside her, then two, before I pulled out and held up my glistening fingers for her to see. "Looks like it's not a myth after all - you're aroused by a man."

"It doesn't mean a thing," she defended herself, but I just laughed and licked my wet fingers with her nectar before I pulled her pants all the way down.

"It means that you're attracted to me and you want me to fuck you."

"No, it doesn't," she objected but she didn't move away when I grabbed her thighs and moved her ass closer to the edge of the table.

"Either way, I'm taking you right here and now." My voice was resolute and my promise backed up quickly when I opened my pants and freed my hard cock.

"Don't," she said, but I ignored her and pushed inside her with a deep growl. Holding on to her knees I pressed all the way in, enjoying the way she closed her eyes and bit her lip.

"Mine," I growled again and that made her eyes fly open.

"What did you say?"

"You're mine, Christina," I repeated loud and clear and slammed inside her again. "My wife, my woman."

"I don't belong to you." She tried to sit up but I wouldn't let her.

"You belong to me and I to you," I said firmly.

"Stop it, Boulder, you're freaking me out," she cried.

"Just stating the facts," I said and squeezed her knees tighter. The sound of our fucking was arousing to me, my hard flesh meeting her moist insides. She was incredibly wet and her face flushed red with arousal; there was no hiding it from me.

"Lie back and let me fuck you," I ordered when she tried to sit up again.

"But I..." she panted, still trying to get up.

In a swift move, I pulled her up on my hips again, holding one arm under her butt and one arm around her waist, lifting and lowering her on my hard cock.

"Ohhh," she said as I impaled her all the way.

"Put your hands around my neck," I instructed and made a satisfied sound in my throat when she complied.

I kissed her and this time she returned my kiss, our tongues dueling for control.

"Say, it Christina," I ordered. "Say my name."

"No," she panted.

"What do you want?" My voice was low as I held her still with only the tip of my cock inside her.

"I don't know."

Lowering her to the floor, I turned her around and pressed at her from behind until she leaned over the dining table, her lovely ass pushed back at me.

With patience I didn't know I had in me, I slid my cock up and down her soft folds, watching her body prepare for my next attack.

"What do you want?" I repeated.

She lifted on her toes and arched her back slightly.

Oh, yeah, she wants me.

176

"I don't know," she repeated.

Leaning over her I rested my cock on her ass and nuzzled her nipples. Her face was turned, her eyes closed, and she licked her lips again.

"Alexander," she whispered in a needy way.

"Yes, beautiful?" Deep male satisfaction filled me at the sound of my name and with a hand on my cock I placed it right at her entrance. Immediately she pushed back but I moved back too.

"Please," she whispered.

"Please what?"

"Alexander, please," she begged.

"Say it, Christina – say the word."

"I want…"

"What do you want?"

"You."

"What do you want me to do?"

Her breathing was ragged and she turned to look at me with half-lidded eyes. "I want you to take me."

"You want me to fuck you?"

"Ye… yes," she stammered.

"Then say it." I looked down at my tip, dripping with precum, and couldn't resist inserting it just a little bit.

"I already did… I said that I wanted you."

"Say: Alexander I want you to fuck me," I pressed her while circling her clit with my thumb.

"Ohh, yes… that's feels so good," she moaned.

I moved my finger and used my cock to play with her clit instead.

"Say it, beautiful, I want to hear you say it."

"Fuck me, Alexander."

Red light blinded me as my head exploded with the most insane lust. Christina had used the F-word for the first time in her life, and I knew that only absurd arousal could have gotten her to do something that unnatural to her.

"With pleasure," I groaned and gave her what she had asked for. Filling her up, swiveling my hips, riding her hard, I took her with my fingers boring into her hips and got off on the way she cried out her ecstasy.

"Ohh... yes, yes, yes," she panted out loud.

An intense feeling of pleasure hit me and I looked down to understand what was happening. It was like her insides were cramping and milking my cock. I had read about this but never had I known what it would feel like in real life.

"Alexander, it feels so gooood," she moaned.

My head fell back and I roared out my own orgasm. "FUUUUCK!!!!!"

I spurted inside her and held on to her in an iron grip, instinctively making sure she didn't pull away before I had emptied myself inside of her.

One spurt, two, three, four – I stopped counting and gave in to the exquisite sensation of my semen pumping into her.

We were both making incoherent sounds and panting, and just like yesterday, I stayed inside her as long as she would allow me.

To spare her pride I didn't make any more teasing comments about her arousal. I had proven my point and regained a bit of dignity after her insult of not finding me attractive. Instead, I showed her to the bathroom and gave her time to collect herself before we left my house and took up the second part of teaching her to fly my hybrid.

CHAPTER 21
Athena's Return

Christina

"So remember, you only have ten to fifteen minutes maximum to get out and get going, okay? There's no time to be afraid or fly slowly. You *have* to push the accelerator if you want to get Athena to the border before we catch up to you," Boulder said in a solemn tone.

"Okay." I nodded with a serious expression.

"And Christina..." He placed both hands on my shoulders. "When we catch up to you, I'll be in a furious mood. Don't be scared, it's for show."

I understand.

"But if you wreck my hybrid and something happens to you, I'll be furious for real, do you understand?"

"Yes. I'll be careful."

"Good. Be careful but *fast*."

"Got it!"

"All right." He drew in a sigh and we flew the last stretch in silence. Boulder was back behind the panel to avoid anyone's knowing what we'd been doing.

He parked the drone with the nose to the road, making it easier for me to get away fast.

"Let's do it," he said and shot me a serious glance.

We walked in together and up the staircase to our room. Making sure no one was close we took a turn and headed toward Finn's room, and quietly knocked on the door.

Finn opened it and took a look at both of us. "Hey," he said.

179

"Hey, Finn," Boulder leaned a hand against the doorframe. "Christina wanted to visit Athena; maybe we could give them a minute to talk. I brought you a beer."

Finn looked at the beer and smiled. "I can't say no to that, but I'm afraid Athena is gone."

"Gone? What do you mean she's gone?"

"Magni took her back to the Momsies."

Yes! It was like sunbeams and rainbows were dancing around his head. "That's wonderful," I exclaimed. "I'm so happy for her."

"Yeah, Khan took an offer from the council," Finn said.

"What offer?" I asked eagerly.

"They haven't found Laura, but one of your council members took Athena's place."

"What?" My joy evaporated. "Who?"

"I don't know. I didn't see her. She's in Khan's office."

I turned around and ran down the corridor with Boulder at my heels. My feet wouldn't move fast enough down the stairs, and he caught up to me. "Stop, Christina."

"No, this changes nothing. I won't allow an innocent woman to be held hostage," I hissed, low.

"Think for a moment. You can't barge into Khan's office without a plan."

I was too upset to think rationally and stormed ahead, Boulder cursing loudly behind me. I didn't knock on the door or wait for permission to enter, I just walked right in to find the least likely scenario.

Councilwoman Pearl and Khan both looked up at me to see who the intruder was. They were sitting quietly opposite each other with a chessboard between them.

"Councilwoman Pearl," I cried out. "What are you doing here?"

Khan gave me an annoyed glance but Pearl stood up and moved to take my hands. "May peace surround you," she said and looked into my eyes.

"May peace surround you too," I replied and poured all my worry for her into that look.

"What happened?" Boulder asked from the door.

Khan waved him closer. "Pearl here offered herself in exchange for Athena.

"Would you mind if I talked to Pearl alone?" I asked Khan.

"I suppose you could do that, but not until our game is over. It shouldn't take too long. Chess is a man's game, after all."

I caught the minuscule smile on Pearl's face and felt easier at heart when she met me with a calm and relaxed expression. "Lord Khan is right, it won't take long. Maybe you could show me the park after we're done here; it's a beautiful day."

Boulder and Khan exchanged glances.

"We'll see about that," Khan said.

"Tell you what." Pearl smiled softly. "If I win, you'll allow me a walk in the park with Christina."

He was amused. "I like your optimism, but you won't win."

"Then it should be an easy promise for you to make," Pearl said sweetly.

Boulder and I pulled back but didn't leave the room as the two rulers returned to their seats and quietly resumed their game.

I never played chess, so all I could do was count the number of pieces that stood on each side of the board. She had seven of his pieces and he had nine of hers.

Khan was quick to make his moves while Pearl took a little longer. When she took his queen, he squirmed in his seat but didn't say anything.

The game went on for five minutes until he proudly said. "Check."

"That was a nice move," Pearl acknowledged in a friendly tone.

"I know." He looked over to us and smiled with satisfaction. "Told you it wouldn't take long," he said.

"Checkmate." The word came soft and unhurried but made Khan swing his head back to the board and frown.

"What?" he spat out.

Calmly Pearl pointed to her move and he grew visibly paler.

"Beginner's luck, I suppose," Pearl said. "I'm sure you were just distracted."

Khan pushed his chair back and stood up with his lips in thin lines. "I wasn't paying attention."

Pearl turned toward me. "Should we take a cup of tea in the park?"

"Tea sounds lovely." I smiled and bit back a chuckle.

Taking my arm Pearl glided gracefully out of the room and spoke over her shoulder. "May we ask for some tea and a bit of privacy?"

Khan pointed to Boulder. "You follow them and make sure they don't do something stupid."

With a nod, Boulder followed us – offering us enough distance to have a private conversation.

"It's so nice to see you again, Christina," Pearl said and squeezed my arm. I couldn't understand how she could look almost delighted in this grim hostage situation.

"I want to say the same, but given the circumstances, I'm not sure," I admitted.

Pearl's brows dropped. "We couldn't let one of our priestesses be here against her will."

"But surely you could have imposed harder sanctions and used your political powers, couldn't you?"

"Yes" was her short answer. "We might still do that."

With eyes scanning the area, I lowered my voice to a whisper. "I was going to help Athena escape today, and I can help you."

Pearl stopped and seemed to be thinking.

"We'll take Boulder's drone and fly to the border before they find out. I've planned it all out and learned how to fly his hybrid manually."

"I'm impressed," Pearl said softly. "But there's no need."

"No need?" I asked incredulously.

"I chose to come, and I stand by my word that I'll take Athena's place. Khan won't harm me, I'm sure of it."

"You don't know him," I warned. "He might be cordial and even charming at times but he's ruthless and barbaric. He'll watch men kill each other and find it entertaining. The man has no heart."

"No heart?"

"No. You can't trust him."

"And Boulder, do you trust him?" She gave a discreet glance in his direction.

My answer came quickly and surprised us both. "Yes. I trust him."

Pearl furrowed her brows. "Why?"

"He protects me and he…" I couldn't say it.

"He what?"

"He likes me," I forced out.

"Christina, what is your relationship with that man?"

I chewed on my lower lip, unsure how to tell her. "Maybe we should sit down first," I suggested.

The weather was nice, and warm enough that we didn't mind the breeze. We found a place to sit and thanked the man who brought us tea.

"It needs to sit for a few minutes," he said with a smile and walked away. Boulder leaned against the mansion wall and lifted his face to the sun. He was too far away to hear our conversation but close enough to keep an eye on us.

"In order for me to do my work and be safe, I was informed that I needed a bodyguard when I first arrived,"

I started. "They never realized that I was a woman until I actually arrived, and at first they wanted to send me back."

Pearl listened attentively.

"I didn't fully comprehend what they meant by a bodyguard until I had to choose my champion. You see, Khan arranged a tournament where the men fought each other to show their bravery and strength to me."

Her eyes narrowed but she didn't interrupt me.

"Some men died and I was horrified, but in the end, I was left with four men to choose from. Boulder was out because he broke his arm so I chose a younger man, who looked like a suitable bodyguard, but then he started referring to me as his wife, and I realized they had tricked me."

"Go on," Pearl said, lost in my story.

"They were all strangers, except Boulder, whom I had spent three days with." I looked down. "I told Khan I would never marry in my life and he said I was free to leave, but that he doubted I would make it to the border without protection."

"He *didn't*," she breathed.

I nodded. "He did, and so I hid behind Boulder, who only knew one way to protect me."

"How?"

"He married me and made me untouchable to anyone but him."

Pearl gasped. "You're *married* to that man."

I closed my eyes, realizing how horrible it must sound to her. "Yes," I confirmed.

It took her a moment to regain her composure but when she did she asked, "And how is he treating you?"

"He's…" I thought about it. "Different, but nice."

"Different how?"

"Well, for one, he curses a lot and he has bad manners. He eats meat and he… well, look at him. He's not very concerned about his appearance, is he?"

184

"I don't know. They all look kind of scrubby to me," Pearl mused. "Maybe that's how they like to look."

"I've seen a few without beards and some with braids but most of them look savage," I said and waved a fly from my face.

"I agree." Pearl frowned. "I was picked up on the border by a man that scared me a lot. His name was Magni and he introduced himself as Khan's younger brother."

"Magni is Laura's husband. The woman who ran away," I explained.

"Ah, yes, I understood that much."

"Have you found her?" I asked worriedly.

Pearl's eyes looked back to Boulder and in an almost-whisper she said: "Of course."

"How?"

"Did you think we don't keep an eye on the border? Laura walked right up to the checkpoint and was handed over to the right people. We're trying to help her acclimatize to her new surroundings but she's fine."

"But if you know where she is, why are you here?"

Pearl blinked at me. "My dear, we couldn't in good conscience return her to a place where none of us want to live, could we?"

"But then why not simply tell Khan that Laura doesn't want to be returned?"

"Because that would set his brother off, and Magni seems volatile enough as it is. Besides, this has given us a great opportunity." Pearl lifted her hands to brush back her blonde hair and rolled it into a loose bun.

I scrunched up my face. "To do what? Beat Khan at chess?"

She chuckled. "Did you see his face? I have to say I rather enjoyed winning."

"I saw."

While I was speaking to Pearl, I noticed her piling the sugar cubes on top of each other in the large sugar bowl.

"What are you doing?" I asked.

"You asked what opportunity I was referring to so I wanted to explain it to you."

"Okay."

"In the beginning of the twenty-second century there was a woman named Martha Beck, who came up with a theory which you might have heard of."

The name Martha Beck rang a bell, but I couldn't remember the name of the theory.

"The pyramid represents the kind of power structure that ruled the world for thousands of years and still rule here in the Northlands. The people on top," she said and pointed to the highest sugar cube, "are the ones with the highest ability to force, harm, dominate, kill, amass wealth, and hold power over others."

"Lord Khan," I said and stared at the pyramid as Pearl continued explaining.

"Martha was one of many to point out that rebellions will never work as they only serve to create a new pyramid of power."

"Okay, so what are you saying?"

"My colleagues in the council and I would love nothing more than to include the Nmen in our society. It's silly that we can't all live together and that we have millions of men living isolated up here."

My eyebrows arched upward. "But we have rules that men can't be in power, and I don't think you understand how different they are from us. They practically break all our laws on a daily basis."

Pearl smiled. "I know. It's understandable with centuries of separation that we will be very different culturally."

"So what do you plan to do? Take out Khan and force the men to be part of the Motherlands?"

"Oh, Mother of Nature, no!" she exclaimed. "We are pacifists and peacekeepers. Violence and oppression is not our style."

"Then what?" I asked confused.

Pearl picked up the teapot and poured a cup for me and her. "Our society is the opposite of a pyramid. We have a flat structure where everyone has value and no one is above others." She pointed to my cup of tea. "Our society is flat like a pool of water. No one is above or below others, and our system works because we are like concentric circles of waves that energetically connect and overlap." She held up the teapot and let drops from the spout form rings in the surface of the tea to illustrate what she had just said.

"I know this," I said. "But the men aren't interested in that sort of life. They compare it to communism and think we're being treated like children with all our protective rules. I guarantee that they won't give up their hierarchy easily. They look down on us, Pearl. I know they do."

She smiled. "So let's say that they see us as inferior, as nothing; we'll start from the lowest point." She held the pot of tea over the sugar cubes that she had formed into a pyramid. "Do you know what happens when a pool of water forms around a pyramid like this?"

"No."

"Then observe." She said and poured the tea around it. "All we need is a group of people to become enlightened and from the bottom up dissolve the power structure."

I watched the sugar cubes soak up the brown tea and melt.

"It's the people on the bottom who are more likely to give up their old way of living first, because they have less to lose. The pool of enlightened people won't destroy the pyramid," she said and tilted her head while looking at the pyramid of sugar cubes tilting down as the sugar melted. "We just absorb the people around us because we're made

187

of inclusion and love. We're not planning a revolution, more like a dissolution, an inclusion."

I sat quietly and stared at the dissolved pile of sugar where only a few cubes were still melting away.

"The ones on the top," Pearl said quietly, "are usually the last ones to know what is happening."

"But how?" I asked in a low voice. "How do you plan to do this?"

"With patience and time. My being here and your being here represents a great opportunity to shine a beam of enlightenment, wouldn't you say?"

"But then why did you come instead of Athena? If anyone is enlightened it should be a priestess."

"True." She tapped her lower lip. "But Athena didn't choose to come and we worried about her."

"Have you met her?" I asked.

"Only when I crossed her by the border."

"She's a strong woman and very wise," I said.

"I'm glad to hear it; maybe she has planted a few seeds in the time she was here."

"Maybe." I paused. "But how will you get access to the people on the bottom as you talked about? Seems to me you're dealing with the highest point of the pyramid."

"For now. But I'm sure Lord Khan will get tired of playing my host and hand me over to some guards that I can influence."

"No. He'll find a protector for you. Probably one of his powerful friends." I sighed with frustration. "Let's just hope you get a nice protector and that Khan won't pester you too much."

She smiled. "Remember what I said. Powerful people tend to underestimate you if they see you as inferior."

"If you planned to make him believe you were inferior, you shouldn't have beaten him in chess, Khan would be a fool to underestimate you now."

"He would," Pearl said with a soft smile. "But he's a man blinded by greed and pride, and I can work with that."

"So you don't want me to free you?"

"No, I don't," Pearl answered firmly. "I have important work here."

I sighed and raised the teacup to my mouth. "Well, in that case, welcome to the Northlands. I'm glad to have you join me here."

Pearl raised her own cup and we respectfully looked into each other's eyes when we drank.

"Thank you, Christina. And now, tell me about your project."

CHAPTER 22
The Ruler's Headache

Boulder

I watched the women drink tea and talk. Bloody hell, that councilwoman used a lot of sugar. I saw her dig into the sugar bowl at least ten times.

After I'd stood in the sun for half an hour Magni and Khan came out to join me.

"Are you going to be her protector?" I asked Magni with a hand shielding my face from the sun.

He scoffed. "I would be happy to. That would give me a chance to pressure that woman like a grape until she admits that they know where Laura is."

"Which is why you're not going near her," Khan said in a low, grumpy tone. "She says they don't know."

Magni hissed back, "And I told you that it's a fucking lie. Of course, they know. Give me an hour alone with the blonde and I swear I'll get her to talk."

I got the feeling that my brothers had argued about this before coming here.

Rolling my shoulders and neck, I asked in a nonchalant tone of voice, "So, if Magni isn't her protector, then who is? Finn?"

Khan crossed his arms and straightened up to his full height, which was only a tiny bit shorter than me. "I am."

"You?" My jaw fell open in surprise.

"Why not?"

I grinned. "Is that a joke?"

"Do I look like I'm fucking joking?" he asked dryly.

"No," I answered at the same time as Magni leaned closer and made a threat.

"You'd better watch her closely, brother. If I find that councilwoman alone, I *will* do what it takes to make her talk."

Smack! The sound of Khan's fist hitting Magni's cheek sounded loud, and I immediately stepped in to get between them.

"Go, Magni, just go," I said and pushed the large man back. Magni's hand was on his cheek, his eyes flashing with anger, and I sympathized with him. I couldn't even imagine how I would feel if Christina had left me without a goodbye. Since Laura ran away, Magni had become a laughingstock, and jokes were being told about how he was so bad in bed that his wife would rather be with a Momsi boy than him.

"Don't hit back – just go," I insisted, knowing full well that if I unleashed Magni on Khan it would be bloody. Khan was a great fighter, but Magni was bigger, stronger, and pumped with lethal anger that was just waiting for a target.

"Think, Magni, fucking think," I shouted and desperately held on to him.

Angrily, he shook his arm free from my strong grip and pointed to Khan. "You're lucky there's an audience, but know this; if you ever fucking hit me again," he snarled at Khan, who scowled back at him, "I will hit back so hard you'll need dental implants."

"You fucking deserved it. If I had threatened Laura you would have done the same thing. So don't think for one second that you get to threaten a female under *my* protection."

Both men were scowling at each other.

"You've done enough damage kidnapping the priestess," Khan reprimanded him.

Magni growled in frustration but left us without responding; and sure enough, it took Khan only a few seconds to regain his calm presence.

"So," he said, brushed off invisible dust from his leather shirt, and shot a glance toward the women who were now looking over to see what was going on. I raised a hand and waved to signal everything was fine.

"You finally claimed your right as a husband."

I stiffened. "What do you mean?"

"You fucked her," Khan said without shame. "Too bad you didn't do it in the daylight so I could have seen more clearly."

My jaws tightened. "You have no right to spy on us."

He just shrugged. "You promised her something; what was it?"

My heart started beating faster. "What?"

"You were whispering so I couldn't hear you, but it sounded like she wanted something from you and you agreed if she had sex with you."

"Oh, right." My brain was running in circles. I had been so sure we had whispered too low for him to hear, but there were only two scenarios. Either he knew what we had spoken about and was waiting to see if I would admit it freely, or he really didn't know the details.

If he knew I was lying to him, I would be in deep trouble.

"Christina wanted to learn how to fly my hybrid," I said – which was true in a way.

"Really?"

"Yeah, they only have automated drones and she's fascinated that I fly mine manually."

He wrinkled his nose and looked in Christina's direction. "And she was willing to sleep with you to fly your machine?"

"I think it was just an excuse. She's been ready for a while."

"Huh." He smiled at me. "So, how was it?"

A smile erupted on my face too. "There's nothing like it."

"Hmm… you seem all smitten with her." He looked me up and down. "Don't let her get inside your brain."

"I won't."

"Good. I need you to keep a sharp mind. We've got work to do."

"What kind of work?"

With a secretive smile, he gave a discreet nod toward the women. "Why do you think I'm protecting the councilwoman myself?"

"I don't know."

"Because this is a great opportunity." His eyes lit up and he lowered his voice into a conspiratorial mutter. "Wouldn't you say it's time men returned to power in this world?"

"Definitely."

"That woman…" he gave another minuscule nod toward Pearl, "…holds influence with the council. I'm going to learn as much from her as I can, and before she knows it, she'll be doing my bidding."

"How?"

He laughed, low, with a cunning grin. "Leave that to me, my friend. That poor woman doesn't stand a chance against my superior intellect. When she goes back to make changes, she'll think it's all her idea."

"So you're going to brainwash her," I clarified.

"Something like that." Khan gave a last long glance in Pearl's direction before he left me again with a final order. "Take Pearl to my private bedchamber and tell her I will kindly share my bed with her tonight."

My hesitation made him arch a brow.

"What?"

"You're not thinking about taking her by force, are you?"

Khan looked over in Pearl's direction. "That won't be necessary. My tongue is my sharpest weapon and I will find her weak spot. Maybe she wants to learn how to fly a hybrid too."

Shifting my balance, I furrowed my brow.

"Oh, for the son of the devil, just do as I tell you," he ordered with a slight fit of temper.

I nodded. "Understood."

Khan waved a hand over his shoulder when he walked away. "I'll see the three of you for dinner in an hour."

Christina

Boulder approached our cozy spot in the park, and Pearl and I immediately grew silent at the sight of the large, intimidating, and brooding man.

"Khan asked me to take you to your room. Dinner is in less than an hour and he thought you might want to freshen up," he said a bit stiffly.

Pearl rose gracefully from her chair. "Thank you. I don't think you and I have shared a proper greeting." She smiled. "Forgive me, my manners seem to suffer when I'm out of my comfort zone." With a few decisive steps Pearl walked to Boulder and reached out both hands to him. His eyes flew to me and I signaled for him to take her hands.

It was a peculiar sight to see Boulder frown down at Pearl, who leaned her head back and smiled up at him. "May peace surround you," Pearl said softly.

His face softened too and he mumbled, "Yeah, same to you."

When the ten seconds were up Boulder let go of her hands and pulled back. I had to stifle a laugh when he gave me a quick glare, as if to be sure I was really okay with him touching another woman.

"He has kindness in his eyes," Pearl whispered to me when we followed him inside the house.

Her comment made me smile because somehow it validated that it was okay for me to be friends with this man. Of course, I hadn't told Pearl that our friendship had developed into a physical relationship.

The direction Boulder took when we got inside the house brought me out of my ruminations. We didn't go up the staircase as I would have expected, but instead walked into a part of the mansion I didn't know.

"Where are you taking her?" I asked Boulder, but he didn't answer until we got to a set of double doors that had two guards posted outside.

"This is the room you'll be staying in, Pearl," Boulder said and one of the guards activated a locking mechanism, making the doors swing open.

I gaped at the opulence of the room. There were thick oriental carpets that had likely been fabricated before the war, high ceilings, and an odd mix of modern details and antiques. The room was bigger than the apartment I lived in with Kya back home. Both our bedrooms and the bathroom could have fit into this suite at least four times.

"This is very nice," I commented and looked at Pearl, who was gazing around the room.

"Come in." Boulder waved us closer and pointed ahead. "Your bags have been brought here already."

"Thank you," she managed to say.

"The bathroom is over there and dinner is in forty-five minutes, so we'll be back to pick you up." Boulder led me out with a hand to the small of my back.

Turning my head, I called to Pearl, "At least the room is nice."

Boulder stopped and looked back at Pearl too. "I should probably mention that you'll be sharing it with your protector."

"Oh?" Pearl said distractedly, still looking around in the large suite with the huge bed and two seating areas. "And when do I get to meet my protector?" she asked.

"You already did. This is Khan's room."

"Khan?" I shrieked beside him.

That got Pearl's attention and she fixed her eyes on Boulder. "Are you saying Khan will personally protect me and share his accommodations with me?"

"Yup, that's what he told me."

Her eyes went to the bed, and it wasn't hard to guess what was on her mind. With a frown, she moved closer to one of the sofas and muttered, "I'll sleep here, I think."

Boulder shrugged. "I'll leave the details for you and Khan to figure out, but I'll give you this bit of advice: stay away from Magni."

"Why?" I asked next to him.

"Because he's convinced that Pearl knows where Laura is." Boulder lowered his voice and turned to look at Pearl. "I would strongly suggest that you avoid him as much as possible."

"Do you think he would harm me?" she asked.

"I would like to say no, but Magni is a desperate man who wants his wife back, badly."

Pearl nodded to Boulder. "Thank you, I'll keep my distance."

"See you in a little while," Boulder told Pearl and gave me a last nudge to get me out the door.

"Why Khan? Couldn't Finn do it?" I asked worriedly when we walked away.

"No."

"Why not?"

"For several reasons."

"Explain them to me," I insisted.

Boulder didn't stop but took the stairs two steps at a time, and only when we got into our room did he face me. "Pearl is a councilwoman, which is equal to a ruler, so it makes perfect sense that Khan shows her the highest honor by protecting her himself."

"No, it doesn't," I protested. "He has a country to rule; he doesn't have time to look after her."

"He'll make time."

"What aren't you telling me?" I pressed him.

"How much did you see today with Magni and Khan?" he asked in an exasperated tone.

"They had a fight."

"Yes. And that fight was over Pearl. Magni wants to interrogate her and pressure her."

Understanding dawned on me. "Ahh, so Khan is protecting her from his brother?"

"Yes. Magni is the second in command in the Northlands. It would be hard for Finn to deny him access if he wanted to speak to Pearl. Only one person outranks Magni."

"Khan," I breathed, my eyes wide. "But will he treat her kindly?"

Boulder huffed out air. "Who knows? He has little experience with women and he's used to getting his way."

"But he won't hurt her, will he?"

Boulder wouldn't meet my eyes and it worried me.

"Talk to me," I pressed him.

With a look of frustration, he finally sighed heavily and walked close enough to whisper into my ear. "Let's just hope she doesn't rile him. Khan can be a real ass."

"Why are you whispering?" I whispered back.

"For no reason." With a sigh, Boulder stepped away and stripped out of his shirt, revealing his hard abs. I stared in fascination and was a little ashamed of my reaction to him.

He was the epiphany of masculinity: something I'd been raised to see as a bad thing. But my body was reacting and I felt my cheeks heat up and a hotness in my lower regions. Men had almost destroyed our civilization, and Nmen were certainly brutal and primitive in many ways, but there were a few redeeming qualities about them. At least when it came to Boulder. The way he made me feel when we were physically together was nice. Very nice!

"Do I have something on me?" he asked and looked down at his chest.

I jerked my eyes away from him, flushing red. "No, I was just thinking about Pearl," I lied.

He frowned. "Don't worry about it. She's going to be fine. Khan isn't..." He stopped himself but added. "I mean he has a good side."

I scoffed, my ingrained politeness overruled by my frustration. "He's the worst!"

Boulder ignored my outburst and found a thin charcoal gray leather shirt to put on.

"You can't wear that." I pointed out to him.

"Why not?" he asked and continued to put it on.

"It's offensive," I complained. "You're wearing the skin of another being. What if someone killed and skinned you to wear you as a shirt?"

Boulder rolled his eyes. "Quit the drama, Christina, this is my favorite shirt and I'm fucking wearing it."

"But Pearl will find you barbaric."

He tilted his head and stepped closer. "And that bothers you?"

I met his gaze.

He asked his question again but a little differently. "You want her to like me?"

My chest rose in a deep intake of air. "I guess so."

The edges around his eyes softened and he caressed my cheek with his fingers. "You're falling for me."

"No, I'm not," I defended myself.

With a small grin Boulder placed a kiss on my forehead before he turned me around and smacked my butt. "Then find me something to wear that will make you proud."

Stunned by the itching pain of his palm on my behind, I took a few steps before I found my voice. "Did you just hit me?"

A chuckle came from behind. "No, love, I smacked you lightly."

Confusion filled my mind. Boulder had clearly hit me on my behind. It was a known fact that domestic violence had been an issue of the past, and I would have sworn that if any man ever laid his hand on me, I would report him instantly.

While I stood flabbergasted trying to reconcile his use of the word "love" with his act of brutality, Boulder snaked his arms around me from behind. "I'm flattered that you want Pearl to like me," he whispered by my ear.

"You *hit* me," I said again, unable to get past that offensive behavior.

"Only a coward would truly hit a woman, Christina. I just smacked your butt playfully because my hands are drawn to that amazing ass of yours." He nibbled on my earlobe while letting his large hands knead my buttocks in greedy movements. "I could just undress you and bite into your creamy skin, it's that delicious."

"First you hit me, and now you want to *bite* me," I said and tried to push him off me.

"Did it hurt... or did it excite you?" he teased in that deep voice of his.

Oh, no – the warm moist feeling between my thighs had returned and I was mortified. At the University, I had taken part in discussions about the enlightenment of modern society and argued that women had evolved from the days when we would allow men to dominate us. I had even argued that women from the past had suffered from general low self-esteem, and that would explain why they had allowed men to oppress them with sexual violence.

Boulder had hit me and now he was biting my earlobe while squeezing my breasts. This could be classified as

199

sexual violence, couldn't it? So why wasn't my body reacting to it with disgust? I should be repelled, but instead my body was humming with a fire that made no sense.

I'm sick! Closing my eyes, I let the shame roll over me and then I did something desperate to salvage my pride and restore balance between us. I bit him back. *I'm not as evolved as I thought I was, but at least I can dominate him back.*

Boulder reacted very differently from what I had expected. He made a low sound in the back of his throat and fisted his hands into my hair, pushing my head back and meeting my eyes full on. "You wanna play rough?" he asked excitedly.

"No, I..." I blinked a few times and didn't have much time to react before he'd picked me up and carried me to the bed with a grin. "Bite me again," he said encouragingly and followed me down to kiss me deeply, sucking on my lower lip.

"I'm not a violent person," I said, disturbed by his suggestion.

With mischief pouring from him, he tickled me until I laughed. "Come on, beautiful, fight me."

"I'm not going to fight you," I got out in between his tickling attacks.

"If you can get on top of me, I'll shave my beard off," he tempted me, and it instantly made me stare at him.

"You will?"

"Uh-huh," he said with a grin. "But you have to fight for it."

Adrenaline was pumping through my body and with an intoxicating feeling I let loose a side of me that I had never explored. I bucked him off me with determination. He got up on his knees and lifted his hands to grab my shoulders. Amusement flared in his eyes when I rudely pushed at him to get him down on his back. He was too big and strong for that and didn't budge.

"You gotta use more than your hands," he challenged. "Use your whole body if you want to succeed."

Narrowing my eyes, I got up, standing with my hands on my hips looking down on him. With me standing and him on his knees, he still reached my chin.

"So what are you gonna do?" he asked.

I had no plan and acted from instinct when I jumped him and pushed at him, placing my hands on his shoulders and using my entire body weight to get him down on his back. He laughed and the minute we hit the bed he rolled me under him. "So close." He grinned from ear to ear. "Now what are you gonna do?"

With a small cry of battle, I bit his earlobe. It was hard but without drawing blood.

He retaliated by twisting my nipple painfully and it made me let go of his earlobe to cry out.

"Come on, tiger, fight me," he encouraged and ground himself against me, letting me feel how aroused he was. My heart was drumming, my blood boiling, and I bit my lip unsure how to deal with these surreal emotions of raw desire that our fight brought out in me.

"You can do better than that," he encouraged and with a new scream I rambunctiously bucked him off me.

Boulder kept on top of me, panting, and lowering his head to kiss my collarbone. His hand was still under my shirt and squeezing my breast. I used the dirtiest trick I could think off and pulled his hair.

He didn't scream in pain, but he growled low when I combined my pulling his hair and bucking him off.

And it worked. With a cry of victory, I scrambled up to straddle him, holding him down with pressure on his chest.

We were staring into each other's eyes, out of breath and with our mouths open.

"You will shave off that beard," I said triumphantly.

"I will." Boulder's smile looked confident and satisfied – as if he had won and not me.

"And you'll take off this shirt," I said and lifted my hands from the soft leather.

His hands found my hips and he pressed his groin against me while moaning low. I didn't move away but closed my eyes for a second, overwhelmed with the tingling of butterflies taking up flight between my ribs.

"I don't want to go down for dinner," he whispered. "I would much rather stay here with you."

Part of me wanted that too. To be exact: my body wanted that. I opened my eyes enough to see him.

Boulder's gray eyes were fixed on my puckered nipples, which showed through the shirt. My skin was on fire when his right hand slid up under my shirt and cupped my breast.

With hooded eyes and shallow breathing, I let my hips swivel against him slowly, pressing against his large erection, meeting his rhythmic bump and grind.

"Fuuuck, you have no idea how sexy you are right now," Boulder muttered low with half-lidded eyes of his own.

While my body was giving in, my mind was holding on to the last part of my self-control. "We have to go down. Pearl needs my support," I said but made a small moan myself when his erection pressed at my most sensitive spot.

"I just wanna stay here and play with you."

"Play with me?"

"Tussle with you and make love to you," he whispered and weaved a hand into my hair, pulling me down for a long explorative kiss that felt amazing.

"Go shave," I said and finally pulled away from him, my hands shaking from what we had just done. I had never done anything remotely as violent as pushing and biting a man.

"All right." He groaned and got out of bed. "But just so you know," he said and walked close enough to pull my back against his chest and lean his head on my shoulder. "When we get back here, I'm burying myself inside of you."

"Maybe," I said and froze when he lovingly kissed my neck. *It's just an experiment*, I reminded myself. *Nothing more than a first-hand experience of a physical relationship between men and women. It means nothing.* Yet, I couldn't take my eyes off him when he walked to the bathroom, stripping out of his shirt on the way and showing off his broad muscled back. Before he closed the door, he gave me a killer smile and teased, "Are you sure you want me to shave it off?" He was touching his beard.

"I'm sure," I said with conviction.

CHAPTER 23
Civil Dinner

Christina

When Boulder emerged from the bathroom completely clean-shaven, I gaped at him. It was like seeing a different man. He arched a brow at me and crossed his arms across his wide naked chest. "I can't believe I did this. I look like an adolescent boy."

"No," I breathed. "You don't."

He touched his face. "At least it'll grow out again."

Flustered by his good looks, I held out the shirt I'd picked out for him. "I like this one," I said.

Boulder moved closer and took it from me. "What's wrong?" he asked.

"Nothing," I said too quickly and without looking at him.

"You don't like it either?" he concluded with disappointment in his tone.

"No, I *do* like it," I corrected him. "You look..." I cleared my throat, "...handsome."

"Christina?" Boulder lifted my face and looked into my eyes. "Are you okay?"

"Yes, of course, I'm just hungry."

"Oh, okay."

I was quiet when we walked downstairs, a new realization growing in me that I was still trying to deny. *I can't have feelings for him. That would be ridiculous. The man is an Nman. A brute who brings out the worst in me.* Since arriving in the Northlands I had read forbidden books, used improper communication, and engaged in fighting with him. It really was disturbing how easily I had been corrupted by his bad influence.

There was no need for us to escort Pearl, as she was already in the dining room.

"You're late," Khan exclaimed with irritation when Boulder and I walked in.

"Yeah, sorry about that. I lost a bet," Khan explained.

Magni, Erika, Finn, Pearl, and Khan were already seated at the table. They all looked up to study the change in Boulder's appearance. Finn broke into a deep belly laugh, Magni shook his head, and Khan scrunched up his face.

"What the fuck, Boulder?" Khan finally said.

"It suits you," Pearl complimented him with a smile and looked at Erika. "Don't you think a clean shave looks nice on a man?"

Erika looked thoughtful. "A summer shave is all right, I suppose. But personally, I've always preferred a man with a beard."

"Hmm," Pearl tilted her head. "A few of our men have beards too, but they trim them in beautiful designs."

"Momma's boys." Finn covered his comment with a cough but both Pearl and I heard him.

"Our men are not boys, Mr. MacCumhail," Pearl corrected him. "Many are highly enlightened, with great intellect and emotional range."

Magni gave her a look of disgust. "Are you trying to pick a fight?"

"Certainly not. I'm just pointing out that true masculinity is not measured in the size of muscles or the length of beard."

"You're right," Magni leaned over the table with a fake smile. "It's measured in his size of cock."

Pearl paled while Finn roared in laughter. "I wish!"

"Must you be so crude?" Erika reprimanded her son.

Magni snorted and opened his mouth to speak but Khan cut him off.

"I'm curious, Councilwoman Pearl. What does masculinity mean to you?"

She put down her cutlery and took a minute before she answered. "This may surprise you but gender plays only a small part in our society. We put much more emphasis on personality and charisma."

"Is that why you women aren't attracted to your men anymore?" Boulder asked. "Because there's no difference between men and women?"

Pearl tilted her head. "What makes you think men and women aren't attracted to each other anymore?"

Boulder shrugged. "Christina told me."

"I have to disagree," Pearl said softly. "We have many couples living together and our men are wonderful, thoughtful, caring, and emotionally intelligent beings that are fully capable of attracting partners if desired."

"Great!" Magni squeezed the knife in his hand tightly. "My wife is without protection and now you tell me that your Momsiboys are a threat to her?"

"Your wife is safe in the Motherlands. No one will harm her, but obviously..." She trailed off.

"What?" Magni said aggressively.

Pearl looked down. "Nothing."

"What?" Magni raised his voice and slammed his hand with the knife down the table.

"Calm the fuck down," Khan told his brother.

Pearl sighed and lifted her face, giving Magni a look of great empathy. "It must be difficult for you. I'm sorry if I made it worse."

"Just finish your fucking sentence," Magni demanded, low and threatening.

"If you insist," she said. "Laura is safe and no one will harm her, but obviously, there's the possibility of her falling in love with someone. It can be a rush to be treated with kindness and respect if you're not used to it."

That set off Magni, who jumped up, knocking his chair back. "Are you saying that I didn't treat my wife with kindness and respect? I fucking fought for her and protected her until that little bitch over there filled her with fairytales about the Motherlands." He pointed a finger at me, and that made Boulder get up from his chair roaring at Magni.

"Apologize!"

"No!" Magni roared back. "Laura would still be here if not for that bitch of yours."

Boulder was at Magni's throat before he had finished the sentence. "Nobody talks about my wife that way," he said in a low and menacing growl. "Apologize or you and I are going outside to settle this like men."

"Go die in a fire," Magni spat back at Boulder.

"Calm the *fuck* down, both of you!" Khan shouted, hammering his fist upon the table.

Pearl's eyes were huge and she was holding her hands to her chest. Over the last two weeks, I had been conditioned to these sorts of outbursts, but she had never experienced anything like the vile talk, the testosterone filling the room, and the hateful glances between Boulder and Magni.

I met her gaze, trying to signal that it would be all right.

"Finn." Khan snapped his finger. "I think my brother needs a night out to blow off some steam."

"Any place in particular?" Finn asked and was already pushing his chair back.

"Whatever he wants. Booze, fights, sex-bots."

Magni pushed past Boulder and muttered, low and hostile. "Enjoy your wife while you have her."

"Is that a threat?" Boulder growled.

"Just a friendly reminder that she's going home soon," Magni hissed low and stomped out of the room while Finn snatched the steak from the plate before him, took a big bite, and followed.

An awkward silence filled the room before Boulder raised Magni's chair from the floor and returned to his own seat.

Khan followed suit. "I apologize for my brother's loss of temper. As you can see, he is not taking Laura's disappearance well,"

"Has he talked with anyone about his anger issues?" Pearl asked with a troubled look.

"Anger issues?" Khan asked in annoyance. "What are you talking about?"

Pearl blinked in confusion. "He's full of rage. Surely inner peace would be much more pleasant for him and the people around him."

"Inner peace?" Khan leaned back. "Who the hell can be peaceful if their spouse disappears?"

"I can understand he's upset, but to express that level of anger..." Pearl trailed off.

"He's got every right to be angry. His wife disobeyed him and now he can't keep her safe," Boulder interjected.

"But to call Christina a..." Pearl cleared her throat. "I'm not even going to say a word that awful."

Khan raised his voice. "Then don't! But don't judge my brother either. When you're in the red zone there isn't always enough oxygen for rational thought."

"Which is why anger doesn't serve him well." Pearl challenged. "He should get some help to communicate his emotions better. That way we could have a civil dinner without shouting and fighting."

Khan gave her a hard glare. "Maybe you're the one who needs help."

"Excuse me?" she said.

"Magni communicated his emotions perfectly clearly," Khan argued. "I don't think anyone else at this table has any doubt that he was pissed, angry, and frustrated."

Pearl closed her mouth and didn't respond to that. She and I were the only ones not eating steak. Instead we addressed ourselves to our salad, potatoes, and bread – in silence.

CHAPTER 24
Impregnation

Boulder

"Just so we're clear, if I win, you don't get to give me shitty assignments to punish me," I pointed out before I moved into the arena to spar with Khan.

Christina and I were still living at the Gray Mansion, and sparring with Khan was something I did often. I sparred with Magni too, but ever since he called Christina a bitch, our friendship hadn't been the same; the last time I sparred with him, he had been downright brutal and mean-spirited.

Khan gave me a wicked smile. "Protecting the archeologist didn't turn out to be such a bad assignment, did it?"

"No," I admitted.

"You're screwing a real woman and experiencing something that is very rare."

"True," I admitted.

"So why are you scowling?"

"Why?" I picked up the thin training gloves that would protect my hands and put them on. "The excavation is coming along fast. And it worries me."

"Because you don't want Christina to leave you?"

I gave a sharp nod.

"So what are you gonna do?" he asked.

"I have several plans, but you wouldn't like any of them," I told Khan, who was moving around me with the grace of a boxer.

"So come up with a better one."

"What if she's pregnant and leaves me? I'll always wonder if I have a kid out there."

Khan's face fell into deep frown lines and he stopped to look at me with a solemn expression.

"If she leaves, I'll go crazy from wondering, you know?" I said through gritted teeth.

"You think she's pregnant?" he asked

"I don't know. But it's been two weeks since I first made love to her and we've done it daily ever since."

"And she lets you come inside her?"

"Yes. At first it was a mystery to me why she would risk it, but now I think I know why."

"Why?"

I lowered my voice and leaned closer to him. "The other day, Christina was talking about the clinics women go to when they want to become a mother. Did you know that they have parenting units where adults who want to raise children live together?"

Khan didn't confirm it, but I knew he had more insights into the culture in the Motherlands than any of us; after all, he and his father had gone there for peace meetings on occasion.

"According to Christina, a child always has a primary mother, but beside that there's a number of people that love them."

"So?"

"So, apparently, men no longer have sperm strong enough to impregnate women. That's why they go to clinics."

"Ahh," Khan nodded. "And she thinks you can't impregnate her either."

"I assume that's what she thinks, and I'm sure as hell not going to tell her that women here are impregnated the old-fashioned way."

"Good."

"Anyway, she was commenting that it was lucky for Laura that she hadn't been to a clinic yet because pregnant women aren't allowed to train in martial arts."

"Christina thinks Magni can't get Laura pregnant," Khan mused.

"Yes. And maybe she's right. I mean, they've been living together for almost a year."

"My brother can impregnate his wife just fine." Khan defended Magni. "These things can take time."

"Right." I backed down. "But Christina thinks he can't and that I can't either."

"Interesting!"

"Why do you think their men have such low sperm counts?"

Khan shook his head. "I can't be sure, but I'll bet that being oppressed by women and downplaying your masculinity isn't healthy. Men in the Motherlands look and behave so feminine it makes you wonder how much testosterone they even have left."

I shuttered. "Thank fuck that I was born a free man."

Khan looked thoughtful. "Yeah... now all we have to do is liberate all the other men."

"You think we can make them real men again?" I asked.

"Maybe not, but hopefully we can work on raising the next generation to be more masculine."

"I like the sound of that," I said and raised my arms. "And talking about less feminine, how about I kick your ass a little to get you into shape? I think you're starting to get man boobs."

Khan resumed circling me. "Say that again and I'll knock your teeth out, pretty boy," he retorted and winked. "Have I told you, you look like a girl without your beard?"

"Fuck you!"

He grinned. "Let me give you a piece of advice. Next week when you go to visit your mine, don't bend over. It's dark there and the engineers might confuse you with a woman."

Smack! I landed my first clean hit and he stumbled back.

"Shaving is a small price to pay if it makes Christina stay. You have no idea how addictive sex with a real woman is."

Khan rolled his jaw and raised his arms again. "No, I don't," he said grumpily. "But I'm considering it."

"What? With Pearl?"

He didn't comment but made a swing that I avoided.

"I didn't think she liked you."

"Who says she needs to like me to have sex with me?" I laughed. "You really have no clue."

He took advantage of my lowered guard and hammered into my ribs five times.

"You bastard," I moaned.

He grinned. "What? You look like a girl and you fight like a girl. Maybe you *are* a girl."

My right hook came resolutely and had him sinking to his knees. I bent forward speaking low and sardonic. "In that case, a *girl* just knocked you down."

I took off my gloves while he scrambled to his feet again.

"Where are you going?"

I gave him a smug grin. "I just knocked you down and I think I'm going to go and knock my wife up."

"Very funny," he panted.

"See you later, my friend," I said and left him.

CHAPTER 25
Flash Drive

Christina

The library that we excavated turned out to be part of an old university. We found a sign with an overview of the campus that gave us an impression of how large an area the university had covered.

Looking around the now lush area with forest and fields, it was hard to imagine that four hundred years ago, students and professors had walked here at what used to be the University of British Colombia. I tried digging for more information on the Internet, but after four nights of searching I gave up. If I'd been back in the Motherlands, I could have searched the Wise-Share, but I doubted I would have found any information there either.

Most of what we dug up was so deteriorated that we couldn't use it, but there were some gems that we'd saved. Bruce Lee, one of my team members, found a glass jar with different things inside it and almost discarded them as rubbish. Luckily, I came by and spotted something I'd seen once before, albeit with a different design.

"Can I see that?" I asked and picked up the small thing when he handed it to me.

"What is it?" Bruce asked.

"It's a device to store digital information," I explained and turned the small thing in my hands. "And this one is in incredibly good shape. There was a logo on it that read UBC.

"How does it work?" Bruce asked me.

Carefully, I removed a cap and showed him what was inside. "Look," I pointed to a small connector. "They would insert this part into a computer and that way they could read whatever information was on it."

"Ahh," he nodded and broke into a shy smile. "I have to be honest with you – I really wasn't happy when I was ordered to help out here, but I'm starting to be intrigued. It's like a treasure hunt of sorts."

I smiled brightly. "Exactly. Back in the day, archeologists lived amazing lives full of dangerous adventures."

"They did?"

"Yes, they were considered heroes by many and people even made movies to honor them."

"Wow, that's something. I wish someone would make a movie about me." He smiled at me and I flashed him a grin.

"Maybe if you become the new Indiana Jones, they will."

"Who?"

"He was a celebrated archeologist from the twentieth century and I'm a major fan of his work."

"All right." Lee looked down at the small thing in my hand. "So is there any way to find out what's on it?"

"Uh-huh," I said with excitement. "I brought a converter that we use when we come across things like these, but it's back at the mansion."

"Well, can we go and get it? I'm curious," Bruce leaned in to see it better and his shoulder touched mine.

"What's going on?" Boulder's voice was low and menacing.

Bruce and I both whipped our heads toward Boulder and an audible gulp came from Bruce.

"Why the fuck are you rubbing against my wife?"

Lee had already moved away and shook his head. "I didn't, we were just looking at..."

"Boulder," I said – cutting off Bruce. "You're being unreasonable. Bruce made a promising discovery and we were merely discussing it."

Boulder's gaze fell to my hands. "What is it?" he asked.

"I'll explain it to you on the way back. I need something from our room." I was already up and walking toward the hybrid, turning my head back to Bruce and the others. "Carry on, I'll be back later."

"What is it?" Boulder asked again when we were in the drone and flying back to the mansion.

"It's called a flash drive."

"What's a flash drive?"

"An old-fashioned device to store information."

"And how does it work?"

"Good question." I held it up so he could see it. "What's your first thought? How would this work?"

"I don't know."

"Guess."

"Okay. I'm thinking there must be a way to activate the projector that shows the content."

"There's no projector in this thing."

He frowned. "So how do I see what it has stored?"

"Try again."

"Is it one of those water hologram things?"

"No."

"Then tell me."

I smiled smugly. "People carried this around but it was useless without a computer."

"What do you mean? I'm still confused. Are we talking implants?"

"No. Before that. These things were used back when computers were something with screens and keyboards."

He nodded but kept his eyes on the road. "They should have never done implants," he said quietly.

Around fifteen years before the Toxic War, implants had been rolled out as a must-have item. People had jumped on board and paid huge sums to have computers implanted in their brains. It offered them the ability to speak more languages and access all the information on the Internet without the use of a device. Of course, none of those people back then truly understood the price of their upgrade until years later when the war broke out.

By the time hacking of implants really took off, people were frantically trying to get rid of them, but only a few succeeded and the rest died horrible deaths.

"The young people are getting implants back home," I said.

"You're kidding?" he asked with surprise.

"No, they say they're safe, and it's been so long since the war that nobody thinks it could happen again."

"Yeah, well, I'm going to pass on having anything implanted in my brain."

"Me too." I held up my wristband. "I like the old simple days better." Releasing a deep sigh, I held up the flash drive. "Cross your fingers that we find good stuff on this thing. It will make the whole journey worthwhile for me."

Boulder grew quiet and his jaws hardened. Maybe he wanted me to say getting to know him had been my highlight, but saying something like that would just give him hope that I would stay.

I couldn't stay! Could I?

No, the thought was ridiculous. I had a life to get back to. My roommate and my friends were probably missing me like crazy. There was no way I could stay.

But I'll miss him, a small voice peeped inside me – one that I quickly silenced.

Back at the mansion I almost ran to our room and fell to my knees, searching through my bags for the converter. I gave a small shriek when I found it and brought it to the coffee table.

"You wanna see?" I asked him.

"How could I miss it?" he said sarcastically. "After all, this is the *highlight* of your journey here."

Ignoring his comment, I plugged the flash drive into the converter and projected the content up in the air.

"What is this?" Boulder asked in confusion.

"It's the coding. Don't worry, I've got this." I muttered and navigated to get an overview of the content. "I see some videos, images, and text files. This should be interesting."

"What videos? I don't see anything."

"Give me a second, I have to find a way to play them." It took me a few moments but I finally got the first video to play.

A young woman came into view, her hair in a short bob, her nose big, and her eyebrows pierced by a ring. The camera shook slightly and her face scrunched up in concentration. "Smile," she said and leaned against a young man who looked up at the camera, pushed his square glasses in place, and squinted a bit. He had stubble, unruly hair falling down his forehead, and a shirt that was wrinkled.

"I'm getting tired of all your selfies," he said with a hint of annoyance, before he flashed a smile that didn't reach his eyes. "Wait, you have it on video."

"Oh, sorry." The clip ended with the girl frowning.

"I hope that wasn't the highlight of your journey?" Boulder said dryly.

"No." I pushed the next video: a noisy food hall with young people sitting, standing, and walking around. "Hey, Mom." A quick flash of the girl from before showed that she was filming. She waved at the camera. "Let me show you our fine dining restaurant here at campus." The camera was turned around for a panorama of the dining hall. "Say hi," the young woman called out to a group of young women at a table.

"Are you putting it on Facebook?" one of them asked with a stiff smile.

"No, It's for my mom."

"Oh, okay." Two or three of the women gave small waves. "Hey, Nicole's mom," one of them said politely.

"And this is the feast I'm eating," the woman who had to be Nicole narrated, and zoomed the camera in on her plate.

Boulder reached out to enlarge the picture flowing above the converter. "Meat!" He pointed to the two drumsticks on the plate that lay neatly next to a baked potato and some salad.

"Shh," I said and kept my full attention on the film.

"So you see, Mom?" Nicole's face came back into view. "I won't starve, in case you're worried about that, and I know you are because you worry about everything. Remember I love you and I'll shoot some more video from my room later." She blew a kiss. "Bye, Mom."

Boulder crossed his arms while I eagerly brought up the next video. It showed Nicole in her room, and she introduced her roommate, a shy-looking young woman with lots of black make-up and blue hair.

"Wow, you think that was the fashion back then?" Boulder asked me. "The blue hair, I mean."

"I don't think so. I didn't see any other people with blue hair in the dining hall."

There were other short videos of Nicole showing her mom around the campus, and every one of those videos was a treasure to me. Then there was a music video with something that made me blink from the heavy use of the bass.

"This is great!" Boulder grinned and rocked his foot to the rhythm. "The girl has good taste in music."

"She's not a girl, but clearly a young woman," I corrected him, "and I don't think that awful music has any positive vibrations." I reached out to stop the music but Boulder wouldn't let me.

"I wanna hear it."

After three minutes suffering through the rock music I moved on to the next video.

"Hey, Mom, I hope you're doing better and that the doctors will let you come home soon. I miss you so much and can't wait to see you in a few weeks, but here's a treat for you. It's my favorite poem by Hera Bosley, and I hope it will speak to you as it does to me. It's called 'The Army of the Chosen Ones.'"

The video changed to a new setting. This time a pretty woman with long brown hair sat in a living room with a candle burning behind her. When she began speaking it sounded melodic but it wasn't singing. It was spoken poetry and I leaned closer, taking in every word.

Grateful, but in the same breath, inadequate.
How could I ever possibly live up to the task at hand?
You see, my soul is not ascending.
My soul has descended to come here and live out this life.
Old soul is not an adequate description of me.
No, I am ancient.
I am beyond time and space.
I am beyond words and black and white definitions.
I am ethereal and I am light.
I am sound and I am vibration.
I am you and you are me.
We are the chosen ones.
We have been called here to transmute and transform.
What an honor,
Oh, but, what a fucking mess.
There are days where it would be easier to go back to higher dimensions from whence I came.

No, I cry, this is too hard. This is beyond repair. This hurts too much.
Why did I choose this?
Why would I have picked this time in history to come back?
Back to the ugliness and rampant racism.
Back to the sexism and the misogyny.
Back to the desecration of our mother earth.
It is so hard to watch but I am trapped.
Trapped between the veil of my soul and my human skin.
Paralyzed by fear.
Fear of not being enough.
Fear of never living up to the demand that has been placed upon my soul.
The massive undertaking of which we all have a part to play.
The destruction and the dissolution.
The rise and the fall.
The crumbling and the crusade.
The heroine's fucking journey.

Boulder laughed. "Did you hear that? She said fuck..."
I held up my hand and shushed him, wanting to hear it all.

It's hard. And it is so dense.
It is up and it is down.
It is amazing and it is frightening.
It is everything and it is nothing all at the same time.
The reality of this reality is sometimes unbearable.
How do I witness without falling victim to it?
How do I surrender and take action?
How do I flow and stay grounded?
How do I honor myself and stay in service to others?
How do I balance the intensity of this duality?
The light and the dark

221

The love and the hate
The inspiration and the ignorance.
The enormity of what I've been called here to do is
enough to swallow me whole.
And some days it does.
But not today.
No, today I am here.
Today I am ready.
Today I am filled with a reverence.
Unafraid and unabashed.
No shame, no guilt, no fear can hold me back now.
No, I have arrived at the feet of my destiny, my
dharma, my purpose.
I was made for this. Quite Literally.
My skin, my mind, my cells, every fiber of my being was
called here to this life.
To witness the rise, no, to actively participate in the
rise.
The heroine's journey.
I am you and you are me.
We are the chosen ones.
We shall stand in the face of this madness and we shall
rise up in spite of it.
We shall give birth to a new generation of beings.
A generation with brilliant minds,
To inspire inventions that will counteract all the greed
and all the hate.
A generation that will push back against the
patriarchy.
A generation that honors the feminine and the
masculine within us all.
We are no longer asleep nor are we afraid.
We are an army of chosen ones here to create change.
Unsure of what the future holds, but I stand steady in
my grace.

The enormity of what I've been called here to do is enough to swallow me whole.
And some days it does,
But, not today.
Today, I rise.
Today, I fight back against all that has pinned me down.
Fight back? They say. A lightworker doesn't need to "fight back"
And to that I say fuck you.
My journey does not need to look like yours to be effective.
We all have a part to play in this orchestrated madness.
My eyes are open to the light and the dark.
The winter of my soul would bring you to your knees, trust me.
Do not look at my fists of rage and judge me.
I look back at my life and see exactly when each finger was pulled down,
Fist forming,
Anger brewing,
Belly full of hot fire.
How did we get here? Where the WOMEN are looked at as less than?
As second class citizens?
The Women? The life givers? The portals? The mystics? The truth tellers?
Who decided this? When did this come to be?
I've been in other lifetimes where we were honored and revered.
Where the blood that we menstruated was considered sacred,
Not shamed and hidden away like a dirty secret.
Not looked at as gross but honored in rituals for its literal life force energy and power.

223

I do not know how this came to be, but I am here, and I will fight back.
With a belly full of fire and a heart full of light,
Because I am allowed to be a beautiful juxtaposition of compassion and rage.
You see, we are all playing our part, our role,
and I'll be damned if I bend myself to fit in your mold of what that should look like.
No, I have been bent and distorted,
I have been held back and I have made myself small,
I have walked on eggshells,
And I have bitten my tongue.
I have kept my opinions to myself for far too long.
I stand here with my scars and my broken limbs,
I stand here with my love and my anger.
My voice may tremble and my hands may shake,
But I refuse to sit on those sidelines any longer.
I stand here as a representative of the army of chosen ones
Here to create change.
The enormity of what I have been called here to do is enough to swallow me whole.
And some days it does,
But not today.

I swallowed hard, choking down emotions from the power in her voice and the knowledge of what this woman would have seen in her lifetime.

"What a bunch of nonsense," Boulder muttered beside me, but I was too much in awe of this battle cry from a time long past to answer him.

I wasn't sure exactly when this had been recorded. Nicole's and Hera's clothing, the flash drive, and the surroundings indicated some time between the years 2010 and 2020.

"I have to show this to Pearl," I said softly, my heart beating like a drum from the excitement of finding such a treasure.

"What's so special about it?" Boulder asked. "Except that it's painfully long and boring."

I looked up from my position on the floor. "Did you even listen to her?"

"Yeah, I did."

"And what did you hear?"

"A lot of fancy words." He sighed with annoyance. "She looks like one of those hesitators."

"Hesitators?" I drew my brows together. "What are you talking about?"

He crossed his arms. "You know, one of those people who sit and do nothing in quietness. Feeling all big and mighty because they're sitting and hesitating. As if that's somehow better than getting stuff done."

I tilted my head. "Do you mean meditating?"

He shrugged. "Is that what it's called?"

"Yes, Boulder. And meditating is not the same as hesitating."

"Looks the same to me. They don't do shit. Just sit there and roam around their feelings and emotions or whatever. It's all bullshit to me."

I got up from the floor. "Have you ever tried meditation?"

He snorted. "That's for Momsies."

His answer provoked me, and already fired up from Hera's feisty poem, I faced him. "Thank you. I know you mean it as an insult, but if you're implying that you're incapable of mastering your mind and it takes female power to do that, then I'll take the compliment. Although, just for the record, it's untrue. There are plenty of deeply spiritual men who master meditation. Nmen are just not disciplined enough to stay quiet for that long."

225

"We could," he defended himself. "We just don't want to. It's a waste of time."

"You know what's a waste of time?" I said without looking at him. "Discussing this with you. You're not evolved enough to appreciate something as fine as that poem or meditation."

"Hey, where are you going?" he asked when I gathered up the converter and the flash drive and moved to the door.

"I'm going to see Pearl, and I suggest you give me some space."

"Space – what's that supposed to mean?"

I made a frustrated sound in my throat and closed the door hard behind me. For a month, I had spent day and night with Boulder, and right now he was getting on my nerves. First his macho behavior with Bruce for touching my shoulder, and now his criticism of something I found beautiful.

We're incompatible, that's why. And it's a good thing really. It would have been terrible if I'd fallen in love with him or something stupid like that. Thank Mother Nature that I haven't.

Below my inner dialogue there was an emotion, as if a small part of me was trying to get a word in, but I pushed it down, refusing to examine what stirred down there.

CHAPTER 26
Eavesdropping

Boulder

Slamming the door hard, I got Khan's attention. He was standing in his office, talking quietly with Magni, and they both looked up with deep frowns.

"I need your help," I exclaimed, pointing to Khan and walking quickly to where they were standing. "Do you have your own room tapped as well?"

Khan's nostrils flared slightly, and I got the sense he didn't want Magni to know about the surveillance, but he gave a small nod.

"Good, because Pearl and Christina are talking in your room right now and I want to know what's going on. The bloody guards at your door wouldn't let me eavesdrop."

Magni's lips pursed and he leaned back, folding his arms comfortably over his chest. "Yes, brother, let's hear what the women have to say. Maybe Pearl will reveal where Laura is."

"She doesn't know," I said harshly. "I've asked Christina to find out and she insists that the council doesn't know."

Magni laughed bitterly. "Oh, geez, you're so fucking blinded by that woman, Boulder. The bitch has been lying to you from day one."

My temper flared up. "I warned you," I sneered at him. "Don't you fucking call her that."

Khan touched his wristband and four images appeared in front of him. Four different angles of his private chamber were showing, and we could see Christina and Pearl kneeling down and watching the recording of that long poem I'd just watched with Christina.

"What are they listening to? I don't understand it," Magni said.

"It's poetry," I answered.

"*Poetry?*" Magni coughed. "Are you fucking kidding me – who has time for poetry?" He had his nose wrinkled as we listened to the words. "Did she say juxtaposition?" Magni asked. "Please tell me that's something dirty and sexual." He poked me. "Did you and Christina ever try the juxta position?"

Khan rolled his eyes. "It's not a sexual position, you dumbasses. A juxtaposition is two things with contrasting effect."

"Showoff." I bumped my elbow into Khan's ribs but he was too busy looking at the women to retaliate.

"I hate poetry," Magni groaned.

"Me too, but according to Christina it's because I'm not *evolved* enough to appreciate something as fine as that poem."

Magni snorted. "She calls that *fine?*"

"Shit," Khan muttered when Christina and Pearl got up from the floor and walked toward the doors to the balcony. "The sound is bad on the balcony."

Luckily the women stayed inside and only opened the balcony door to let in some fresh air.

"We have to show this to the council," Pearl said, leaning against the doorframe. "It deserves a prominent place, but we'll need to reframe some of the wording to something more appropriate."

"Why? People will know it was written before the big enlightenment. It's art, Pearl. You don't change a painting because the color offends you. Hera speaks the language of her day, and any poem should stay true in its form," Christina argued.

"You have a point." Pearl nodded.

"I swear, Momsies are soft in their heads," Magni groaned.

I shushed him, desperate to hear what Christina was saying, but only caught the last part. "What did she say?" I asked worriedly.

"Something about time to go," Khan answered, and we all listened carefully when Pearl placed her hand on Christina's arm.

"Are you sure?"

"The university is large, and I'll admit that I would like to keep digging to see what buried treasures we could find, but it would take me years to uncover the whole thing and I'm not sure it's healthy for me to stay."

"Is it Boulder?"

Christina lifted her gaze and gave a small nod. "He wants me to stay."

"And you, do you want to stay?"

"No," she said and looked down. "Of course not."

In Khan's office, I fisted my hands and closed my eyes, exhaling deeply.

"Then we should start planning for your return," Pearl said softly. "There are messages I need you to deliver to the council and you need to copy everything from the flash drive. What is found in the Northlands remains in the Northlands; it's part of our agreement. We can learn from our findings and bring home electronic information, but the books have to stay.

Christina tensed up. "You know they have lots of books already, right?"

"So?"

"Even in this mansion there are plenty of antique books. Maybe they wouldn't mind if I bring back a few and study them."

"Maybe," Pearl said thoughtfully. "But you would need to let a librarian classify them first."

"I could classify them," Christina suggested.

"No, Christina, you're still young and impressionable. Reading of violence or passion could bring out unwanted emotions in you."

"You mean like longings?" she asked.

Pearl squeezed both her hands. "Yes, Christina, like longings."

"Those books aren't forbidden here," Christina said softly.

"I know." Pearl let go of Christina's hand and looked out the window. "They didn't used to be forbidden in the Motherlands either."

"So what changed?"

Pearl's shoulders lifted in a shrug. "It's confidential, but since I sense that it hasn't happened to you and you already declared that you're going home, I'll tell you."

"Turn up the volume," I instructed Khan.

"In the beginning of the twenty-third century a young woman wrote a series about the Nmen. It was pure fiction of course, but she made them sound like amazing, virile heroes and had millions of women starting to swoon at the idea of being with one of them." Pearl shook her head. "Of course, the council back then tried to spread the word that it wasn't true and nothing but a fairytale, but women made their way to the borders trying to get across."

Khan, Magni, and I exchanged glances. "What the fuck," Magni muttered. "I didn't know that."

"And then what?" Christina asked.

Pearl let out a deep breath. "Obviously, the council couldn't allow it and needed to take radical measures to protect the women. All of them were sent back home, and after that laws were made to prohibit people from speaking about the Nmen and sharing pictures or stories about them. Not only were the books that had started this dangerous situation banned but so were all books that involved sexual passion or violence. It's been that way for more than two centuries now and we still enforce those laws to prevent something similar from happening again."

"But if someone wanted to come here and stay voluntarily, why couldn't they?" Christina asked with her head tilted.

"It's not safe here. What do you think would happen to us if we weren't protected in this mansion? Nmen are not like our men. They have high levels of testosterone and are prone to violence."

"True." Christina looked down. "But Boulder has been very kind to me."

"That's good, but for all we know, he might be an anomaly, Christina; we can't know for sure. And there's the obvious concern."

"Which is?"

"What would happen if women came here and the population grew, with more females being born?"

Christina shrugged. "They wouldn't be so desperate?"

"No, I'm talking about the threat to us. To the Motherlands."

"You think women would be a bad influence on the Nmen?"

"No, you're getting it wrong. Today we have a peace treaty and we hold a powerful position because we're supplying them with enough boys to sustain their numbers."

"Right."

"Christina, it's not our choice to isolate them up here, but surely you understand that we can't let them grow in numbers. It would be a catastrophe if they were to attack us."

"Because we don't know how to fight?"

Pearl shook her head. "We can defend ourselves perfectly well, but we're pacifists and we don't want to kill to protect ourselves. Being forced to do that would be horrible."

"Yes." Christina nodded. "But you said the council would like nothing more than for the Nmen to join us."

Pearl sighed heavily again. "I did say that, but maybe it's just wishful thinking. Enlightenment takes time and Khan is..." She shook her head.

"Khan is what?"

"A genius," Khan said dryly and gave me a "What?" expression when I shushed him again.

"I'm trying to make him see things our way, but he's a stubborn soul and very limited in his thinking," Pearl said thoughtfully.

Khan snorted and arched a brow. "Limited in my thinking – ha, look who's talking, I can't tell you how annoying that woman is."

I kept my eyes on the image of the two women.

"All right," Christina said. "I'll leave the books here then. Maybe *you* can categorize them," she suggested. "Unless of course you worry that it will affect you and make you vulnerable to one of the men here."

Pearl laughed. "Not likely. The only one who is slightly attractive is Boulder, and only because he doesn't hide behind a huge beard."

That made me square my chest and grin silently when Khan shot me a scowl.

"It's funny," Christina said. "I can remember how intimidating I found all the men when I arrived here, but my time with Boulder..." She trailed off.

"Yes?" Pearl asked.

"It has changed me," Christina breathed. "I feel safe with him, and as annoying and primitive as he can be, he can be funny and sweet too."

Magni tousled my hair. "Such a sweet boy," he teased.

"I think you're right, my dear," Pearl said solemnly. "It's not safe for you to stay. You're becoming too attached to him."

Christina nodded. "I know. Can you imagine me and Boulder being a *real* couple? It's ridiculous, right?" A fake laugh escaped her, but Pearl didn't laugh. "I would have to give up my entire life," Christina said, and her words made me heave up my chest in a deep intake of air.

"It's not like I could take him home to visit my friends and family. They would think I'd lost my mind and would be scared of him for sure."

"They would!" Pearl confirmed.

Christina looked down. "So it's best if I just go."

The way Pearl pulled Christina in for a hug and held her close made me jealous. I wanted to do that. To hold Christina and to tell her that she should stay.

They stood like that for at least a full minute until Christina pulled back and dried her eyes. "I'll tell him tonight then."

"You do that. I'll prepare the letters that I need you to deliver for me. And, sweetie..."

"Yes?"

"It's going to be very lonely here without you."

The two women stood slightly apart, both with sunken shoulders.

"I'll stay if you ask me to," Christina said and I willed Pearl to speak the words, but she didn't.

"I could never ask that of you."

"But how long will you stay here?"

"Until I decide otherwise."

"Laura probably feels guilty," Christina told Pearl.

"If you meet her, tell her that I don't blame her and that I'm fine." Pearl looked down. "As fine as I can be under the circumstances."

"I will," Christina assented and left the room.

"Aha – see?" Magni exclaimed triumphantly. "I knew it. Pearl knows where Laura is. She just admitted it."

"No, she didn't," I said. "She said *if* you see her, and that doesn't mean they know where she is."

"I agree with Boulder," Khan said and pointed to the image of Pearl. "Did you hear what she said about staying until she decides otherwise... Ha, the woman is crazy if she thinks she can escape from here. I don't think she fully understands what being a hostage means."

While Khan was talking, Magni spun around and raked his hand through his hair, making sounds of frustration.

"Give me ten minutes with the councilwoman and I'll have her spilling all her secrets," he almost shouted.

"No!" Khan shook his head. "I won't allow you to interrogate Pearl or frighten her further."

"What are we waiting for?" Magni exclaimed. "I can't just sit here and do nothing. I want Laura back."

Khan had that expression on his face: the one that signaled that he was about to explode. Being called limited in his thoughts by Pearl and hearing that she found me more attractive than him had to be a blow to his male pride.

Magni and I both knew the expression and normally Magni was smart enough to back down, but this time he didn't. Instead he kept pressing for time with Pearl until Khan slammed his fist down on his desk.

"When are you fucking gonna accept that Laura is gone? Your wife didn't want to be with you. She left you. Do you hear me? *She left you!*"

Magni stumbled backward as if Khan's words were a physical blow. "But she's my *wife*."

"I know, brother, I know."

The sorrow in Magni's eyes tore at my heartstrings. After hearing that Christina was leaving me too, I felt like looking at my future self. A protector without anyone to protect. A husband with physical needs and no one to fill them. I would never be able to be fulfilled by sex-bots after experiencing the real thing, and I didn't even know what to do with all the emotions I had for Christina. I had no memory of my mom. Like other Nmen, I had been three years old when I came from the Motherlands. The only physical connection I had experienced, until Christina came, was fighting other boys and men.

The despair I felt in my belly, just thinking about going back to my old life without her, made me feel aggressive and irrational. I could relate to Magni's desperation.

"I'm going to keep her here," I muttered.

"What?" Khan swung his head from Magni to me. "What did you say?" he sputtered.

"Christina – I can't let her leave."

"The fuck you can't. It's bad enough that we have a councilwoman as hostage, we're not taking Christina hostage too."

"That's easy for you to say. You're the only one with a woman in your bed," I sneered back at Khan.

"A woman in my bed?" He narrowed his eyes at me. "What I do with Pearl isn't your fucking business."

I arched a brow. "So you can watch me fuck Christina but what happens in your bedroom is a secret?"

"What are you talking about?" Magni interjected. "When did you see Boulder and Christina?"

"He spies on us," I explained. "Maybe he spied on you and Laura too."

Magni pinned Khan with his gaze. "Is this true? Did you?"

"What?"

"Spy on me and Laura?"

"No, of course not."

I was walking toward the door, growling in frustration. "This is all a fucking mess."

Behind me the brothers were still arguing.

CHAPTER 27
Last Night Together

Boulder

I was on edge!

Rationally, I knew I should enjoy the time I had left with Christina, but I couldn't think straight. I was so scared of the end that I wasn't myself when Christina confronted me that evening with the words: "Boulder, we need to talk."

No, we don't I wanted to scream because I knew what was coming, but I sat down with a knot in my throat and listened when she started her rehearsed speech.

"Look, I want to thank you for everything you've done for me. I know it was inconvenient that I came and took you away from your normal routine and your business dealings, but I appreciate that you've kept me safe and been my friend."

I turned my head, unable to look at her when she spoke the dreaded word. "I've decided that it's time for me to go home."

Even if I had wanted to object, I couldn't have. My throat burned as if hot lava was running down it on the inside.

"I know you want me to stay, but it's really for the best, Boulder," Christina said and this time our eyes clashed. I didn't give a shit that she saw the disappointment and pain in mine.

"Please know that I've enjoyed my time with you," she whispered and teared up.

I fought my own tears. There was no way I would be a wuss and sit here and cry like a little boy. My pride wouldn't let me.

"Do you have anything to say?" she asked after a long silence.

I swallowed again and again, trying to find my voice, but only managed to croak out: "When?"

"Tomorrow evening. I'll go to the digging site tomorrow and instruct the team how to proceed from here. I don't think we'll find much more in the library but they may want to proceed with other parts of the university."

"Okay," I said brusquely and stood up

Christina leaned her head back to look up at me. "Okay?" she asked.

I made an angry shrug that beat falling to my knees and pleading with her to stay. "What do you want me to say?"

"Nothing... I mean, I just thought that maybe..."

"What? That I would beg you to stay?" My voice was shaking with emotion.

She reached out to me but I stepped back. "You made your choice."

A minute later I locked the door to the bathroom and watched myself in the mirror. I used to think myself handsome and worthy. Now I could see nothing but my flaws. Tomorrow I would be in the same boat as Magni. A public failure whose wife had left him.

I dried away an angry tear and shamed myself in my mind.

You really thought you'd be enough to make her want to stay? As if you were ever smart enough, attractive enough, sexy enough, enlightened or evolved enough.

My head fell forward, my shoulders sinking. What did it matter that I was one of the best fighters and most successful businessmen in the Northlands? I was just a big unsophisticated brute in her world. Tomorrow I would be alone again, and somehow that was worse than never having had a wife in the first place.

I knew what it felt like to have someone to protect, the pride of being chosen, the pride of having what other men would never have.

I knew the delirium of having a woman spread her legs and invite me to enter her.

I knew the salty taste of her skin after a day of work and the warmth of her body in my bed at night.

I knew what crazy ideas she had and how she made me reflect on things I'd always considered normal.

I knew what it felt like to laugh with a small woman who tilted her head and asked me questions like I mattered to her and was the most interesting person in this world.

And tomorrow I would know what missing all of it felt like.

I had seen old movies with break-ups but at least back then there were other women to move on with. There would never be another woman for me. That was certain, and even if there was, how could anyone affect me the way Christina had?

Acute nausea made me hold a hand to my mouth and widen my eyes in panic. *Not that!*

With frantic movements, I turned on the shower before I leaned down over the toilet bowl and threw up. My stomach convulsed in painful cramps until I had nothing more to get rid of.

To cover my tracks, I flushed the toilet, cleaned my mouth, and showered quickly. The time in the shower gave me a chance to collect myself before facing her again and when I did, I acted as calm as possible. My plan was simply to get through tonight and tomorrow with my pride intact.

Christina

Boulder took the news much more calmly than I'd expected. He didn't ask many questions or try to convince me to stay.

Except... From his hard expression, I almost got the feeling that it didn't matter much to him, and I wondered if it was our argument from earlier that had caused this change in him.

I don't know what I had expected or hoped for. Maybe a sign that I was more to him than merely the first woman he had been intimate with. Or that I wasn't the only one who felt an emotional connection between us.

After our talk, Boulder took a shower before he joined me in bed. We lay quietly looking up at the ceiling, not speaking a word for a long time.

"This is our last night together," I finally whispered.

"Uh-huh," he responded quietly.

"Are you okay?"

"I'm fine."

I turned my face to see him in the soft light.

"Will you miss me?" I asked him softly.

Slowly he turned his body and met my eyes. "Will you miss me?"

There was such a heaviness to the atmosphere in the room that I tried to lighten it up with a smile. "I'll miss being with you at night."

"And at day?"

"Nahh, you're a pain," I said ironically. Surely, he knew I would miss him.

Moving my body closer, I kissed him gently. "Do you want to be with me one last time?"

To my surprise he hesitated and didn't hungrily roll on top of me like he normally would have.

"Is that what you want?" he asked in a controlled voice.

Sucking his lower lip into my mouth and releasing it with a pop was my way of answering him affirmatively, but he still didn't get into action. "Yes," I clarified. "I want us to have one final night together."

He didn't say a word when we undressed, and the sex was very different than usual. More cold and mechanical, as if he was holding back. I tried to kiss him, but he kept the kisses short and would hardly look at me.

I didn't come, and I learned that night that sex without an emotional connection is no better than being with a sex-bot. Or maybe even worse, because with a bot you have no expectation of anything beyond a physical release.

After we were done, Boulder turned his back to me and the quietness resumed. I had never felt so lonely in my life. He was right there next to me. I could reach out and touch him, but I didn't. Emotionally he was closed off and maybe it was for the best. Tomorrow we would be strangers again. Strangers living different lives in different worlds. Strangers who shared memories, but nothing more. A colossal sense of loss overwhelmed me and I cried, pulling the cover over my head to drown the sound of my shaky breathing.

I needed to go home and curl up, and somehow make sense of all that had happened in my life these past six weeks.

Once I get home, my mind will clear up and I'll be happy that I didn't stay, I comforted myself.

CHAPTER 28
The Return

Christina

My roommate, Kya, was overly excited that I had returned. She kept hugging me and asking a million questions.

"You know I'm not allowed to speak about the Nmen," I told her with a sad smile.

"You'd better," she said. "I'm dying from curiosity."

"Well, they're big and strong like you've heard and they swear a lot."

"So they speak English?" she asked.

"Uh-huh, with a slight accent and more gruffly than us, but I understood them just fine."

"Did any of them hurt you?"

"No, I made a friend." As I said it my face fell. "His name was Alexander Boulder and he protected me."

"He protected you? From what?"

"Any harm that could come to me."

"So you *were* in danger?"

I sighed. "It's a place where women are a rarity and desperate men do desperate things."

"So how did he protect you? Did he carry a weapon of some kind?"

I frowned. "No, only the guards carried weapons. Nmen seem very honor bound, and once it was decided he was my protector other men just backed off."

"Wow, good for them. So, if they have honor they can't be as bad as we've heard. And here we thought they were brutal savages."

I bit my lip. "Actually, they *are* brutal, and I witnessed them fight and argue several times. Alexander even broke an arm fighting for me."

"Fighting for you," Kya scrunched up her face. "What are they, Vikings?" She laughed at her own joke.

I laughed with her. "They kinda look that way with their beard and hair, but most of all with their clothing."

Kya wrinkled her nose. "Don't tell me they wear fur."

"Oh yeah, they do, and lots of leather. Luckily for me, it was still summer so I didn't have to see them in fur coats."

"Oh, it makes me so mad that they would kill innocent animals." Her curly hair bobbed from the way she shook her head.

"I know, but you can't discuss it with them." I sighed. "Trust me, I tried. They think we're the crazy ones and will argue that it's the natural order of things and that humans have always hunted and eaten animals.

"So much for the big enlightenment." Kya shook her head.

"I know – somehow they managed to avoid that wave of raised awareness."

"God, it sounds like you traveled back in time or something."

"No, they have modern amenities. But yeah, culturally, I think it was like traveling back in time."

"So you loved it?"

I looked down. This was so typical of Kya. To see right through me.

"I mean, what archeologist wouldn't like to travel back in time? Tell me…" I felt her eyes burning on my face. "What part of it did you like the best?"

Meeting her curious eyes, framed by her impossibly long lashes, I swallowed hard. On my way back from the Northlands I'd convinced myself I would never let anyone know the details of my relationship with Boulder, but I had been delusional thinking Kya wouldn't sniff out that something big had happened to me. And more importantly, the truth was burning in my belly like a hot piece of coal that needed to be cooled down or it would consume me and destroy me.

"Boulder," I admitted quietly. "Boulder was the best part."

Kya waited for me to elaborate.

"You can't tell anyone about this, do you promise?"

"I promise."

"Please don't hate me or report me for being unstable, but Boulder and I..." I pressed out the last words. "We had sex."

Her hands flew to her mouth, her eyes wide in shock.

"He didn't rape me!" I hurried to say. "It was more like a social experiment. I was curious and wanted to experience what it would be like to be with a man like him. Someone who is so much like men used to be."

Her hands lowered from her mouth. "And?"

A shy smile spread on my lips. "And it was amazing."

"What do you mean?" She moved closer on the sofa.

"It's so different. I mean *he's* so different. Tall, muscled, strong, and almost animalistic in the way he would take me."

"Animalistic?" She tilted her head.

"Yeah," I laughed. "Sometimes he would literally growl while having sex with me. There was so much passion in his eyes and his movements. It's something that I've never experienced before, and I envy women from the old days if sex was like that for them."

"Holy Mother Nature." Kya pulled her knees up and wrapped her arms tightly around her bent legs. "And here I was so worried about you. I never imagined sex with an Nman could be a pleasurable experience for any woman."

"Look, I think I know the answer, but Kya, have you ever had sex with a man?"

"A living man?"

"No a dead one," I said sarcastically.

She wrinkled her nose. "No, just male sex-bots."

"Yeah, that's what I thought." I sighed. "Anyway, I have a lot to think about and process, but one thing is for sure. I'll never forget Boulder." I looked away so she wouldn't see the sadness I felt.

"I almost regret becoming a teacher," Kya said in a light tone. "You archeologists have all the fun."

"I know." I was grateful that she didn't dig deeper.

Playing with my hair, Kya gave me an empathetic smile. "At least you're back home with good memories. It would be worse if you returned all traumatized."

"Good point," I said softly.

"And..." She held up a hand. "They have a new sex-bot down at the pleasure parlor. Ann was raving about him. They let you take him home to sleep with and..." She wiggled her brows. "To have sex with, of course."

"Ann took him home?"

"Yes. And she was raving about how good it was to have him for a whole night. He does this thing called spooning."

"What's that?"

Kya furrowed her brows. "I'm not sure, but it's something about sleeping in his arms all night."

"But why do they let him go home with people?"

Kya shrugged. "It surprised me too, but after seeing how excited Ann was, I signed up to have him for a night of my own. You want to get your name on that waiting list because it's growing fast."

"Okay," I said distractedly, thinking about how Boulder had held me in his arms at night. Yeah, I could see why Ann would have liked that. I had too.

Christina

Days turned into weeks. I had delivered all the messages Pearl sent with me, and my thoughts went to her often. For some reason, it was a secret that she was a hostage in the Northlands. The situation made me reflect upon our society and all the times Boulder had accused the council of treating us like children.

"They decide what books you can read, what movies you can see, what truth you're being told. It's like an old-fashioned religious sect – that's what it is," he had argued and I'd thought him crazy.

But the more I thought about it, the more I started questioning our way of life. I could see the reasoning behind the laws, and it was undisputable that in general people were happy and thriving. But the poem with Hera Bosley stood out to me because of the conversation I'd had with Pearl about it. Her first instinct had been to censor the poem and replace the curse words.

Three months ago, I would have agreed, but not any longer. Boulder was right. Words only held the power we gave them and I was strong enough to handle swear words without feeling traumatized. My guess was that so was everyone else.

We just weren't given the choice.

If I hadn't gone to the Northlands, I would have never known passion, desire, or fear. I would have never experienced raw emotions like the Nmen expressed them.

Our priestesses always spoke about being authentic but somehow I was starting to doubt that we had any room for that in the Motherlands. We weren't authentic. We were molded into positive clones that were taught how to suppress any human emotions that didn't benefit us and – more importantly – didn't benefit our community.

My nights were the worst. Insomnia kept me awake thinking about my decision to come back here.

When I made that decision, I had naïvely thought I could return to my old life, but I had underestimated how much my time with the Nmen had changed me and not realized that the new me didn't fit into the small, secure mold I'd been in before I left.

I thanked Mother Nature that I had Kya in my life. She saw me cry and didn't report me for being emotionally unstable. She asked a lot of questions, and I opened up and told her almost everything – except the part about Athena and Pearl and the rather important detail that I'd married Boulder. I couldn't betray Pearl's trust, and the part about my being married would surely freak Kya out.

Every day, I pulled myself out of bed and put a fake smile on, but I was miserable on the inside.

"You're grieving," Kya said with sympathy. "You lost a good friend who meant much more to you than you knew."

She was right about that part. I hadn't understood or appreciated what Boulder and I shared together.

One morning, I had woken up with a smile on my lips and sweet dreams of Boulder still filling my mind. He was holding me close, teasing me and tickling me. But as the dream faded and reality came into perspective I opened my eyes to find my empty bedroom in a city where Boulder could never be allowed access.

I wanted to claw out the ache in my belly. I wanted to scream out my frustration. But an emotional outburst like that would get me on the radar of the authorities and call for an evaluation.

At some point, I even considered voluntarily going to a place of reflection. Maybe I needed time to space out and find my inner balance again, but the hope that tomorrow would be better made me go on, thinking that soon Boulder wouldn't be the first thing I thought about when I woke up and the last before I fell asleep.

I wondered how he was doing and if he missed me. I imagined him in his large house, being with his friends, walking the park by the gray mansion, or flying his black hybrid while listening to that awful music he liked so much.

I wondered if he'd grown his beard back and if he wore his favorite leather shirt now that I wasn't there to object.

"How much weight have you lost?" Kya asked me with a troubled look, three weeks after I'd returned.

"Not sure."

"Look." She sank down on my bed next to me. "It's getting to the point where I'll have to do something. You're not eating, you're not sleeping, you have bags under your eyes, and I haven't seen you smile for weeks."

"I know," I said and sighed.

"You spend most of your time at home in bed. It's not normal, Cina." Kya was the only one who insisted on using that nickname for me.

"I'm sorry. It's just that..."

"You miss him. I know." We sat quietly for a while, her on the edge of my bed, me against the wall with my legs pulled up and my head drooping on my knees.

"You've been crying again," she said matter-of-factly.

I couldn't deny it; my eyes were red and puffy.

"What are you gonna do?"

I covered my face with my hands. "You're not going to like it," I warned her.

"Will it be worse than seeing my best friend in misery for weeks?" she asked.

"I'm going to request the council to send me back."

Kya didn't seem as surprised as I'd expected. She nodded slowly. "Okay."

"Okay?"

"I would rather that you're happy up there than miserable here," she said rationally. "You should do it."

"You mean that?" I felt so much lighter with her approval.

247

"Yeah." She bit her lip. "Doesn't mean I won't miss you."

"I'll miss you too." We hugged and again I thanked the stars that Kya was my friend.

Fueled by a surge of energy, I sent in my application that same day and started smiling again. Instead of grieving over my loss of Boulder, I was starting to visualize his surprise when I returned to him.

And then doubt filled me. What if I overestimated how he felt about me? He had been cold to me the last day, and I was suddenly questioning our whole relationship.

No, Boulder asked me to stay many times. He wouldn't have if he didn't care about me, I reminded myself. *But then again, he would have been happy with any woman; he has nothing to compare it to. If he'd had a choice of women, he wouldn't have picked me.*

I started looking at other women, wondering if he would prefer them given the choice. Probably Kya, with her caramel skin color and gorgeous eyes and voluminous hair.

It took a full week before I got my reply. As with the last time, I was asked to come in for a meeting, and I pedaled my bike with great gusto, creating energy for the network and feeling optimistic.

My bags were already packed, and with the approval I could leave tonight.

I meet a clergywoman this time. She was old, wrinkled, and partly deaf, which made me wonder why she hadn't gotten that fixed. Hearing and vision were easy to fix but some people were just in denial, I guessed.

"Your application to go back to the Northlands has been rejected," the woman said and looked down at her arm where her wristband projected my application.

My face fell and my heart skipped a beat.

"Why?" I muttered.

"There's been no request from the Northlands for an archeologist at this point. We have no reason to send you."

"No, but I didn't finish the project they asked me to help them with," I hurried to say.

"You didn't?" She lifted her brows. "Hmm."

"I *have* to go back." My jaw felt like rubber and my words were shaky.

"I'm afraid the council doesn't agree, but you can re-apply in six months."

"Six months?" I shrieked. "I have to go back *now*."

The old woman leaned away from me as if afraid that my frantic energy was contagious. "Go in peace, Christina Sanders, and may I suggest that you lower your voice."

I fisted my hands and looked down. Disappointment and a deep sense of powerlessness filled me with despair.

My dreams of Boulders and my reunion would be only that – dreams.

"Wait!" I got up and ran after the old hag who had just destroyed my future happiness.

She turned and eyed me disapprovingly. "Your voice, Christina," she said in a scolding tone.

"I'm sorry, but could I at least send a letter to someone in the Northlands?"

"You know that's not possible," the woman said stiffly, but with a fake smile.

"It *is* possible," I insisted. "Don't forget that I've been there." My alarm bells were ringing loudly. My hard tone of voice and my narrowed eyes would be considered hostile by the clergywoman.

"If I were you," she said with that ugly fake smile that didn't reach her eyes, "I would accept the council's answer and forget about the Northlands. There is nothing for you there, my dear."

I hated her endearment in the end and felt belittled like a child. She was wrong! There was something for me in the Northlands. Boulder was there and I needed to see

249

him again. I needed to know if he felt as miserable without me as I did without him.

Standing in the foyer at the community hall, my senses were taking in the serene sound of the water fountain meant to add a tranquil atmosphere to the large room. But there was no peace or tranquility inside of me. There was only dark despair.

Closing my eyes, I roared out my powerlessness like a cornered animal and screamed at a woman who passed me, wishing me eternal bliss. There would never be any bliss in my life. I had known bliss but failed to recognize it for what it was. Now I knew. Now I understood that to me bliss came in a large, primitive, brutal package of a man with the name of Alexander Boulder. A man who could make me pant with want and scream out his name in orgasmic euphoria. A man who brought out emotions in me that no one else could. Bliss to me was feeling *alive*, and no one made me feel more alive than him. I screamed all that at the woman, but luckily only on the inside of my skull. Thirty-one years of indoctrination had taught me to hold my tongue.

Suffocating from emotions pressing in my chest, I hurried outside and desperately breathed in a large gulp of fresh air.

I biked home, blinded by tears, and when people called out to ask me if I was okay, I responded that I'd hurt my elbow but would be okay. Physical pain was accepted. Emotional pain would concern them more, and before I knew it I would be in the hands of well-meaning advisors who would help me find my balance again. The very thought of my finding my balance and living a full life was offensive. I had screwed up the most amazing thing that had ever happened to me and every year I lived without Boulder would be a year half-lived.

CHAPTER 29
Khan's Secret

Boulder

Parking my hybrid outside the gray mansion I looked for Magni's ride, but didn't see it.

Instead I found Khan in the park in a heated discussion with Pearl. He looked like he was close to strangling her but the woman fearlessly stared up at him with her head held high.

Pausing, I almost didn't approach him because of the tension between them, but then Pearl turned her back on him and Khan strode off with a huff of annoyance.

"Hey, Khan, hold up," I called out and ran after him.

"Boulder," he said grumpily. "You lucky bastard."

"What do you mean?" I asked because if there was one thing I didn't feel like, it was lucky.

"You got rid of Christina. I swear, Momsies are the most frustrating creatures on this planet. They have no logical sense and live in a fairytale world." He stopped abruptly and pointed a finger at me. "I'm the ruler of ten million men, but I can't get one single woman to do my bidding. Can you explain that?"

"No." I looked back at the woman in question. "But to be honest, I don't think Pearl is the norm when it comes to Momsies. She seems..." I thought about how to put it, "...unique."

"Unique?" He glared at me. "If by unique you mean stubborn and inflexible, then yeah, she's fucking unique."

"I meant more like – uniquely strong... you know, for a woman."

He huffed out air and started walking briskly again. "I can't *stand* the woman."

"Are you sure you still want to be her protector?" I asked.

"Don't ask me that," he hissed. "Right now, I'm tempted to boot her all the way to the border. The woman is infuriating."

"So your plan about brainwashing her isn't going too well?"

He didn't answer me, and I decided it was time to change the subject.

"I came to see Magni. Have you seen him?"

"No." Khan frowned. "He hardly speaks to me anymore."

"That's because he doesn't agree with your decisions regarding Laura. It's been almost eight weeks since Pearl arrived; don't you think it's time to put pressure on her?"

"Laura is gone!" He scowled. "And if I ever see her again, I'll fucking strangle her myself for all the drama she's caused between Magni and me. She destroyed my brother and made me look like a fool." He flung his hand back toward Pearl, who was looking in our direction. "If not for Laura, I would be a happy man who didn't have to protect the most awful woman in history."

"So *do* something about it," I suggested.

"What?" He raised his voice, his eyes burning into mine. "What exactly would you have me do, Boulder? You want us to go to war because of a woman who didn't value her marriage?"

"I don't know, but I get why Magni is upset with you. You have no idea what it's like, but I do." The last three words came out pained.

Khan's eyes softened a bit and he looked down, taking in a calming breath. "I know, my friend. I know you miss her, but there's nothing I can do about it." He patted my shoulder. "Give it time and you'll forget her."

252

"No, I won't. It doesn't work that way. And the worst part is that I have these obsessive thoughts that she's pregnant with our child," I said.

"Who's pregnant?" Pearl asked behind us and it made us both swing back to face her.

"Eavesdropping now?" Khan accused her. "And you blame me for having bad manners."

Pearl ignored Khan and focused only on me. "Who is pregnant?"

Clearly Khan was angry with Pearl, but she was the closest thing to Christina right now and I was hoping that maybe she knew something I didn't, so I spilled my heart. "Christina and I had sex for weeks before she left and I can't help thinking that she might be pregnant with our child. It's driving me mental not to know."

Pearl paled. "You had sex with Christina?"

"Yes." I furrowed my brow. "She didn't tell you?"

"No." She looked thoughtful. "She was probably too ashamed to tell me."

"Ashamed? What the fuck are you talking about? She's my wife; why would she be ashamed of having sex with me?" I asked, offended.

"I thought your marriage was a practical solution only." She tilted her head slightly. "But now it all makes sense."

Shifting my balance, I shot her a pleading look. "What does? Pearl, I'm begging you, can you find out if she's pregnant?"

Khan crossed his arms and scoffed. "Don't let her fool you, Boulder. Even if Christina is pregnant Pearl will tell you that she isn't. The Momsies protect their own."

Raking my hands through my hair, I cursed. "If I'm to be a father I want to be part of the child's life."

"And I respect that about you," Pearl said softly. "But Christina chose to leave and if she's pregnant the child will stay with her. You wouldn't want a baby to be torn from its mother, would you?"

"No, but later… when the child is old enough to come here – if it's a boy, I mean – I could take care of him and train him," I rambled.

"Oh, for fuck's sake, Boulder, don't turn all mushy because of a kid. You've probably fathered several already."

I froze and stared at Khan. "No, I haven't. I've only ever been with Christina, you know that."

Pearl looked down and Khan closed his eyes like he had said too much.

A queasy feeling spread in my gut. "What?" I barked. "What children have I fathered?"

They exchanged a long glance before Pearl spoke. "If we tell you, can we trust you to keep it secret?"

"Yes," I said quickly, eager to hear what the hell Khan had meant.

"Most men in the Motherlands are sterile." Pearl started slowly. "It's something we're trying to change, but the massive pollution our ancestors fought after the war has left us with a medical predicament, and children are no longer produced naturally."

"But your numbers are rising." I said because Christina had told me this.

"Yes, they are." She nodded solemnly, "but only recently. Seventeen years ago a deal was made between the Northlands and the Motherlands. We trade."

"I know," I said with a frown. "I own mines and logging companies, I know this."

"Yes, but what you might not know is that the greatest export the Northlands has is sperm."

"Excuse me?" I glared at her. "Did you just say sperm?"

Khan let out another deep sigh and pressed his lips into a fine line.

"We get sperm from the ten million men living up here in the cleanest and most unspoiled natural surroundings that the world has left."

I dropped my chin. "How? I've never heard a single guy mention he donates sperm. How do you get sperm from us?"

"Simple," Pearl said. "Every sex-bot has a core designed to contain and freeze the sperm that is ejaculated into it."

"You... you steal our sperm?"

"Certainly not," Pearl said in defense and looked to Khan. "Tell him."

"It's a bargain that my father made and I renewed," Khan admitted. "Since the first peace treaty was struck centuries ago our boys were always bred on Nmen sperm. It was one of our conditions for entering the agreement in the first place. How do you think it is that we're so big compared to the men of the Motherlands?

"Because we eat meat and build our muscles from childhood," I answered, because that's what I'd always been told.

"Yes, but there's a genetic component to it too." Khan shifted his balance and drew a deep breath. "Since the beginning the robots have been designed to evaluate the male they're with. When a man who doesn't fit the criteria of a breeder is with the robot his sperm is disposed of, while a man like you will be selected as a breeder."

"A man like me?"

"Tall, muscular, and fit," Khan said matter-of-factly. "But now that the Momsimen are almost incapable of producing their own offspring we've accepted donating our genes."

"We?" I asked incredulously. "I don't remember being asked."

"Boulder, this is bigger than you," Pearl argued. "This is about the survival of the human race. The Nmen sperm is being used in different corners of the Motherlands as we speak."

"So all your men are sterile, are they?" I asked harshly.

"No, luckily we still have men capable of reproducing, although over the years the fertility among our men has dropped alarmingly, to the point where only one percent of our men can reproduce and only with help from specialists. We prefer genes from our own men, but there's simply not enough."

"That's insulting," Khan bit out. "You should be fucking honored to get our strong genes."

"Who else knows about this?" I asked, my heart pounding in aggravation.

"Only a selected few. For the most part, everyone thinks the core of the sex-bots are being changed constantly for hygiene purposes. There's a man in charge of collecting and shipping the sperm and he and his team obviously know, but they've signed non-disclosure agreements."

"And the women?" I asked Pearl. "Do they know Nmen are fathering their children?"

"Of course not," she said.

"And you?" I looked to Khan. "Have you donated too, or did you stay clear of coming inside the sex-bots?"

His eyes shot to Pearl and she folded her arms across her chest with an expectant smile.

"That's none of your business," he bit out.

"Did you donate?" I asked again and pinned him with a challenging glare.

"Of course I did," he said. "I have excellent genes, and who wouldn't want to father as many children as possible?"

"And not see them? Not know what became of them?" I asked incredulously.

Khan shifted his balance. "Don't be so melodramatic. I would much rather that *my* genes got spread than those of some Momsiboy who is more woman than man."

"Oh, please." Pearl shook her head. "Enough of this name-calling; our men are highly intelligent and wonderful men."

All she got was snorts from both me and Khan.

"Boulder, listen." Pearl drew back my attention. "It's unlikely that Christina is pregnant. Many women are sterile too. But in case she is, think of how wonderful it will be for her to know the father of her child. That's very rare."

"You don't get it," I said. "That baby and Christina – they're my family. My responsibility."

"Family." Pearl gave a small laugh. "What an odd thing to say. We're all family."

"No." I cut an arm through the air. "A family is a man, his wife, and their children."

"You Nmen are so unbelievably old-fashioned," she said and threw her hands up in the air. "It's not about that. It's about forming a bond and a community with people you care about. If you could look beyond the traditions and challenge your minds to find beauty in other configurations you would understand why the Motherlands is such a success."

"A success?" I gaped at her. "You limit your people and control them like children. I'm done listening to your shit." I walked off determined to find Magni, and I didn't stop to take part in the argument that Pearl and Khan continued as I left.

CHAPTER 30
Papa Hunt

Boulder

I found Magni at a bar in the nearest town. He was sitting with his head drooping and an almost empty beer.

"Hey," I said and took a seat next to him. "I've been looking for you."

"Oh, yeah?" His voice sounded so unlike the old Magni I knew.

"Can we talk?" I asked quietly and signaled to the bar-bot that I wanted what Magni was having.

The bar-bot had the design of a pretty female bartender and was quick to deliver me my beer with a smile and a wink. "Here you go, handsome, a well poured lager, never goes out of fashion."

"What do you wanna talk about?" Magni asked without lifting his head.

"How did you get into the Motherlands?" I asked low.

Slowly, Magni turned his head to look at me. "Why?"

I took a long sip of my beer and met his eyes. "You know why."

A slow smile pursed his lips. "Told you, didn't I?"

"Yeah, you did and it fucking sucks."

Magni was tipsy and his movements slow when he lifted his hand to pat me sympathetically on my shoulder.

"So how did you get in?" I asked again.

"You wanna go after Christina?"

I looked around the room before I gave a discreet nod. "I have to."

"She doesn't want you," he slurred slightly. "Just like Laura doesn't want me."

"It doesn't matter, I still need to see her." I sighed and fired my next question. "Do you ever wonder if Laura was pregnant when she left you?"

"Fuck yeah, all the time." Magni rubbed his face. "We had sex the same morning she left me and now I wonder if she was lying there planning how to make a fool of me. She must have known that she was leaving. It's not something you do on impulse, you know?" he looked absolutely horrible. His eyes were glassy, his cheeks sunken.

"Did you ever tell her that you loved her?" I asked and swallowed a large gulp of beer as if somehow that could numb the self-blame I felt for my last night with Christina. Maybe if I had told her how much I cared and made love to her instead of the awkward séance that took place between us, she would have changed her mind about leaving. Maybe if I hadn't been too proud to beg her to stay...

"No," Magni finally said. "Those words don't come easy, do they? And Laura sure as hell never told me either." His nostrils flared from his deep intake of air. "And now I know why."

"Why?" I asked.

He scrunched up his face. "Because she didn't love me of course."

"Do you regret fighting in the tournament for her?" It was a question I'd thought about a lot, but every time I asked myself that question the answer was "no." I would have preferred a lifetime with Christina, but the weeks I got were the best in my life and I wouldn't give them back for anything.

"Sometimes," Magni said. "When someone picks a fight and calls me names and ridicules me, then I curse her to hell for picking me as her champion." He rested his head in his hand. "But mostly, I just fucking miss her. You know?"

"Yeah, I know!"

"So?" He gave me a scrutinizing glare. "You're going after Christina, are you?"

"That's the plan."

"And if she rejects you again?"

"I don't want to think about that. Just tell me how to get into the Motherlands."

"Okay." He nodded solemnly. "But I have one condition."

"What?"

"I come with you. Maybe this time I can find Laura."

"Deal." I stretched out my arm to shake his hand. "Let's go find our wives."

Boulder

Magni took me on a journey to a small town I'd never heard of.

"When you see him, don't stare," Magni had warned me, but I still took a double glance at Papa Hunt when I saw him. The man was missing an eye, and his mouth and right cheek were severely disfigured from a large angry scar running from his jaw to his hairline. The way he had let his beard grow around it made him look even more asymmetrical because he had a perfectly normal beard on the left side while the right side had chunks of hair mixed with bald spots.

"Hello, boys," he greeted us with a deep rusty voice that sounded incredibly hoarse.

"We meet again, Papa Hunt," Magni said and shook the man's hand.

"You think you'll have better luck this time?" the old man, who had to be close to sixty, asked.

"I'll take my chances," Magni muttered and introduced me. "This is Boulder, he's a friend of mine and he's going with me."

Papa Hunt gave me a once-over. "I know who you are. You're that fellow who won the archeologist and let her go again." He shook his head. "What the hell were you thinking?"

I scowled.

"If she was mine, I'd've kept her somewhere safe and knocked her up with a few babes to make her stay. Women are softies for babies," he said as if he had the fucking manual on how to make women happy.

"We didn't come for relationship advice," Magni interjected. "Can you get us over or not?"

Papa Hunt reached his hand out. "What's in it for me?" he asked.

Magni leaned closer, "How about we don't tell my brother about your smuggling across the border. Does that sound like a good deal to you?"

Papa Hunt scrunched up his face and looked like he wanted to negotiate, but Magni's tapping his shoe impatiently made him give a shrug of resignation and move to the door. "I hope you've learned from last time and that you'll fucking take my advice this time."

"Yeah, yeah, fine, we'll do it," Magni said.

"Do what? I asked.

Papa Hunt grinned. "Last time, I told your friend that he had to use a disguise but he refused to shave and cut his hair, and what happened?" He answered his own question. "The moron got spotted, panicked, and stole the first woman he saw."

"I said, we'll do it," Magni said through gritted teeth.

"Good. My contact on the other side of the border will be there tonight and he'll take you home and change your appearance. He'll whine about it, of course, but that's how they are: fucking whiners all of them, and completely

261

under the thumb of women." Papa Hunt spit on the floor as if the idea left a foul taste in his mouth. "Don't worry, I'll pay him handsomely – and he's a greedy bastard if there ever was one. He'll help you."

There was a tunnel under the border that was normally used to smuggle whatever was easy to sell. Papa Hunt was a businessman, and did his best to protect his operation by asking us to be blindfolded when he led us to the location of the tunnel.

Magni and I, both bigger and much stronger than him, quickly convinced him to forget that idea.

"Hop in," he said and got in a small wagon. "This will take us through the tunnel in only twenty minutes."

"How long is that tunnel?" I asked, a bit worried. The idea of being underground didn't sit well with me.

"Don't worry," he reassured me, "I built it myself and I never do anything by halves. The tunnel is well supported and safe."

"How come the Momsies haven't found it?" I asked.

"Oh, they have." He gave me a lopsided grin. "The drones can detect caves and tunnels and report it straight to the nearest border patrol. Of course, I didn't know that when I built it. Long story short, I got caught red-handed about eight years ago on one of my first test runs."

"So how come you still use it?" I asked.

"Because David, the man who caught me, didn't report it. In fact, he made sure the system thinks this tunnel was destroyed and he has overruled the program to make it overlook this tunnel."

We drove slowly in the tunnel, and I figured the low speed was to avoid making any noise or vibrations above. "David is my partner now. Him and two of his friends."

"But Momsies aren't interested in money," I said in surprise.

"True, but it's human nature to want the forbidden, and we're their only source to beer and whiskey, which they love as much as the next man. Besides, the men are fascinated by us *real* men and love to hear tales of our lives on the other side of the border."

"They don't consider themselves real men?" I asked, skeptical.

He scoffed. "Sure they do. David and his pals think they're real badass rebels for running a smuggling business right under the nose of the Momsies." He pointed ahead. "Now duck your heads."

Magni was slower than me and I had to pull him down when we entered into a lower part of the tunnel. He had sobered up on our flight here but I wished he hadn't been drinking before our journey into this uncharted territory.

"Pay attention," I whispered in his ear.

"I am," he muttered back.

Papa Hunt's contact, David, met us at the other end of the tunnel, which ended on a hillside with trees and plants covering the exit. He gaped at Magni and me. I'm not sure if it was our size or the determined expressions on our faces that made him step back.

"Who... who are they?" he stammered.

"These are two of our finest warriors," Papa Hunt said. "They have both won great glory and the ultimate prizes." He grinned. "But then they went and fucked it all up and now they need your help."

"M... my help?"

"Yes, they're going to retrieve their wives but they can't very well travel through your lands looking like that, can they?"

"No." David held his hand to his heart as if to steady the pace of it. It wasn't that he was tiny per se. He wasn't. The man was at least five-foot ten, and somewhere in his early to mid-forties, but he just looked so different from us. I leaned in to study him closer. "What's wrong with your eyebrows?" I asked.

His hands flew to his brows. "What do you mean?"

Papa Hunt nudged us forward. "We don't have time for that now. David, I'll get you your deliveries tomorrow; these two big boys took up the space in the wagon."

"But I... I..." David looked completely overwhelmed.

"It's okay. I know it's a change of plans, but consider this a personal favor to me and don't worry about paying me for tomorrow's delivery, it's your payment for guiding these two fuckers."

"Guide them where?" he asked horrified.

"To their wives, of course."

"O... okay, but where are they?" David asked.

"They can tell you." Papa Hunt got into his wagon again and pointed at us. "I can't wait to meet the women who would inspire two such magnificent warriors to do something this stupid." With a shake of his head he drove back the same way we'd come.

"All right, David." Magni leaned into the man. "The first thing we need is a way to blend in. You think you can help us with that?"

"I... I can try," he got out, clearly intimidated.

"Good, lead the way." Magni patted the man's shoulder and David's knees almost buckled under the force.

It was dark but David knew his way around the hillside and guided us to a drone that he had waiting.

Carrying a bag with him, he didn't say much.

"What's in the bag?" Magni asked.

"My payment to Papa Hunt."

"What do you pay him with?"

"Different things that you don't have in the Northlands."

"Oh, yeah, like what?"

"Like beauty products."

Both Magni and I swung around. "Did you say beauty products?"

David nodded his head, looking like a fucking turtle with the way he crammed his shoulders up in fear.

"Who the hell wants beauty products?" I asked.

"I don't know, but Hunt says there's a market for it."

"What kind of products?"

"Hair removers are popular."

"What the hell for?" Magni shot me a confused glance.

"Well, the one I'm bringing tonight is especially designed to permanently remove hair in your lower regions without pain."

We were both staring at him as if he spoke a different language.

"It's practical and more hygienic," he stated.

"What, to look like an adolescent boy?" I grumped.

"The removal of your pubic hair makes your shaft look bigger," David stated and got in the drone.

"Yeah, that's a Momsiboy problem," I grinned "We don't need our cocks to look bigger, they already scare the women."

Magni shot me a sardonic grin.

"But surely you can see the advantage to at least removing the hair from your other part," David said dryly.

"What part?" I asked.

"Do you mean our butt crack?" Magni asked bluntly.

We grew quiet as he nodded and talked about the advantages and then Magni grabbed the bag from the floor and started rummaging through it. "Is it this one?" He held up a package and David nodded.

"Here." Magni shoved one into my arms and grabbed one for himself. "Put them on Papa Hunt's tab."

David just nodded and took us to his small home, which was very modern in style.

"I don't know if you'll fit my clothes," he said and looked us over, "but we'll have to do something." He pointed to Magni's leather vest. "That has to go, and the belts for both of you. Leather is illegal here." We stripped down and got into some of David's clothes; luckily he had some jackets that hid our bulky muscles pretty well.

265

"Now we've got to do something about your hair and beards," he said and walked around us for a while until he made a decision. "I'm going to have to take a chance here."

"What?" I asked.

"If I cut your hair, it's going to look awful, and no man with any sort of pride would walk around that way. Maybe I could braid it, but I really think your best shot would be to call in someone who knows what they're doing."

"And who would that be?" Magni's eyes narrowed.

"My friend, Jonah. He's a barber."

"Can you trust him?"

David only hesitated for a second before he gave a firm "Yes."

"How can you be sure?"

"Because he's one of my distributors and he's kept secrets for years."

"Okay," I said. "How fast can he get here?"

CHAPTER 31
Momsi Fashion

Boulder

Jonah, the barber, came half an hour later.

Never had I seen someone look so ridiculous. The man was about my age and had a hairdo and a beard that had me seriously doubting his sanity. It was cut to look like what can best be described as an open-mouthed shark, ready to attack.

The sharp point of hair on his forehead was mirrored by his beard cut into the same pointy "teeth" look.

"Oh wow, you truly weren't exaggerating," Jonah breathed to David and looked us over with curiosity.

"No, these are real Nmen," David said. "The question is, how do we make them blend in?"

"Leave that to me, I've always loved a challenge," Jonah said excitedly and pointed to me. "You," he commanded, "we'll start with you."

I exchanged a glance with Magni, silently telling him that I didn't appreciate being bossed around by a Momsiboy and that I didn't feel comfortable with Jonah's style.

"Make it as simple as possible," Magni said. "Aren't there any normal-looking men here?"

"Normal-looking men?" David asked. "I'm pretty ordinary, I think."

"You look like a boy with that flawless skin, and how come you don't even have a stubble? Did you just shave?"

"No." David shook his head. "I had my beard removed permanently."

"You did *what*?" He might as well have told me he had his dick removed by surgery. What kind of man would do something that absurd?

"It's standard here; actually, Jonah's having a beard is uncommon," David explained.

"Well, I don't want eyebrows like that." I pointed to David's fine lines that curved unnaturally and returned my gaze to Jonah. "And I don't want my hair to look like sharp teeth like yours. Just make it simple."

"Oh my, aren't you a big dictator," Jonah purred, and his feminine way of flicking his eyes at me made me take a step back.

"Come on, darling, take a seat." He pulled out a chair and I hesitantly moved to it.

Bending forward and letting his hands run along my jaw, Jonah said, "I would looove to go crazy on you but since you won't appreciate my art, I guess we're doing it the boring way."

"Yes, as boring as possible," I agreed.

"We'll need make-up," he muttered and frowned. "You both have scars and that's rare to see here. We take really good care of our skin, and we have excellent surgeons should we be unfortunate enough to get a scar."

With a hand under my chin he moved my head from side to side. "You have nice bone structure; we could do an elegant cut that would enhance that – hmm, maybe go with a vintage look."

"What's a vintage look?"

"Undercut in the neck and over the ears and longer on top," he explained. "It's a classical hairdo that was popular back in the day and one you can still get away with, although most would never dream of doing something *that* boring." He gave another long speculative glance at me. "Or I could braid your hair in the butterfly style. That would look pretty."

268

"Cut it," I said. To me this was about more than blending in. I wanted Christina to find me attractive, and maybe cutting my hair would have the same effect on her as the time I shaved for her.

My hands clenched the armrests of the chair tightly when Jonah went to work. I didn't have a mirror but felt my long hair fall to the floor indiscriminately.

I can grow my hair back, I kept telling myself, and truth be told there were men in the Northlands who preferred their hair short. It was rare, but not as uncommon as it had been when I was a child.

A childhood memory played in flashback – when the master at the school I grew up in had once shaved off all my hair because of problems with lice among the children. If I had been the only one it would have been humiliating, but he did it to all thirty of us and that left all the students in the same boat. I vaguely remembered the feeling of running my hand over the short hair back then and liking it.

"*Voilà*," Jonah exclaimed after a while. "Boring, but still much better than the messy nest you had on your head before."

I stood up and brushed hair off my shoulders before I moved to the bathroom and looked myself in the mirror. The front of my hair fell down in an edgy way but the sides and my neck were completely short.

"Do you like it?" Jonah asked behind me, meeting my eyes in the mirror.

"It reminds me of something from an old movie I once saw," I commented.

"Yeah, like I said, it's vintage." He tilted his head. "With your full beard you kind of look like an old-school hipster, but it won't work here. The beard has to go, or I could cut it in an elegant pattern if you'd like. How about waves, or little hearts?"

I looked at his hideous beard again and made a quick decision. "I'll shave it off.

"Good. But turn around first."

I did and Jonah, who was almost a head shorter than me, lifted his hands.

"Bend your knees, giant, I need to do your eyebrows and I can't reach."

"Don't mess with my eyebrows," I said again.

"Come on, big boy, trust me, will you?" Hoping that he would do something boring and old-fashioned like he had with my hair I bent down so he could reach.

It took him only a minute and then he signaled that he was done. "I just made them less bushy."

He hadn't made them into fine lines like David's, and I almost sighed with relief when I saw that they looked fine.

"Good. So, project number one, you'll shave while I go and take a look at project number two."

"My name is Boulder," I told him. "And my friend is called Magni."

"Nice to meet you, Boulder," he said. "I'm Jonah, as in Jonah and the whale," he pointed to his hair. "You get the reference from my design."

"No," I said honestly. "I don't."

He opened his mouth and bared his teeth dramatically. "You know, like a big white whale."

"Ahh, you mean a white *shark*?"

"No, a whale," he insisted.

I crossed my arms. "You do know that whales didn't have teeth, right?"

"Of course they did. How else would it eat Jonah?"

I shook my head. "Jonah wasn't eaten, he was swallowed."

"Says who?"

"The Bible," I answered calmly. "Don't you learn anything in school here?"

"Oh, I've heard of the Bible." He nodded. "My class focused on Greek mythology but I had a friend who learned about Christian mythology, and he was the one who told me about Jonah and the whale. They were terrifying creatures that could eat a man whole."

"They didn't *eat* people."

He waved a hand dismissively. "You would understand if you saw a picture."

"I've seen pictures and I'm telling you that whales didn't eat people; you're thinking of sharks.

"How would you know?" Jonah said, slightly offended. "Have you ever seen either of them in real life?"

"That's a stupid question since they're extinct," I pointed out dryly.

"They were *almost* extinct, but I've heard there are still some left and not to brag or anything, but we've brought back lots of extinct animals so I bet the oceans will be full of them again soon."

I gave up arguing with the small man and went to watch him give Magni a makeover.

"Braids or haircut?" Jonah asked.

"Braids," Magni said after looking at me. "I'm not fucking cutting my hair like that."

"Wonderful, I'll make you really pretty." Jonah eagerly started combing Magni's hair. "By Mother Nature, have you ever heard of hair products?" he complained. "Your hair desperately needs a deep impact treatment."

Magni had his eyes closed and I was sure he was trying to refrain from saying something vile.

"And your beard?" Jonah asked when he was done. I had to look away to swallow my laugh. Jonah had braided blue ribbons into Magni's mane and created what he called a butterfly braid.

"What do you think?" he proudly asked me.

"It's… lovely," I said, my lips twitching from my suppressed grin. Magni got up with a scowl and moved to the bathroom, where I heard a deep groan.

When he was clean-shaven and we had both suffered through Jonah's fashion tips and been schooled on what colors worked with our complexion and shit, I looked at Magni, who was wearing a blue scarf that complimented the blue ribbons in his hair.

"I love it," Jonah said and clapped his hands with excitement. "The turquoise color truly makes your blue eye pop out, and you…" He turned to me holding up two different scarves against my face, biting his inner cheek over what looked like the toughest question of his existence. "I think we're going to go with golden. Yes, those piercing gray eyes of yours can use the warm contrast."

I had to stand still while Jonah arranged the scarf in a fashionable way and when he finally announced he was done, Magni pulled me close with his eyes narrowed.

"I swear, if you ever tell anyone about me dressing this way, I'll use that hair remover I took from David tonight and make sure you live the rest of your life without eyebrows."

"Right back at you," I groaned. "And just so you know, I don't think I would stop with the eyebrows."

"So we never speak of this," Magni stated firmly.

"No." I didn't point out that if we were successful our wives would see us in this pitiful state.

"So, where is it that you need to go exactly?" David asked us.

"My wife is a professor at a university called New Berkeley; do you know it?"

He nodded, "Yes, it's down in Old San Francisco, but that's hours away"

"So?" I challenged him. "You have a drone."

272

"It's not *my* drone. It's a public drone and a trip like that would cost me all my energy points." He sighed and looked at Magni. "And *your* wife?"

"I don't know where she is."

Confusion spread on David's face. "You want me to guide you to your wife but you don't know where she is."

Looking tormented, Magni tensed his jaw. "That's right, I don't know where she is. Her name is Laura and she's a Northwoman."

"Wow..." Jonah whistled. "Talk about impossible odds."

"We'll go to find Christina, and look for Laura on the way," Magni ordered.

"All right." David looked at Jonah. "Thank you for your help. May peace surround you my friend."

"No, no," Jonah chuckled. "I'm coming with you; this is too exciting to miss out on."

David lit up. "You sure?"

"Yeah, we can use some of my energy points too. I've never been on a guys' trip before – this is like a real adventure, right, boys?" Jonah was smiling from ear to ear.

"We're men, *not boys*." I said firmly and didn't miss the irony of my first meeting with Christina when she'd felt offended because I called her a girl.

"Let's go," Magni ordered and led the way to the drone.

CHAPTER 32
Victor

Christina

"Hey, honey, I have a surprise for you." Kya's voice sounded from the other side of my bedroom door.

"What?" I asked tiredly and lifted my head from my pillow.

She opened the door softly and popped her head in. "Can I come in?"

"Sure," I pushed myself up, not bothering to cover my naked breasts since we'd been roommates for years and seen each other naked plenty of times.

"I know you miss you-know-who and that you're depressed that you'll never see him again."

Her words alone made tears rise in my eyes.

I'd asked Kya not to mention Boulder's name because hearing it was like a knife stabbing into my heart every time.

"Oh, honey." Kya empathetically took my hand. "It's horrible to see you this way."

"Don't call anyone," I reminded her and dried a fat tear from my cheek.

"I already promised I wouldn't, but maybe you should get some help. Don't you want to be happy?" Her eyes were moist too.

I didn't answer that.

"Anyway, I wanted to do something really nice for you so I brought someone here to comfort you." A nervous smile erupted on her face and then she looked to the door. "Victor, you can come in now."

My eyes expanded when a beautiful man appeared in my doorway, smiling at me and opening his perfect lips. "Are you Christina Sanders?"

My hands snatched the cover up to cover me, suddenly very aware of my nakedness.

"Yes, I'm Christina Sanders," I said and blinked in confusion. "And who are you?"

"My name is Victor." Without an invitation, he walked into my room and sat down on my bed. "I'm here to make you feel good."

My eyes darted to Kya. "What is he talking about?"

"Sweetie," she said. "You haven't had sex since you came back and Victor just wants to please you. It's unhealthy to deny yourself sexual gratification. You could really use the oxytocin and endorphins that a good orgasm will release in your body. Don't forget, sex is a stress reliever and you're definitely stressed out," she said matter-of-factly.

"I can't be with him," I whispered frantically. My forehead wrinkled in deep frown lines. "I'm not ready to be with *anyone*."

Victor reached out and caressed my legs through the cover. "Don't worry, we'll take it slow. We've got all night."

Kya stood up. "You may not like this, but I'm your best friend and I can't just do nothing when you're hiding in your bed feeling depressed. Either we get you some help or you enjoy a night with Victor to feel better. He won't hurt you and you can just pretend that he's Boul... I mean you know who. Victor will be okay with that."

"Yes," Victor said with a flirtatious smile. "You can call me any name you'd like. All I want to do is please you."

I closed my eyes and when Kya left the room, I exhaled in a deep sigh of resignation and took a minute to study Victor. He looked harmless and pretty with his fine features and flawless skin. He was nothing like Boulder and had never been in a fight or fought for a woman's hand in marriage, that was for sure.

"I heard you're having a hard time," he said softly. "I really just want to help and I'm a good listener."

"Thanks."

"Why don't we lie on your bed and I'll hold you while you tell me what troubles you. I promise you'll feel better, and as Kya said: if you want to pretend I'm someone else, I'm okay with that."

It would never be the same as lying with Boulder, of course, but then again. I would never get to lie with Boulder again.

"Okay," I said and moved to the side, signaling for him to join me under the cover.

Victor smiled and stripped out of his clothes before he crawled onto the bed. A few months ago I would have thought he was male perfection but now he looked boyish with his hairlessness and lack of toned muscles.

I turned my back on him, unwilling to see him or smell him. I would just imagine he was Boulder.

"Do you like to spoon?" he asked softly and positioned himself up against my back and behind.

"Is this spooning?" I asked.

"Yes." He kissed my nape.

"Yeah, I like spooning, but can you be quiet, please?"

"Of course. Just let me know when you're ready to receive sexual pleasure and I'll be happy to provide it."

"Place your hand on my breast," I said quietly, because whenever Boulder and I had "spooned" his free hand had always found my breast.

Without hesitation, Victor complied and I sighed contentedly, holding on to the memories of a large, virile Nman behind me, insisting that I was his wife.

A smile spread on my face as I reflected on how repulsed I'd been by the title "wife." I had associated it with someone oppressed, obedient, abused – and yet

276

being married to Boulder had been nothing like that. If anything, I had felt supported, protected, and loved. I tasted the word "loved." Had he loved me? I would never know for sure, since no such words had been exchanged between us. Yet the memories of his tireless lust for my body and his need to be close to me even in his sleep had made me feel wanted, desired, even revered.

Another tear from my seemingly endless internal well ran down my nose and dripped onto the mattress. I clung to happy memories of falling asleep in Boulder's arm, sated from our love-making and feeling cocooned in his safe arms.

Boulder

The trip to New Berkeley took forever. The drone was incapable of flying fast like ours. Clearly they didn't live their lives on the edge much.

When the sun rose in the early morning hours I took in the Motherlands with fascination and was surprised at how different it was from what I'd imagined. Whenever I thought of this place, I pictured it like an ant farm with people living in impersonal cubicles and dressing like clones.

I was wrong.

Everything was clean and inviting, with every building covered in flowers or greens. They had bike lanes all over and David explained that not only did the bikes produce energy but the lanes themselves were designed to suck up energy from the sun. We didn't have anything like that. We went from place to place in drones or hybrids that would fly over water, gravel, fields, or mountains if needed. Outside the towns, there was no need for roads in the Northlands.

People here had a lot of pets, it seemed. I saw a lady walking five cats, a man jogging with both a dog and a mini horse, and I saw a child with a rabbit under his arm.

"Stop the drone," I barked when we passed a group of mothers with babies on their arms. I'd never seen a real baby. Boys came to us when they were three years old, and I'd never been lucky enough to see one of the few babies that were born in the Northlands.

"What's wrong?" David asked.

"I want to see the babies," I said with my nose almost pressed against the window.

Magni leaned forward by my side. "Hard to believe that we all start out that small and fragile," he said, but he quickly resumed scanning the streets for Laura.

"Remember," he said to Jonah and David. "Laura is about five foot nine, large blue eyes, long red hair, and cute freckles across her nose."

"You've told us a billion times," David muttered.

"I need to eat soon," Jonah exclaimed. "I get really cranky when I don't eat."

"Girl," Magni muttered low.

"Say sorry," Jonah insisted.

"For what?" Magni didn't even turn his head to look at Jonah. His eyes were scanning the streets.

"You made an attempt to insult me."

"So?"

"Apologize."

Magni rolled his eyes. "I'm sorry you're such a whining pussy who needs food not to be grumpy."

Two loud gasps came from David and Jonah.

"Look," I interfered before Magni got us in real trouble. "It's just how we talk. Don't be offended, we're just more crude than you are."

"And tougher," Magni muttered low.

I slammed his shoulder hard. "Shut the fuck up. They are helping us, so cut the crap and leave them alone, you miserable fuck."

David's and Jonah's jaws were hanging open and when they finally spoke their voices were shaken. "I've never heard anyone talk that way," Jonah said and whistled. "My friends won't believe me when I tell them about this road trip."

"You can't tell them," David reminded him. "It's forbidden to speak about Nmen."

Jonah lowered his brows and gave David a sideways glance before he looked to me and Magni. "Talk about forbidden, I know a crude joke," he said conspiratorially.

"Oh, yeah? Then let's hear it," I encouraged him and saw his lips twist in a wicked closed-mouth smile. "Why is a man the smartest when he is having sex?"

"Why?"

"Because he's plugged into a woman." With an expectant smile he waited for our reactions.

"What the fuck?" Magni breathed and shook his head at me. "Do they even understand how fucking disturbing it is to hear shit like that from someone with a dick?"

I leaned forward. "You need to work on your repertoire," I told Jonah. "Next time you tell a crude joke, tell this one," I said. "How do you know when a woman is about to say something smart?"

"How?" Jonah asked.

I smiled. "When she starts her sentence with, 'A man once told me...'"

They laughed. "Do you know anymore jokes?"

"Sure, why did the woman cross the road?"

"Why?" David asked.

"Who cares? What the hell was she doing out of the kitchen in the first place?"

Jonah and David frowned in confusion.

"Ahh, forget it," Magni grunted and waved a hand dismissively in the air. "They have no sense of humor."

"We have a sense of humor," Jonah insisted, "but what's funny about a woman in the kitchen?"

"It's a sexist joke suggesting that a woman's place is in the kitchen to serve her man."

"Ahh," they said but still looked puzzled.

"Look, I'm hungry too, so let's take a break and find something to eat," I suggested.

"I could eat a big juicy burger," Magni sighed wistfully.

"Do you want one too?" Jonah asked me.

"We can have burgers? But I thought meat wasn't allowed." I grinned in surprise.

"Of course it is." Jonah gave me a what-do-you-take-me-for look and walked off to a group of shops nearby. The rest of us stayed by the drone.

I was drooling when he returned with four small containers of food, and I couldn't believe my eyes when I unwrapped my burger and saw it had actual meat inside. I took a big bite and chewed with a sound of appreciation."

Next to me, Magni nodded his head, chewing and speaking with food in his mouth. "This is good beef."

I opened my burger, taking off the bun and poking at the patty to make sure it was real. It was cooked just right and had that pink center that I preferred.

"I thought you were all fucking vegans," I said and took another big bite. "Like against eating animals and all that nonsense. I can't tell you how happy I am that you're not feeding us some stupid kale-shit but an actual burger."

"This is cultured meat," David explained. "You know, produced as part of cellular agriculture."

Magni stopped chewing and his "What?" was muffled because of his full mouth.

"We don't actually kill the animals to eat their meet. My friend is a farmer, and all they do is take some tissue from cows, from their muscles to be exact, and then they extract the stem cells and grow muscle under tension to bulk it up. That's the meat that is then minced and turned into burgers." He smiled. "It's good, right?"

Magni and I looked at each other for a long second and then he shrugged and kept chewing. "Yeah, it's good if you don't think too much about it being grown in a fucking lab."

I finished my burger and we continued for another forty minutes, Magni and I constantly scouting the streets for Laura while David and Jonah chatted like women.

I rolled my eyes when they talked about a male beauty competition they had both seen last night, and I tried holding my tongue when they analyzed my joke about women in the kitchen.

"Don't they know how relaxing and rewarding cooking can be? Why would the Nmen *not* want to be in the kitchen?" David said softly to Jonah.

"I don't know." Jonah shook his head, signaling that the whole thing was a puzzling matter to him as well.

"You're missing the fucking point," I said. "The joke is only funny because it infuriates women – and just to set things straight," I said and leaned toward them, "women can be as violent as men."

Jonah's eyes grew big and round.

"What?" I asked him.

"If your women are so violent, Boulder, then why would you let them near the kitchen?"

I shook my head. "What? No, our women aren't..."

"Yes, I agree with Jonah." David cut me off in support of his friend and continued with a troubled expression. "Clearly it's not the brightest idea to let a violent person into a kitchen when that's where all the sharp knives are kept?"

"Magni, is your wife violent as well?" Jonah asked and Magni, who hadn't been paying attention to our

281

conversation, looked at him with a big question mark virtually visible above his head.

I thought it safer to change the subject to something I'd been wondering about.

"Look, can I ask you two the obvious question?" I said.

"Of course."

"So, how many women have you been with? I mean with one man per fourteen women, surely some of them are still interested in you guys."

They exchanged a glance before Jonah turned his chair around to face me. "I'm not attracted to women."

"You're gay?"

"Uh-huh."

"But I like women," David said quickly and added softly, "and men."

"Wait a minute," Magni barked out. "Are you two fuckers telling us that you have access to unlimited numbers of women but that you prefer men?" He scowled at them. "I fucking knew it."

"I'm not gay," David argued. "I'm attracted to a person and not their gender."

"So how many women have you had?" I asked David but got distracted by Jonah's laughter.

"I don't think you understand how our women work. Sex isn't high on their list."

"I've had a few," David said and puffed out his chest. "Women have a thing for me."

"Why?" I asked, genuinely curious, because in my mind a woman would have to be a lesbian to be attracted to someone as feminine as him.

He smiled smugly. "Because I've got a smooth move that works every time."

"And what is that?" I asked intrigued.

"My magical hands." He lifted his palms as evidence. "I offer them a massage and once they're relaxed, I pleasure them with my hands, and then when they're ready for more, I give it to them."

Magni leaned closer. "Is that all it takes?"

"Uh-huh."

"We fucking have to kill to get our hands on a woman and you just rub their neck."

"Well, some aren't interested," David said. "But as you pointed out: with fourteen women per man there's always someone open to a massage.

When we finally reached the university that Christina had said she worked at, my heart was pounding like crazy.

"Now what?" I asked and looked up at the building.

Jonah opened the door. "Now David and I go talk to people while you two stay here."

Magni and I sat for at least an hour, watching the two flutter around like butterflies talking and smiling with a bunch of different people until at last they came back.

"Christina doesn't teach here anymore," Jonah said. "But one of the woman told me she's famous for riding an antique bike with flowers in front."

"Is that all you've got?" I asked.

"No, someone else said he'd seen her at the senior center a few days ago."

My heart instantly leaped. "Really?"

"Yes, so maybe they know where she lives."

At the senior center a receptionist confirmed that Christina taught in the evenings sometimes, but she didn't know when she would come next and she wasn't allowed to give out her contact information.

She did, however, allow us to meet a few of Christina's students and ask them questions.

David and Jonah told us to stay back in the drone, but I refused, not trusting that they would ask the right questions.

"Stay quiet," Jonah warned me as we walked down the corridor. "They'll hear your accent."

"Marie and Martha," the receptionist said when we reached an open area where two old ladies sat. "These gentlemen are looking for Christina Sanders; do you know when she'll be back to teach her next lesson?"

One of the old ladies lit up in a bright smile and signaled for us to come closer. David stayed by the wall, while Jonah and I walked closer.

"Are you friends of Christina?" the little woman asked.

"Yes," I said quickly before I remembered to shut up.

"That's good." She nodded. "She was just here a few days ago and she'll be back next week at the usual time."

I cursed inwardly. I couldn't wait until next week.

Jonah took a seat opposite the women. "Do you have any idea where we can find Christina?"

"Is she in trouble?" one of the older women asked.

"No, Christina isn't in trouble." Jonah explained. "But her friend is trying to find her. They share a special bond."

"Oh, that's nice." The smaller of the women turned to the other. "Martha, didn't Christina live with that teacher friend?"

Martha leaned her head back, thinking. "That's right. I remember her. She had funny hair and she sniffed her food."

"Right. I had forgotten about that, but where did they live?"

Martha was quietly shaking her head as if to say she didn't know.

"I'm sorry." Marie held her hands to her head. "My memory isn't as good as it used to be."

We prodded them for a few more minutes, asking them about the bike, which was our only clue.

"We never see her outside, only in here, and no one bikes indoors," Marie explained patiently.

My shoulders fell when I realized we had hit a dead end.

"May peace surround you," Jonah said in goodbye to the women before we all left.

My steps were heavy walking back to the drone. Christina was somewhere in this city and I needed to find her *now*.

"We'll just have to circle the area and look for the bike," David said but was interrupted by a female voice from behind.

I turned to see Marie standing all winded right outside the entrance to the senior center, waving her hand to get our attention.

Quickly I ran back to her. "Did you remember something?"

She nodded and waved me closer with a crooked finger.

I leaned in.

"Closer," she said with a twinkle in her eye and when I complied, she said, "I apologize for being such a forgetful old woman, but there was a time when we made a beautiful quilted blanket for Christina's birthday."

"And?"

"And we wanted her to have it on the day so we had it brought to her."

I held my breath. "Please tell me you have her address?"

"I do." She smiled. "And I'll give it to you, if you do two things for me.

"Anything," I said quickly and smiled.

Three minutes later, I was back in the drone facing Magni, who gaped at me.

"What the fuck was that?" he asked with his hand in the air.

"I don't want to talk about it."

"Oh, we're gonna talk about it."

"No!" My lips were tight. "I have Christina's address and that's all you need to know."

He shook his head with disbelief but let it rest for now. "It's Magnolia Circle, building seven."

"Got it," David nodded and looked down at the navigation system. "That's three minutes from here."

My body reacted physically to the fact that I was close to her. Butterflies fluttered between my ribs and I could feel my heart racing like a drum. "Be home, Christina," I muttered, "please be home."

Nobody spoke. Not even when we arrived at the long row of small townhouses. Magni, Jonah, and David just got out and looked at me.

My eyes fell on the yellow bike parked outside with a basket in front that had silk flowers. "This is the right place," I mumbled with terror in my chest. What if she rejected me? Or reported me?

Taking a deep breath, I stepped up to the door and knocked on it.

Thump, thump, thump. The sound of my heart was in my ears when the door opened and I looked into the eyes of a beautiful brown woman with clear cognac-colored eyes and the most voluminous curly hair I'd ever seen.

"May peace surround you," she said politely and looked past me to the three men still standing by the drone.

"My name is Alexander," I said softly as not to scare her. "I'm here to see Christina."

Understanding spread on her face. "Boulder?" she asked and when I gave a sharp nod, she lowered her voice and looked up and down the street. "Are you crazy?"

She ushered me in while pointing to Magni. "You too – hurry, get in here before someone sees you."

He jogged up the five steps to the door and came in with me.

The brown woman closed the door behind us and leaned against it with her arms spread out as if to shield us from whatever threats were on the outside.

"You came all this way?" she said, staring at us.

"Yes."

"How did you find us?"

"Is Christina here?"

Her eyes flew to a door right behind me and back to my face. "She went to bed early. Give me a minute to wake her up."

I didn't have a minute and barged in through the door she had looked at. The vision I saw made me lose my shit completely.

CHAPTER 33
Murder

Christina

I woke up to the sound of commotion outside my bedroom door and stretched my arms.

"Did you enjoy your nap?" Victor asked and snaked his arm around me to pull me close. I was just about to tell him to stop when the door was flung open and Boulder came through, his eyes taking in me and Victor closely entangled in the bed.

"Boulder," I shrieked in surprise. My instant happiness was quickly replaced by panic when he zoomed in on Victor with pure murder in his eyes.

"Get the fuck away from my wife," he sneered and took a step closer.

Victor removed his hands from me and scrambled out of bed, revealing that he was stark naked and sporting an erection.

I quickly got out of bed too and threw myself between Boulder and Victor, pressing my naked chest against Boulder.

"Don't touch him," I begged again and again.

Boulder looked down and saw my naked chest, hurt flickered in his eyes, and a hoarse sound of pain came from his throat.

"Easy," Magni said behind Boulder and placed a strong hand on his upper arm. "We didn't come to fight."

"Fight?" Boulder barked. "I'll fucking *kill* the bastard for touching my wife."

"Boulder, relax," I pleaded. "Calm down." My hands went to his face and I pulled at him to make him look at me. "It's nothing. *Nothing!*"

Kya pushed into my small, now overcrowded bedroom with questions of her own. "What does he mean by *wife*?"

Boulder didn't even register her; he was solely focused on me and Victor, who stood passively in the corner.

"Who is he?" Boulder growled.

"My name is Victor, and if you do not cease acting hostile, I will report you instantly."

"You can try, you motherfucker," Boulder sneered and pushed forward to get to Victor.

"Out, out," I shouted and pushed Boulder back with the help of Magni.

"If we were home I'd let you kill him, but we're not so you need to calm the fuck down," Magni hissed at Boulder and got around him to block the entrance to my room.

I stood in nothing but my panties in the small entryway with a massive Boulder, fuming with anger.

"Don't talk, just take a minute to calm down," I said in a placatory voice and held out my hands in a sign of peace.

"I'm sorry, but the overnight deal does not apply to more than one person," Victor said loud and clear, and I stretched to see Kya in my room, signaling for her to shut him up. "I cannot partake in sexual orgies," Victor added matter-of-factly.

Magni swung his head around to stare at Victor. "What did you say?"

"I'm merely saying that I'm fully capable of taking male penetration, but you'll have to make a reservation. Would you like me to add you to the waiting list?"

"I don't fucking think so," Magni sneered.

"Would you like to think about it?"

289

"No." Kya stepped in front of Victor with a worried expression on her face. "Victor, have you alerted the authorities?"

"Strong language is to be expected during intercourse – especially when a person enjoys an orgasm. Were you enjoying an orgasm?" His question was directed at Magni, who walked closer to them.

"Geez," Magni muttered low and called out to Boulder over his shoulder. "Fucking hell, he's nothing but a sex-bot."

Kya acted quickly. "Yes, he's enjoying orgasms, a lot of them. You can relax, Victor."

"I'm confused. I'm here to satisfy Christina Sanders tonight. How come you experienced an orgasm too?"

Kya held up a hand, signaling to Magni to be quiet. "It's not you, Victor. This man was with me and we were having a good time together."

"But he just arrived." Victor leaned his head to the side. "How did you manage to get him to orgasm without touching him?"

Kya moved over to snuggle up against Magni, "I'm just talented that way and as you can see, we're just mad about each other, so there's no need to report any of this." Magni stiffened when she rose to her toes, planting kisses along his jaw.

"Thank you for the explanation – I'm happy for you both. Now, if you'll excuse me, I'll find Christina Sanders and satisfy her." Victor moved past Kya and Magni and went straight to my side, completely ignoring Boulder.

"Hello, beautiful," he said with a charming smile. "Would you like me to give you a backrub or some oral pleasure?"

I frowned and ignored Boulder, whose face was lobster red.

"Ehm... sure, Victor," I cleared my throat. "Why don't you go into the living room and wait for me there?"

Victor reached for my free hand and planted a kiss on the back of it. "I would love that, gorgeous," he said seductively.

A low growl sounded from Boulder, who stood close to me, and I increased my pressure on his hand, holding him back.

"Would you close the door, please?" I called to Victor when he entered my living room.

"Yes, darling," he responded and actually winked at me.

"It might be a while. I need to shower and talk with my friends a little," I told him with a sugar-sweet smile.

"I'm ready when you are," he said and finally closed the door.

Pushing Boulder back into my bedroom, I closed the door behind me and confronted them all.

"I can't believe that you're actually here."

Magni was still standing with Kya snuggled up against him, but avoided looking at me, and when Boulder tore the blanket from the bed and covered me up, I understood why.

"Are you pregnant?" Boulder said, turning me around to face him.

"What?" I blinked in confusion. "No, how would I be pregnant?"

"Have you had your bleedings?"

Overwhelmed with his questions and the situation, I was speechless.

"No, I'm not pregnant," I said astonished that he would ask such a ludicrous question.

His shoulders fell. "Christina, I..." He trailed off and took a deep breath. "Fuck. It wasn't supposed to be like this, I didn't expect to find you with..." He waved at the bed. "You know."

"I'm sorry," I mumbled. "But I didn't think I was ever going to see you again and he..."

Boulder silenced me with his hand covering my mouth. "I don't want to know what you did with him. Just tell me that you'll come back with me."

My face softened and I pulled his hand down to smile at him. "You want me to come back with you?"

"Yes!" he said; his anger from before was fading and being replaced with hope. "Will you?"

"I tried to go back," I said.

"You did?"

"Uh-huh, but they wouldn't let me."

"So you'll come." His voice almost broke.

"Yes," I breathed and got lost in his burning eyes, "But how, Boulder?"

"Don't worry about that. Just come with me. Magni and I know how to get back."

I nodded, out of words, and Boulder pressed a relieved kiss to my lips.

Kya cleared her throat. "I'm sorry, but Victor has probably already reported you two for improper communication and violent threats."

"Shit," Magni cursed.

"I can't believe that you two are real Nmen," she said and showed no signs of being afraid of them. In fact, she looked intrigued.

"We're real Nmen alright," Magni confirmed and looked down at her, placing his hands on her shoulders and pushing her gently away from him. "Real *married* Nmen."

"Ohh." She blinked up at him. "Wait – you thought I was coming on to you?"

His perfectly arched brow confirmed that thought.

"That's ridiculous," she chuckled. "I would never."

"Good, because men of the Northlands don't sleep around." Magni's eyes pinned me with his last words and I cringed.

"I'm just floored that people still marry in the Northlands. That's so strange."

"Of course we marry." Magni lowered his brows. "Would you like to get married? We could have a tournament and you could choose your own husband."

"That..." Kya swung her eyes to me silently asking a thousand questions. "Sounds very tempting, but I'm a teacher and we don't really do that sort of thing."

What an odd thing to say. No one did that sort of thing in the Motherlands, but I didn't blame her for coming up with a polite excuse on the spot – weak or not.

Magni blew out a breath. "What a shame. You're a beautiful woman and so exotic with your looks. Men would have fought bravely to secure your hand in marriage."

"Really?" Kya glanced at me and Boulder standing closely together. "This is crazy," she whispered. "I can't believe you married him and didn't tell me."

"How do you tell something like that?" I asked her softly.

"Christina, have you seen Laura?" Magni asked sharply.

"No, I'm sorry, but I haven't seen her."

Disappointment filled his blue eyes.

"Laura, wait, I've heard of her," Kya said. "Who is she again?"

"My wife," Magni said shortly while I reminded her.

"The woman I met who decided to come here... you know, martial arts." My eyes bulged in my attempt to signal that it was a sensitive subject and now wasn't a good time.

"We need to go," Boulder said. "Get dressed and pack what you need. Our ride is waiting outside."

The men stepped outside my bedroom and Kya helped me fill a bag while I quickly pulled on my favorite sweater and pants.

"I'll miss you so much," I told Kya and hugged her fiercely.

"Will this be the last time I see you?" she asked, her voice choked up with emotions.

"I don't know," I said honestly. "But if it is, I want you to know that I love you."

"I love you too." She sniffled, those adorable expressive doe eyes full of tears.

"Be careful," she whispered when I opened the door. "And call me if you can."

"I will, sister," I said giving her the highest compliment a woman could give another.

"Sister," she whispered back, shoulders bobbing from suppressed sobbing.

Magni and Boulder had the grace not to say anything. They kept quiet as we ran down the stairs and didn't introduce me to the two men waiting by the drone parked on the street. Instead Boulder followed me to the back seat and placed me in his lap, folding his arms protectively around me and kissing me on my hair.

I could have told him the drone wouldn't take off with me in his lap. I needed to be in my own seat, safely buckled in.

One of the men turned and told Boulder that the system had detected an unsafe passenger and that I needed to be next to him instead of on top of him. Boulder told him in Northland style what he thought of that stupid rule.

CHAPTER 34
Home

Boulder

From the moment I got Christina inside the drone we were in constant physical contact. My hands on her thigh, interlacing our fingers, or playing with her long brown hair. We didn't talk much, mostly out of respect for Magni, who sat quietly starring out the window trying to spot Laura.

Our eyes searched the streets too. At least mine did. There was nothing I wanted more than for him to be reunited with Laura and take her back home with us. Hours passed and the closer we got to the border, the more somber he grew.

After a few hours of flying, Jonah turned in his seat and asked Christina. "What did you think of Boulder's new haircut?"

She smiled and looked up at me. "I think he looks really handsome." That brought out a smile on both Jonah's and my face. "But he was always handsome," she added softly and squeezed my hand. "It's just easier to see when he isn't hiding behind his beard and wild mane."

"And the clothes?" Jonah asked.

She wrinkled her nose and pulled at the golden scarf. "It's not really your style, is it?" Her fingers trailed up to my face and she shook her head in disbelief. "And you've got makeup on."

"Of course – have you seen all the scars those two have?" Jonah complained.

"It comes with being a warrior," Christina mused without taking her eyes off me. "It doesn't bother me."

Jonah was still talking but all I could see and hear was Christina. Her eyes were telling me a million things that she didn't want the others to know. My hand slid to her thighs, squeezing her tightly, letting her know that I was never letting her go again.

It felt like we were having a real conversation in our own little bubble, making promises of what was to come.

"Is that Laura?" David exclaimed when a red-haired woman came into view.

"Where?" Magni eagerly leaned forward. "No," he said, his voice dripping with disappointment. "That's not her."

"And you have no idea where she lives?"

He shook his head. "None."

We didn't find Laura, and it was heartbreaking to see Magni retract back into his shell of anger. While we had been on the hunt he had been full of purpose and determination. Now that he had failed for the second time, he fell into a bitter silence and would hardly look at me and Christina.

Papa Hunt met us that same night and took us back through the tunnel, keeping his promise of paying David with a precious amount of smuggler goods.

He didn't give Magni shit about failing again but left my brokenhearted friend alone. I was relieved because I'd already decided that I wouldn't let him taunt Magni.

I kept Christina on my lap in the wagon – there were no safety regulations. Papa Hunt talked to her all the way back, entertaining her with gruesome details from the time he was mauled by a bear and lost his right eye.

We dropped Magni off at the Gray Mansion and told him to let Pearl and Khan know Christina was back. It was long past midnight so I didn't want to stay, but flew us home to my island, fulfilling a dream of mine when I leaned in and said, "Welcome home, Christina."

She had been in my house once during her flying lessons, but never slept here.

"It's so good to have you back," I muttered into her hair, unwilling to let her hand go, even as we were walking up the stairs.

She gave a small giggle that rang sweetly in my ears. God, this house had been empty without her. My life had been empty without her.

"I still can't believe you came for me," she said and turned around when we reached the top. With wonder shining from her eyes, she placed her hands around my neck and kissed me. "It feels like a dream that I don't want to wake up from."

Sliding my hands up the backs of her thighs, I lifted her onto my hips and carried her to my bedroom, placing her on my large bed.

"Let's see if I can do better than Victor."

It was meant to be a joke, but I was still resentful of the way I'd found her.

Christina raised up on her elbows. "I didn't have sex with Victor," she said. "I just slept in his arms pretending he was you."

"Really?"

"Yes, Boulder. I didn't even want to but Kya insisted because she couldn't bear seeing me so depressed."

"You've been depressed?" I crawled onto the bed, getting on top of her, softly nuzzling my nose against hers. "Because you missed me?"

"Yes. Did you miss me?"

"What do you think?" I asked, the edges of my eyes wrinkling in a smile. "I've been losing my mind in this house, blaming myself for letting you go."

"It wasn't your choice."

"I should have..." I trailed my fingers over her dry lips, taking in every detail of her face from the perfect shape of her nose to the left eye that was slightly bigger than the right.

297

"I like your eyebrows," I said and brushed my thumb over them.

"You were saying something," she reminded me. "You said, 'I should have,' but you didn't finish your sentence."

"Ahh." I bit the inside of my cheek, unsure if it was wise to say what I'd been thinking.

"What?" She smiled expectantly at me.

"I've just blamed myself for not telling you how much I cared. I can't help thinking that if I'd told you then you wouldn't have left."

We were nose to nose with me firmly placed between her legs and leaning on my elbows to avoid crushing her. Her hands raced up my spine making me shudder with delight.

"So tell me now," she encouraged in a low, intimate voice. "Tell me how much a man would have to care about me to enter the Motherlands illegally and track me down."

"A lot," I admitted. "He would have to care a *whole* lot."

Just tell her that you love her, I pushed myself, but I was scared of frightening her or maybe more scared to bare my naked soul and not have her say it back.

Kissing replaced talking and with eager hands I undressed her. "I'm sorry about our last time together, I wasn't myself," I muttered against her neck.

"It's okay."

"No, it wasn't, but I was fucking breaking inside knowing it was my last time with you."

"Shhh." She stroked my hair. "I'm here now."

To fully understand that she was real I sniffed in the sweet fragrance of Christina that I had missed so much. "I missed your smell."

"And my kisses, did you miss my kisses?" she asked with humor in her voice.

Entangling my hands in her hair I kissed her deeply, entwining my tongue with hers and getting high on the glorious feeling of my woman pressed against me.

"I missed all of you. Your company, your touch, your softness – everything about you." I kissed her again. "More than you'll ever know."

"Can I ask you a question?"

"Of course, anything."

"Do you think if you had a free pick of every woman in the Motherlands that you would have picked me?"

I furrowed my brows trying to understand where this question was coming from.

"Or do you think you like me so much because I was the first woman you had sex with?"

"Honey…" I took a deep breath. "I've just been to a place with more women than men and I didn't see a single one that compared to you."

"You mean that?"

"Yes, I'm serious. From the first time I saw you wandering on that small road from the border, I've found you gorgeous."

"So you're happy I ended up as your wife?"

"Of course." I smiled and kissed the tip of her nose before I homed in on her last piece of clothing and slid down her panties.

As I soaked up the sight of her naked body, my hands roamed over her shape and concern filled my chest "You've lost weight."

"I've been mourning," she said softly and waited for me to look into her eyes. "I only understood how much you meant to me after I left and I thought I'd lost you forever."

The tears in her eyes made me blink back my own emotions. "You never lost me," I said, my voice shaky.

"I thought I did."

"I'll make the pain go away," I promised and pressed myself against her.

She spread her thighs to give me access.

I was still on top of her, supporting myself on my elbows so as not to crush her but close enough for our

299

chests to rub against each other when I slowly penetrated her. She leaned her head back and closed her eyes, a sweet moan escaping her.

My hands found hers, silently interlacing our fingers, our tongues, our minds, and our midsections as if we were two electronic components made to come together to recharge.

Our lovemaking started out slow and emotional. She cried and when tears welled up in my own eyes I hid my head against her neck, hating how damn fragile I felt with her. Christina had the power to destroy me, and if she had rejected me when I came to find her I would have most likely ended up a sad shadow of myself, like Magni.

But she was here, she wanted me, and instead of fucking feverishly to make up for lost time, we were more like two people who wanted to eat a cake a crumb at a time to prolong the exquisite taste of it. To me it was all about the connection between us. With my wife back, I wasn't alone anymore. From now on Christina and I would be a team.

"What are you thinking?" I asked when we lay entangled after our lovemaking.

"That this was a beautiful reunion of two lovers who had been miserable without each other," she said. "And I wonder how you found me."

"I remembered the name of the university where you used to teach, so we went there and someone had seen you at the senior center a few nights ago."

"And the senior center gave you my address?" she asked with a tone of surprise.

"No." I looked away.

"Boulder." She turned my face back to her. "How did you get my address?"

"Marie had it." I couldn't meet her eyes and looked away again.

"Yeah, I know Marie – what's wrong? Why do you look so guilty?"

I placed an arm across my face, hiding my eyes. "I did something awful."

"Please tell me, you didn't hurt Marie to get my address?"

"No!" I said quickly, giving her a disturbed look.

"What, Boulder? You're scaring me." She sat up and pushed at me. "Just tell me. What did you do?"

I sat up too. My head hanging low. "I would have never done it if I wasn't so desperate to get your address, and I feel horrible. Please know that I feel horrible."

Her face grew redder by the second and her jaws tightened. "What the hell did you do to Marie?"

My eyes widened with her use of a curse word and I cleared my throat before I admitted in a whisper, "I kissed her."

Christina's jaw dropped and a small triangle formed between her brows. "You did *what*?"

"I'm sorry. I'm truly deeply sorry and I would never betray you like that if I had known any other way."

Christina closed her eyes and then she shook her head in disbelief. "You kissed old Marie?"

I sighed with shame. "I did. But you have to believe me when I say that it meant nothing to me."

I wasn't prepared for the belly-deep laughter that suddenly filled the room. "Did Marie seriously get you to kiss her?"

Confused by her laughter, I nodded. "That wasn't all. She guessed I was a man of the Northlands and asked two things of me to give me your address."

Christina's eyebrows flew up. "Two things?"

"Yes, she asked that I pick her up in my arms and kiss her."

"And you did?"

I nodded. "Right there in front of the senior center."

Humor sparkled in Christina's eyes. "I can't believe that old fox would do that. Next time I see her, I'll have a word with her for sure."

I stiffened. "You're going back?"

"No, Boulder, not unless we can go together." She fell back on her shoulders. "But I would seriously like to have a stern talk with her for coming on to my man." She chuckled low again.

"How come you're not angry with me?" I asked. "I kissed another woman."

She pulled me down and hugged me. "Only to get to me."

I rolled her on top of me, meeting her gaze with a serious expression. "It worries me that you laugh about this. I would never laugh if you kissed another man."

"Not even if he was a harmless old guy?"

"Not even then," I said in a no-bullshit tone. "The thought of anyone kissing or touching you makes me sick."

"You take fidelity very seriously," she said and met my eyes. "So it's a good thing that the only man I've ever been attracted to is you."

"Yeah, that's a very good thing," I said and bit her softly.

We were happy – blissfully so – and just before we drifted off to sleep, I mumbled what we both knew. "We have to go and see Khan."

"And Pearl," she added with a yawn. "I hope she'll understand."

CHAPTER 35
First Steps

Boulder

Christina was extremely nervous when we entered the Gray Mansion.

"I can do the talking if you prefer," I offered.

"No, I think I need to explain this to Pearl myself."

"All right." I took her hand and squeezed it as we walked through the house and to the gardens where we'd been told by servants that Khan would be.

Because of my height, I spotted Khan and Pearl before Christina did. They were half hidden behind some hedges, and my heart skipped a beat when I realized they were too close for a normal conversation. Were they making out?

I was almost about to stop Christina from going any closer but then I heard their voices and they were fighting again.

Christina and I exchanged a glance before we rounded the hedge and faced the strangest sight.

Pearl and Khan were tied together and they were both facing away from each other.

I laughed at the comical sight and Christina couldn't help smiling either but managed to ask, "What's going on?"

Khan and Pearl spoke at the same time, each trying to talk over the other, and Christina held up her hands.

"One at a time."

Khan had his arms crossed and his legs spread as if signaling that he wasn't moving. "I'm sick and tired of her running away," he complained. "I can't protect her when she constantly wanders off, and I have important work to do."

"He wanted to chain me like a dog!" Pearl cried out. "Like a dog."

"But I didn't, did I?"

She pointed to the flexiband holding them together. Because of the height difference it was around her belly and his hips. "Oh, so you think this is any better?"

"At least now I can keep track of you and if I'm not moving, you don't move either."

Pearl clicked her tongue and crossed her arms too. "This is absolutely ridiculous. I demand that you let me go immediately."

"No."

"Well, you'll have to eventually. How else do you suggest we shower and do *other* things?"

"No," Khan said again and Pearl visibly paled before her head swung to us. "Tell him he's insane."

"Khan, you're insane," I said, chuckling. "So since you're not surprised to see us here together I guess that means Magni told you what happened?"

"Yes, we heard," Pearl said and pointed a finger at me. "And I demand to know how you crossed the border. It's a major breach of Motherlands safety and it shouldn't be possible."

"We have invisible drones that your detectors don't see," I said. "We cross as often as we please. We just never told you, but since it looks like you're not going anywhere soon," I nodded to the band, "I guess there's no reason to hide it from you."

"Invisible drones?" Pearl narrowed her eyes and turned to look at Khan. "Is that true?"

He arched a brow knowing full well I was lying, but he didn't confirm or deny.

"How long are you going to keep Pearl trapped like that?" Christina asked with a sympathetic glance at her distraught friend.

"That's no one's business but mine," Khan told her.

304

"It's my business since I'm forced to be close to you – and just so you know, you smell," Pearl said.

"Yeah?" Khan lifted an arm and sniffed his armpit. "It's not that bad, but if you'd like we could go and shower, right now." He took a step forward.

Pearl dug her heels in. "No!" she shrieked. "No, no, no."

"I don't think she wants to shower with you." I laughed.

Khan had that look on his face that I knew too well; I almost felt sorry for Pearl. He could be a real ass when he was in that mood and she was getting the full wrath of his scheming personality.

Her hands were grasping at the tight band that he had secured around them. "Let me go," she protested.

"I will, as soon as you accept that you follow me and not the other way around."

"I'm not your lap dog," she pointed out.

"I was hoping to speak to Pearl alone," Christina said.

"Yeah, well, that might be difficult, as you can see," Khan noted.

"Does that mean you'll allow Pearl to hear all your private conversations too?" Christina mused and turned her head to look at Pearl. "You're really getting to know all his secrets, aren't you?"

Khan scowled, but held his ground. "I'm glad to see you chose to return, Christina. Boulder was a pitiful excuse of a man when he moaned around, missing you."

"Just because he had emotions doesn't make him pitiful," Pearl said. "I thought it was refreshing to see an Nman express how he felt about a woman."

"Really?" Khan stared her down. "If you enjoyed that so much, I'll be more than happy to express how I feel about you. You think that would be refreshing too?"

She actually rolled her eyes at him, and it made Christina and me look at each other. Khan was corrupting Pearl and she was driving him insane. The two of them together were like two chemicals that were fine when kept apart but explosive when mixed.

"We came to talk to you about us," Christina interrupted them."

"That's right," I took over. "Christina and I are staying together. She has moved in with me by her own free will and we won't let anyone separate us," I stated firmly.

In support of my words, Christina placed both arms around my waist and I instantly placed my arm protectively around her.

"Congratulations." Pearl took a deep breath and finally her smile became more genuine and warm. "I hope you'll be very happy together."

"Thank you." Christina sighed with relief. "I was afraid you would insist on my going back."

"No, dear. I'm not blind; I see your infatuation with Boulder. It's understandable, and now that he looks handsome with his haircut and clean shave, I can definitely see his appeal."

Her whole body jerked from Khan's sudden movement when he turned to give her an angry stare.

"Don't you fucking say that in front of his mate."

"I'm not offended," Christina hurriedly said. "I agree that Boulder is very handsome with his make-over."

My whole body was tense and I understood what the women were so blatantly missing. Khan's male pride was hurt that Pearl preferred me over him. He was a vain man, and her praise of me was an insult when he'd given her so much of his time and attention. He might not like her very much but Pearl was a beautiful woman, and Khan would have to be dead not to be sexually attracted to her.

"Don't worry," I said and tried desperately to come up with something to restore his pride. "I'll soon be back to looking like a real man again. This boyish look is for Momsiboys. I just hope Christina still likes me when I grow my hair long again."

"I'll always like you," Christina said and smiled up at me, "but I might cut your hair when you sleep."

"So I figure you didn't meet Laura then?" Khan changed the subject.

"No, we didn't know where to search and unfortunately we didn't bump into her."

The worried expression on Khan's face grew deeper. "Magni is falling apart," he said. "It's hard to watch."

"Yeah, it is."

"Maybe one day Laura will choose to return," Christina said and looked at Pearl. "I tried to return, but my request was denied by the council. I hope that Laura is free to return at any time she should choose to."

Khan made a strained sound in the back of his throat and faced Pearl. "You fucking better guarantee me that no one tries to stop Laura from returning."

"Of course she's free to return," Pearl assured him. "I'm happy to send a message to my colleagues making that clear, but it shouldn't be necessary."

"No, it shouldn't be fucking necessary since Laura is one of us, but with your people's nonexistent logic, I don't trust you – so yeah, send a message just to be sure."

"Are you staying for lunch?" Pearl asked us, completely ignoring Khan's little tirade.

"Nah." I wrinkled my nose. "I think we'll go back to the estate and work on increasing the population on Victoria Island.

Christina shot me a confused glance. "Children? Are you talking about children?"

I grinned down at her. "Uh-huh. A few girls would be nice."

"You like children?" Pearl asked with a new interest in her voice.

"Yes, I do."

"And you have a large estate?"

"Very large."

"Boulder has a whole island," Christina added.

Pearl arched a brow and gave Khan a pointed stare.

He shook his head. "Now isn't the time."

"But…"

"No," he cut her off and gave me a short explanation. "Pearl and I are working on an idea and I'll involve you when I'm ready to discuss it."

"Sounds interesting," I said, curiosity aroused, but he didn't offer any more information than that.

"Come back soon," Khan told us and started walking with Pearl. When she refused to move, he simply lifted her and kept going, telling her that he liked the idea of a shower.

"They're going to kill each other soon," Christina said softly.

"Or realize that they're not so different," I mused.

"Oh, they're very different," Christina insisted. "She's kind and wise, he's ruthless and sly."

I kissed her. "And what am I?"

Shielding her eyes from the sun, Christina broke into a smile that made my entire body buzz with joy. "You, Alexander Boulder, are *mine*."

I couldn't stop grinning when I picked her up and pressed my lips against hers. "I love it when you call me yours."

"Then I'll do it more often." She burst into laughter.

"What's funny?"

"It's just saying that antique word 'husband' in my mind. I can't believe I have a husband and that I'm not miserable."

"I told you, marriage is a beautiful thing when it's two people who don't want to be without each other. The passion and the love is the best part of life."

She tilted her head, her lips still smiling. "The love?"

"Yeah, you know," I looked down.

"Are you trying to tell me something?"

"You know I'm crazy about you," I said.

"Yeah, I know. And the love part?"

I boldly met her glance. "Would it freak you out if I told you that I love you?"

Sunshine spread on her face as she lit up. "No."

"Well, in that case, Christina Sanders, I love you."

She swung her arms around my neck. "I love you too, Alexander Boulder."

Grinning, we kissed and I spun her around in the air before I sat her down. "Do you love me enough to take my last name?" I asked.

Her eyes expanded.

"I want us to be a family and share our name," I said.

"Then you can be Alexander Sanders."

"Not a chance."

"Why not?"

"Because Boulder is more than my last name, it's what people call me."

"Well I'm not Christina Boulder, I'm Christina Sanders."

"Will you at least think about it?" I asked her with a pleading look.

"Yes," she gave in. "I'll think about it."

"Good, that's a start – and you know I always get my way."

"That's not true." She playfully hit my chest.

"See, I've completely corrupted you. You used to be a pacifist, now you're hitting your husband."

"I would never…"

"Of course you would, you just did. But you forget one thing, *wife*," I teased her with mischief welling up inside me.

"And what's that?"

"I'm not like your Momsiboys from home. I'm an Nman and we don't let our wives control us or dominate us. We like to be in charge."

"Oh, yeah?" she said challengingly. "I don't think so!"

I leaned into her and whispered in her ear. "Here's what's going to happen: I'm gonna take you home and you're gonna spend the entire day naked, and every time I want to fuck you, I will. All you have to do is say 'yes.'"

"Ha!" she scoffed. "Not likely."

I grinned as I picked her up in my arms and started walking. "Oh, it's happening and I guarantee that you're going to love it."

She didn't fight me, but held on to my neck as I walked. "You know, Boulder, I probably will love it, because I love everything about you."

"Liar!" I grinned. "But it's okay, I know I can be annoying as hell."

"So can I," she said and nuzzled her head against me. "Maybe that's why we're so good together."

"Just tell me this…" I said and kept walking with her in my arms. "Tell me you can live with someone as crude and primitive as me."

Warmth shined from her and I couldn't decide if her blue eye or her hazel-green eye was more beautiful. "I can," she said. "Because I know what it's like to live without you, and I never want to do that again."

I stopped and squeezed her into a tight hug. "Christina…"

"Uh-huh."

"You're the best thing that ever happened to me and I would fight a thousand men to be your champion."

"You don't have to fight anyone because I'm already yours," she whispered into my ear. "And I'll prove it to you by following orders and staying naked all day at your house."

"Our house," I corrected.

"Okay, our house, but only if you're naked with me."

"Oh, see – now you're just making unreasonable demands on me." I winked.

"But you'll follow my wish?"

"I might, we'll see." We both knew that I would happily be naked with her, but as a proud Nman I couldn't let her think she got to dictate to me.

"We're going to be making a lot of compromises, you know that, right?"

"Sure. Let's make this compromise, shall we?" I bit back a laugh. "I'll make sure you'll never lack sex if you promise to never leave me again."

She laughed. "So I never leave you and I give you as much sex as you want. That's your compromise?"

"Yes."

"How about, I'll never leave you and you'll let me be in charge of your hair and beard?"

"Nope, I like *my* suggestion better."

"Hmm... then let's start with that and we'll work our way up to the rest. After all, we have the rest of our lives."

"I love you!" It flew out of my mouth – loud and clear – as an expression of the fullness in my chest that felt so amazing. "I fucking love you with all my heart."

Her eyes lit up with joy as she flashed me a wide grin. "That's lucky, because I fucking love you too."

This concludes The Protector – Men of the North #1

Enjoy this book? You can make a big difference.

Thank you so much for reading the first story in my new series. Did you like it?

Now ask yourself this: If this was a meal, would you leave a tip? Your review is that tip.
(PLEASE avoid spoilers)

Want more?
The series continues with *The Ruler* where you'll meet
Boulder, Christina, Khan, Pearl, Magni, Kya, Archer, Finn,
and other of the characters from *The Protector* again.

ELIN PEER

MEN OF THE
NORTH #2
THE RULER

The Ruler – Men of the North #2

Four hundred years in the future, women control the world but Khan Aurelius, ruler of the last free men, is determined to take back the power that has been denied men for centuries. Outnumbered by far, he knows that women need to give up their power willingly and with one of their councilwomen as a hostage, he's certain he can influence her with his superior male intellect. She is just a soft woman, after all.

Councilwoman Pearl has sacrificed herself to save an innocent priestess. Trapped in the Northlands, her soft voice and sugar-coated view of the world doesn't impress Khan, who constantly challenges her by playing his mind games to corrupt her and see things his way. It's a battle of words and wills when the two intelligent rulers clash. Will Pearl succeed in bringing enlightenment and democracy to the primitive Nmen or will Khan corrupt her with his charm first?

The Ruler is the second installment in Elin Peer's *Men of the North* series that offers, drama, humor, and romance in a fabulous blend that will have you longing for more.

Don't miss out on a great chance to escape from reality in this riveting story – get the book today!

Check out my website elinpeer.com for an overview of my other books and make sure you sign up for my newsletter to be alerted when I release new books.

Want to connect with me? Great – I LOVE to hear from my readers.
Find me on facebook.com/AuthorElinPeer
Or connect with me on Goodreads, Amazon, Bookbub or simply send an email to elin@elinpeer.com.

About the author

Elin is curious by nature. She likes to explore and can tell you about riding elephants through the Asian jungle, watching the sunset in the Sahara Desert from the back of a camel, sailing down the Nile in Egypt, kayaking in Alaska, and flying over Greenland in helicopters.

She can also testify that the most interesting people aren't always kings, queens, presidents, and celebrities, because she has met many of them in person.

After traveling the world and living in different countries, Elin is currently residing outside Seattle in the US with her husband, daughters, and her black Labrador, Lucky, which follows her everywhere.

Elin is the kind of person you end up telling your darkest and deepest secrets to, even though you never intended to. Maybe that's where she gets her inspiration for her books. One thing is for sure: Elin is not afraid to provoke, shock, touch, and excite you when she writes about unwanted desire, forbidden passion, and all those damn emotions in between.

Want to connect with Elin? Great – she loves to hear from her readers.

Find her on Facebook: facebook.com/AuthorElinPeer
Or look her up on Goodreads, Amazon, Bookbub or simply go to www.elinpeer.com.

Made in the USA
Middletown, DE
29 November 2019